He smelled of man

Aby glided towards the bar, uncharacteristically drawn by the handsome stranger. He was tall, with long legs and cowboy boots. His broad shoulders gave her a shudder and she wondered at his strength. Strong men always made her look twice.

But there was something about the man…something predatory that put her on guard and called to her womanhood. She got a new scent. It was dark, malevolent.

Was he human?

He filled the air around her and went beyond it, as if his aura could not be contained. And Aby was powerless to resist him.

She had no idea who he was, but she'd find out.

MICHELE HAUF

The HIGHWAYMAN

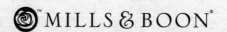

First published in Great Britain 2010
Harlequin Mills & Boon Limited,
Eton House, 18-24 Paradise Road, Richmond, Surrey TW9 1SR

© Michelle R Hauf 2009

ISBN: 978 0 263 88771 6

89-0810

Harlequin Mills & Boon policy is to use papers that are natural, renewable
and recyclable products and made from wood grown in sustainable forests.
The logging and manufacturing processes conform to the legal environmental
regulations of the country of origin.

Printed and bound in Spain
by Litografia Rosés S.A., Barcelona

Michele Hauf has been writing for over a decade and has published historical, fantasy and paranormal romances. A good strong heroine, action and adventure and a touch of romance make for her favourite kind of story. (And if it's set in France, all the better.) She lives with her family in Minnesota and loves the four seasons, even if one of them lasts six months and can be colder than a deep freeze. You can find out more about her at www.michelehauf.com.

This one's for Tara Gavin, my editor, because sometimes I want my men to have lace dripping from their sleeves and she says, "Absolutely not." One of these days, when you're not looking, I will sneak some lace onto my hero's sleeve or collar.

Prologue

Chased by a shadow? Impossible.

But as Jeffrey Raymond scrambled across the tarmac, a dark figment followed. Black and vapory, like a floating shadow.

He glanced over his shoulder. Was it getting darker? More solid?

Slapping his palm to the brick wall, he swung around the corner, only to find a dead end.

He raced as far as he could down the alley, then swung about to face the menace.

No longer a shadow, it had changed into a menacing figure, humanlike and hulking. At the end of the alleyway, the figure stood taller than he by a head, dressed in a long black duster coat. His arms were arced as if prepared to draw six-shooters from hip holsters. Moonlight glinted on a silver ring at his thumb. Mist from a nearby sewer fogged about his legs.

He looked like something out of a summer blockbuster movie—but Jeffrey wasn't choking down the popcorn.

Moments earlier he'd thought a shadow pursued him. Slinking along the brick walls, traipsing across the alleys, Jeffrey had fled the dark sensation of being watched.

Of knowing he would not survive this night.

Now there was nowhere to run.

Stumbling, he slammed a shoulder against a rough brick wall. Escape was up the side of a three-story building. He spied an iron ladder a mere leap from his grasp, but running had exhausted him. This mortal shell he'd nabbed earlier wasn't in any condition to run a marathon.

The Highwayman approached slowly, silent upon the fog.

Yes, he knew this man was the one whispered about amongst his kin. The hunter who stalked the night, brandishing a razored whip against demons, vampires, werewolves, any and all paranormals.

The Highwayman didn't look so imposing. He could take him.

If he hadn't had that seventh Kamikaze while attempting to seduce the blonde at the bar. Misery was his demonic forte, not seduction. But a dude needed to indulge in the mortal pleasure of sex once in a while—which was why he'd stolen this mortal body.

Mist swirled at the Highwayman's boots as he narrowed their distance. Jeffrey hadn't seen him move, yet now the man held something in his right hand.

The whip?

"Hey, dude," Jeffrey tried, hating that his voice trembled. "Let's talk about this. I think you got the wrong guy."

The whip cracked the tarmac. The noise sliced down Jeffrey's spine. He flinched, then realized he hadn't been touched. What were those red glowing things along the braided whip?

He wished to hell he could smoke on out of here. But when panicked, he couldn't shift shapes, and escaping the mortal shell was a bitch. Damn those Kamikazes!

"I never make a mistake," the Highwayman hissed ominously. "You're a misery demon and your head is mine."

"Dude, no, I like my head!"

"Then why don't you use it to manifest peace and acceptance?"

"Peace? That's just wrong, dude. That's not my thing. Hey, why don't you send me back to where I came from?"

"The demonic realm? What's to prevent you from returning?"

"I wouldn't." A lie. He was desperate. "You want to send me away?"

"I want you off this earth."

The whip soughed in the air. The glowing red sigils entranced him. Ah. Demon binding sigils.

Damn.

Razors stung Jeffrey's neck. The first slice burned across his Adam's apple. He enjoyed wearing mortal flesh, but when it experienced pain, man, it really knocked him off his game.

A cry for mercy spurt out on a gush of blood. Before risking entrapment inside the mortal shell, the demon disconnected from flesh and blood. The mortal shell known as Jeffrey Raymond collapsed, left to be found comatose hours or days later by druggies or garbage men.

The misery demon formed, red flesh and muscles, stretched torso and clawed appendages. But in the moments after detaching from the mortal shell, the demon was always disoriented.

The Highwayman's whip found its target.

A sulfurous cloud spilled from the demon's severed head, surrounding the body and buzzing like a plague of insects. Within moments the entire demon dissipated into a pile of dust on the ground before the Highwayman's boots.

A slash of the whip over his head coiled it many times over, then the Highwayman fit it on the holster at his hip. The binding sigils ceased to glow.

Leaving the alleyway, he strode across the street where he'd parked his black '68 Shelby Mustang.

Once behind the wheel, he cranked the tunes and took off in a rumbling peel. On to the next town. The highway was his home, his lover, his destination.

One of these days it would lead him to salvation.

Chapter 1

A charity show wasn't the strangest event Max had ever crashed. He'd been everywhere, seen everything. It took a lot to impress, disturb or even surprise him. A man who had lived over two centuries didn't miss much.

There were days he wished to miss more.

A twenty-story skyscraper jutted up from downtown Minneapolis, three blocks from the bustling City Center mall. The blue-windowed steel spire was nestled between a white stucco building and a multilevel parking ramp.

This was where he'd followed the limo that had picked up the familiar. He spied only a flash of green dress as she stepped out from the limo's backseat and took the hand of a beefy bouncer to be led inside.

Green. Max loved when women adorned themselves with green. It reminded him of wild French meadows and freedom. Few could wear the color as well as this woman. And if she wore spike heels and had bright, sexy eyes, then he was a goner.

Rare was the woman who could truly leave Maximilien Fitzroy speechless.

This one wouldn't have a chance to render him silent. He wasn't here to socialize. He had found the familiar. Now he would convince her to do a job for him.

And then he'd kill her.

The majority of guests filing into the building wore tuxedoes and fancy dresses. Checking his black duster coat and cowboy boots, complete with spurs, Max gave a tug to his black denim jeans and pulled the coat over his hip to conceal the whip he never forgot.

The delivery door was set into the shadows. Striding down the alleyway, Max released hold on his mortal shape and shifted to shadow form. He could shadow for five minutes and still maintain complete control over the demon. Any longer than that and he was headed for a dream walk.

He glided inside the building, following delivery of a massive arrangement of red roses.

Once inside, he clung to shadows in the crevice where floor met wall, until he made the elevator. Inside and alone, he reneged control over the shadow.

Later, he'd have to appease the shadow by allowing it to peer into the dreams of unsuspecting mortals.

Hell, it wasn't all for the demon. Shadowing sublimated Max's basic needs by allowing him to experience them vicariously. It was all he had. He rarely missed a night of dream walking.

At the twentieth floor, the elevator dinged. Max stepped out before two goateed bouncers dressed in tuxedoes and brandishing discerning stares. He wasn't questioned; he'd obviously made it in at ground level.

Never comfortable in crowds, he eased himself into the mixture of bodies, both mortal and, he suspected, paranormal. His attire was lacking, but now he noticed some artsy sorts who wore a range from wildly colored hair to Day-Glo glasses, Earth shoes and military camouflage pants.

More than a few feminine necks and wrists sported sparkling jewels.

I do love the shiny stuff.

The placard on an artist's easel announced the Charity Auction for the Northern Wolf Sanctuary featuring local celebrities, The Fallen and Johnny Lang.

Max strode through a long hall clattering with heightened conversation and clinking crystal goblets. Floor-to-ceiling windows lined the east wall, providing a brilliant view of the half moon. The west side was lined with mirrors, which gave the eerie effect of looking skyward at distorted multiple moons.

He wasn't interested in the art hung before the mirrors by braided silver cables. The pieces were apparently being auctioned off. But as he passed the paintings, he smirked and stepped closer to study a six-foot-tall piece.

"Cheesecake?" he muttered. The entire row boasted cheesecake paintings of scantily clad pinup girls.

"Better than Mondrian," he muttered, recalling an art event in the early twentieth century that had confused and bored him. But it had introduced him to absinthe—one of few pleasures he could yet imbibe.

Max strode through the tightly packed room where guests chattered and cooed at one another. There were many tall model sorts, and he matched a couple of emaciated posers to their nudie paintings as he passed through the clutch.

The women cast him lingering glances. One siliconed blonde in barely-there strips of black leather approached him. Diamonds glittered at her neck

and ears. Her red lips smiled coyly, while her brown
eyes touched him from boots to belt—and there she
stopped.

"See something you like?" Max asked.

"Oh, yes."

He slid a hand along her cheek, touching her
hair, lightly brushing her ear, then returned that
hand to his pocket. "Sorry, not into blondes."

Her smile dropped to a pout and she brushed
rudely past him.

Max could only shake his head. A dalliance with
a gorgeous woman mostly proved frustrating.
Much as he enjoyed indulging, he didn't have the
patience for self-denial tonight. He was here on
business.

Focusing, he headed for the ballroom ahead.
The glass ceiling soared high and white marble
walls and windows glittered. Chandeliers threatened to dribble a rain of crystal droplets, and the
funky blue lighting cooled the complexions of all.

The chrome bar inside the ballroom drew him.

"You have absinthe?" Max asked. The liquor
had only recently been legalized in the United
States.

The bartender nodded. Max laid a twenty on the
bar. That would buy him a sip of the overpriced
Green Faery.

Scanning the room, his eyes fell upon a woman

whose green dress spilled in loose curves to the top of her shapely derriere. Her entire back was exposed, revealing sexy, sinuous skin. From her hips, the green fabric greedily clung to long legs, which ended in black spike heels. Black ribbons, tied about her ankles, begged to be bitten and tugged from their bows.

The line of her body curved and sashayed as she prowled the center of the ballroom, her arms swaying, as if choreographed, to attract all eyes. Short tufted hair emphasized her slender neck.

"Red," Max whispered. Now, redheads he liked.

Not a single jewel or bauble detracted his eye from her soft skin and sleek body. Just as well.

Sucking in a breath, he whistled lowly. Spike heels and a sexy, body-clinging dress. And to top it off, she was a redhead. This wasn't going to be easy on his fickle libido, or his itchy fingers. Max never mixed business with pleasure.

Come to think of it, he would if he could, but pleasure was an elusive beast he sought to capture.

The air-conditioning was overkill. Aby shivered and rubbed a palm up her bare arm. She'd dressed to the nines tonight, green silk dress with a low-cut back. Stilettos held her ankles in bondage with crisscrossing black ribbon.

The artist whose prints they were auctioning off

later, Wesley Aims, was a friend, and this was his first big showing in an art world that normally sneered at pinup paintings.

The charity auction should give him entrance to further showings. Or so he and Severo hoped.

She sought Severo to cozy up to and draw some of his natural male heat over her chilled skin. He'd been out of eyesight since the bigwig in the Armani suit had taken him aside to discuss Severo's investments. His passion was buying land and transforming it into a natural wolf preserve, so she couldn't fault his inattention. Any chance he found to buy land before the vampires could sink their teeth into it, he jumped.

In her peripheral vision, Aby sighted Ian Grim, a centuries-old witch whom she'd been working with exclusively. She tolerated him, but lately he'd been flirting with her before they got down to business. The man gave her stronger shivers than the air-conditioning, and they weren't the sexy kind of shivers.

A step outside into the sweltering July evening appealed to her, but the charity show was on the twentieth floor. And the band was supposed to take the stage soon.

She'd not listened to The Fallen previously, but the lead singer was attractive, and—despite Severo's reservations about hiring a longtooth—a vampire. They'd had some success years ago, but now only played local events.

Aby roamed her gaze across the room. If she didn't leave or at least go sit by the bar, someone would whisk her into another dance. She liked dancing, but the men's hands tended to roam her bare back with an ease that put her off. Hell, the illicit touches put up the tiny hairs at the base of her neck.

She liked to dress sexy, but she was always a little confused how to handle blatant flirtation.

A flash of blue at the bar wafted the bittersweet-orange scent of Curaçao across the room toward her ultrasensitive nose.

Her world was navigated by scent. She never made a move without first assessing the atmosphere. It usually took her but moments to acclimate to new smells, else she'd be dizzy from a melee of odors.

A new smell, beyond the alcohol-laced colognes and grooming products and cigarette smoke, tickled her nose.

Aby smiled at a passing couple, then tilted her head to eye the bar. Running her tongue along her lower lip, she took in the tall man who also scanned the room.

Though the ballroom was filled with eclectic clothing and hair, even the latest haute couture, the man, wearing a long, black duster coat, stood apart.

Not here for the art or to save an abused captive wolf, she suspected. Possibly to hunt out a missing girlfriend? Or maybe he was a friend of one of the bartenders.

He smelled different. But what about him was unique?

Drawing a soft breath through her nose, Aby discerned the faint masculine odor wafting from his direction. That was it. One simple scent. He was clean. No tobacco, alcohol or chemicals that tainted every living being in the world. Not a definitive food odor that usually lingered even on the most fastidious.

"Odd," Aby murmured.

And yet, too intriguing for her curious nature to ignore.

She glided toward the bar, but remained parallel to the man. Gracious as she liked to be to Severo's friends, she didn't approach handsome strangers out of the blue. And this man definitely ranked high on the handsome scale.

Tall, he looked as if he could see over the heads of everyone in the ballroom. Narrow dark denim emphasized long legs. The cowboy boots were perhaps too scuffed for this elite crowd. And spurs?

Maybe he was some kind of Wild West entertainer hired for the evening? Severo did like westerns.

A tousle of brown hair dusted his ears and coat

collar. Broad shoulders gave Aby a shudder as she wondered at his strength. Strong men always tempted her to look twice.

He was definitely not the glitzy charity-ball type. So what brought him here this evening? Was he alone or with a date?

Aby sucked in her lower lip. There was something about a man who absolutely filled the space he stood in—yet went beyond, as if his aura could not be contained and crept out at the edges.

His eyes scanned the room, stopping first at the bar, and then finally, he looked right at Aby.

The room heated measurably, and yet beneath the thin green silk Aby's nipples tightened. His gaze wasn't accidental; rather, it was determined. Maybe predatory. That put her on guard.

Yet inquisitiveness kept her stare fixed on him.

The scent of him heightened. He'd found what he was looking for, and his body reacted by pulsing adrenaline through his system.

Me? she wondered. Had he wanted me?

She had no idea who he was. But she'd find out. Curiosity and the cat thing.

Striding forward, Aby was aware her hips sashayed and her steps moved her like a feline. Of course.

She could track the man with her eyes closed, but he hadn't dropped her gaze, nor did she feel the need to drop his.

It was when a new scent intruded, deep within the tendrils of his clean odor, that Aby paused. It was dark. Malevolent.

Was he human?

He smelled like it. And yet, something clung at the blurry edges of his being. An otherworldly charge. It wasn't enough to make her retreat. She could handle all sorts, and could determine paranormals from humans with ease, though she usually couldn't determine what type of paranormal.

She actually preferred paranormals to humans. They were more understanding of her, as she was of them.

The bartender set a shot glass of cloudy green liquid before the man. A slotted spoon rested over the glass rim, topped with a melting sugar cube.

Aby slid onto the stainless-steel stool beside the one he stood closest to. She loved the smell of anise. He must be drinking absinthe. How decadent.

"And for the lady?" the bartender asked.

"Whatever she desires," the man said in a raspy voice that reminded her of cool winter nights snuggled in a fuzzy wool sweater.

"Cream with a touch of grenadine," Aby said, and didn't turn to face him.

Winter nights? Oh, Aby, you're such a dreamer. The last time she'd gotten some sexy snuggle time was—never.

Six horizontal neon bars gleamed behind the bar in varying shades of blue. Aby didn't like the color, nor, she guessed, did it grant her complexion the best glow.

"Cream," he said. "That's a new one."

"With grenadine," she added lightly. "I like it to be pink."

His smile wasn't at all mirthful. "Name's Max. And you are Aby."

That he spoke her name as fact pricked at the base of her spine.

Perhaps he'd spoken to someone here who knew her. A slim chance. Though she was amiable, she didn't go around shaking everyone's hands and introducing herself.

She scanned her memory for the man's face. Dark eyes, maybe blue, and a strong nose above nicely bowed lips. A shadow of stubble darkening his jaw and upper lip. Scruffy bangs over one brow. Styling products had never seen that head of sexy, carefree hair.

Nope, never seen him before. Which didn't mean much. Aby led a sheltered life.

The absinthe sat untouched before the man.

"Gorgeous dress," he said. "The color suits you. I like green."

Of course he did. If she had been wearing blue, she could guess he'd prefer that color. Just because she wasn't experienced didn't make her stupid.

"I saw your picture."

Aby tilted her head down. Severo had not been pleased when she'd agreed to pose for Wesley, but it had made her feel so free and utterly sensual. "And what did you think of it?"

"Cat's ears and tail, and some sexy slip of black lace? I don't think there's a man in the room who wouldn't find it attractive."

She didn't like his answer. It was less than personal. What did he think?

Aby sipped the pale pink cream from the wine goblet.

This didn't feel right. She should walk away and find Severo.

And yet, the stranger smelled so interesting. A girl could lose her sense of right and wrong from an enticing scent. Happened all the time. Hell, some claimed to fall in love at first sniff.

But Aby didn't know about that. She knew love—the friendly, family kind. Romantic love? That was a mystery she'd like to solve.

"How do I know you, Max? What is your last name?"

"Maximilien Fitzroy. Whatever you've heard of me, don't worry, I'm just here to talk."

She hadn't heard of him, but should she have?

"Just call me Max. I have a business proposition."

"Do you now?" Aby saucily stared into his

deep-blue eyes. No answers there, very emotion-less, in fact. "Seems you know more about me than I you."

"I know you're a familiar, and that's why I've come looking for you."

She was a familiar, and familiars bridged demons to this realm. Which meant…

"Not interested," Aby said abruptly. She should have followed her intuition. He was just another man who wanted something from her.

"You haven't heard what I have to say."

"I know the only reason someone would come looking for a familiar, and I'm not interested."

Because any business he had in mind would mean he wouldn't be available to her on a more personal level.

Standing and extricating herself, Aby slid a thigh against the man's leg as she did so. Taut and firm. Oh, but his clean scent dizzied her.

Which was why she had to move away from him. Now.

The room had suddenly burst into flame. Imag-inary heat licked at her skin. Aby strode toward the mirrored hallway as quickly as her five-inch heels would allow.

He followed. She couldn't shake his scent.

"Will you at least hear me out?"

"Not interested," she called, but he'd already

caught up and now walked at her side. "Find another familiar to do your dirty work."

The tinging sound of an elevator announced an arriving couple, who exited laughing and holding hands. Aby veered left and boarded. The doors closed, but a hand fit between them. Max pushed open the doors and stepped inside, blocking her exit as the doors slid shut behind him.

Mercy, but she didn't like enclosed spaces. Especially small spaces that harbored danger. And his clean scent wasn't natural, nor was the dark edge.

"You're frightening me," she said, trying to stay calm.

Prickles sparked up her spine. Her muscles tensed. Soon her claws would come out.

But eighteen floors to go, and she could flee. She knew a few high kicks, but those only worked on the unsuspecting and the weak. This man was a head taller than she and he absolutely oozed strength.

"I don't mean to scare you, Aby, but I need you to listen to me. To at least hear me out before you refuse me."

He pressed a hand high on the fabric wall over her head. Sensing he would block her in, Aby slinked sideways. He sighed and dropped his head, his back and shoulder to her.

"I need to summon a demon," he said. "I've heard you're the best. I'll pay any price."

Any price? Well, she was the best. Only because her species dwindled daily. Not a lot of competition out there.

"There are a half a dozen familiars in the country who can do the job for a few thousand. Why me?"

"I don't want to piss around with amateurs. I need a guarantee. Someone I can trust. And I don't want to bring in a witch. I'll work directly with you to summon the demon."

"Oh, really?"

The nerve of the man. The prickles pinging her spine persisted. Everything was too sharp, too clear. Her pupils dilated when threatened, which enhanced her vision. But it was too much now.

Fisting a hand at her hip, she stepped up to the towering slayer. "So, what you're asking is for me to bridge a demon, and…you want to have sex with me all night long?"

"Yes. No." He grimaced and shook his head. "Not like that."

"But you know what is required for a familiar to bridge a demon?"

"I know. You have to be sexually sated."

"And you think you're the man to do it for me?"

She scoffed and turned away from him. Twelve more floors to go. Damn, this was a slow elevator.

He'd said he wanted someone he could trust. But he didn't know her! What kind of double-talk was he working on her?

"It's for me," he said. His sigh dusted her shoulder. The warm breath tingled, entered her being and awakened…something. "I need to get a nasty demon off my back."

So that was the scent she detected limning his peculiarly clean odor.

"I'm retired." Aby turned and, leaning against the wall, offered a forced calmness. It was difficult to be too standoffish when the man was so delicious.

Sex all night with this one?

It could never happen the way she'd like it to go. Summoning demons was her job. Sex was a job. And she didn't want to associate work of any kind with this appealing man.

Punching the wall, he startled her. "Listen. Do you have any idea what it's like to live for two and a half centuries?"

His eyes burned now, half lidded and yet so volatile. Aby slid closer to the control panel.

"That's two hundred and fifty years," he reiterated and tracked her movements with a deft sidestep. "I've walked this earth alone and frustrated, unable to satisfy the few basic desires necessary to all men."

The heaviness of his gaze slinked down her face and settled on her shoulders. Aby inhaled. His attention slipped to her breasts, jutting high beneath the thin green silk. It wasn't a lewd look, but rather she felt as if he were giving her something precious. Acknowledgment.

"Y-you're scaring me, Max. What the hell are you?"

"I'm human," he answered easily. "But immortal. There's a demon shadow inside me. I want it out."

"Is that why you can't satisfy your desires?"

He leaned in, hot breath whispering over her breasts. The man tickled his gaze along her neck, as if her flesh were the one thing in this world that could satisfy his unmet desires.

His mouth paralleled hers. Aby's breaths came light and fast. Would he kiss her?

When his eyes found hers, wide pupils darkened his gaze. Desperation frightened her to reality. No kisses, she told herself. Not from a man she didn't know.

Poor guy. Immortality was a bitch. Especially when denied the pleasures most took for granted.

Still. "Look, I can give you the contact information for a familiar in New Orleans. She's very good—"

He slammed his fist into the wall over her head. Aby chirped nervously.

"I'm here," he said, leaning in close to her face. "I've got ten thousand dollars in my pocket."

"You can't buy a screw with me. I said I'm retired." Sort of a lie, but he intimidated her. She didn't like the feeling.

He gripped her by the shoulders.

The elevator landed with an announcing ding. The doors opened, and an angry growl prompted Max to let go of Aby.

She moved, but Max was too fast. He blocked the exit with his broad frame and determined stance. But she needn't see to know who waited in the hall.

The werewolf stepped forward and yanked Max from the elevator by his coat lapels.

"Severo!" Aby cried.

Chapter 2

Max's shoulders connected with the wall. His spurs skidded along the marble floor. The growl from the man who had done the shoving didn't sound human.

Then again, Max knew he wasn't human. He guessed if the man weren't wearing a long-sleeved suit coat the hairs on his arms would be upright.

Max knew what he was. A werewolf. He didn't hate them, but he didn't like them, either. They usually ran in packs and he often found them at biker bars in the summertime. A wise man never turned his back on a werewolf unless he had a pocket full of silver.

What was this one doing at a fancy charity ball?

Protecting a familiar? That didn't compute, because cats and dogs did not mix.

"You bothering Aby?" the wolf said with barely masked vitriol. His dark eyes held a wicked threat Max had seen far too many times—and he never liked it. "You okay, Aby?"

"Yes, Severo, let him down. He was asking me about doing a job. I said I wasn't interested."

Released, Max went for the whip at his hip. He fingered the braided leather handle.

"You touch that, asshole," the werewolf said with a growl, "I eviscerate you."

Max winced. "You're not the friendly sort, are you?"

He slid the hand from his hip, shrugging his shoulders and forcing calm through his muscles. The air hummed with aggression. He wasn't here for a fight. The wolf couldn't handle what Max could give him.

"Who are you?" the one Aby had called Severo asked. "Why are you here when a smart man should know you don't approach a familiar in such a manner?"

"Just trying to talk nicely with her. Don't want to cause trouble."

But please, give me trouble so I can knock you down.

Severo nodded toward the whip. "You use that to remove demons' heads?"

"It'll take off a wolf's head, too."

A claw stopped short of slicing open Max's chin. Aby held Severo's arm, straining to keep him from attack.

The whip unfurled.

The wolf shuffled backward as if he'd been stung. "Hell." He shoved Aby behind him. "You're the Highwayman."

"What?" Aby peeked over the wolf's shoulder.

"The one I've warned you about, Aby." He looked over Max, taking in the whip, his attire. "Am I correct?"

Max tucked the whip at his hip, showing he wasn't about to let this escalate in front of a female. "My reputation tends to precede me."

Aby gasped. "Oh, gods."

Her fingers clutched the werewolf's arm. She'd gone from sexy tease to a frightened little girl in the flick of a whip.

"She said she isn't interested," Severo ground through a tight jaw.

"Who the hell is this?" Max asked the wide-eyed familiar. "Your pimp?"

He hadn't been prepared for the slap Aby delivered with an echoing sting.

The wolf smirked and put an arm around Aby's shoulders. "Familiars don't have pimps, idiot. Now get the hell out of my air. She said she's not interested. And I'm not about to let you harm a hair on her pretty head."

Licking the droplet of blood pooled at the corner of his mouth, Max eyed the familiar. She was involved with a werewolf?

Bleeding cowboys, wonders did not cease.

"I've no intention to harm her."

Yet. That was number three on his list.

"It's what you do, Highwayman," the wolf spat. "Kill familiars. Don't deny it."

Indeed, his reputation was notorious worldwide. Max had figured out about ninety years ago that he could never slay all the demons in this world. But he could go after the conduits who brought those nasty bastards to this realm—the familiars.

But the werewolf's assumption annoyed him. He'd found the familiar—task one complete. The killing wouldn't come until he got beyond the second task. And number two would prove tricky.

"I give you my word no harm will come to her tonight. I just want to talk business."

"Business?" Severo smirked. "You don't deserve a moment of our time. Besides, she works exclusively with Ian Grim."

"Grim? Not the witch who bespelled the werewolf's wife?"

"What?" Aby looked to Severo.

"It's an urban legend," the werewolf reassured

the woman. To Max, he said, "Grim's a good man. For a witch."

"If that's what you want to believe."

Max studied their embrace. Aby's fingers clutched the wolf's arm. Her breasts hugged close to him. The wolf slid a hand along her thigh, keeping her safe from Max, but marking her as his own. They were definitely involved.

As for the witch, he hated to think any woman was involved with Grim, in any way. "Aby, you won't even hear me out?"

The pixie-haired familiar shook her head and slunk against the wolf's side. The mongrel lifted his chin, eyeing Max down the bridge of his nose.

She'd been confident and open earlier, when she had not been in the wolf's presence. Max would get nothing further from her until he could speak to her alone. That is, if he could convince her he'd no intention of harming her.

He could lie with the best of them.

"Sorry to have crashed the party."

He spun and stalked off, taking the steps to the street level two at a time. When he reached the Mustang, parked two blocks down the street, he hopped inside, but didn't start the ignition or switch on the headlights.

Exhaling, he merely dropped his head back against the headrest.

Being alone in the car meant solace. He'd never grow accustomed to the city sounds of mufflers backfiring, sirens blaring, people shouting and industry grinding at gears and grease. The world had gotten so noisy over the past half-dozen decades.

Tugging the diamond earring from his pocket, he examined the sparkle. Two carats, surely.

He shook his head miserably, and leaned over to toss it in the glove compartment. He didn't want to steal; he was compelled to it.

From his other pocket he pulled out a silver coin. The hole in it held bad memories…

Paris—1758

The serving wench flaunted enticing curves designed to steal souls, and sensual bow lips to condemn those stolen prizes. She did not win Maximilien Fitzroy's glance.

Nor did his partner, Rainier Deloche, look away from Max's steady gaze. The two men clashed their pewter tankards of the Green Cat's finest brew.

"To riches," Rainier announced. He swallowed the entire mugful, slamming it on the wobbly wood table with a satisfied grin.

"To riches and fast thinking." Max followed suit.

The beer was stale and warm, yet it was the best thing he'd tasted in days. He called for another round.

The wench poured their drinks, the beer slopping over the side of Max's tankard, but he did not curse her. Instead, he lifted the tankard and licked around the rim.

The wench sighed at the sight of his tongue slurping up the moisture. Yet Max's attention could not be won by feminine wiles this night.

Affronted, she stormed off in pursuit of other prospects.

Max tilted his mug to Rainier. "To adventure."

Agreeing with a nod, Rainier beat Max at the second round. The flat beer was hardly worth the two sous, but neither minded paying. They could afford it.

Reaching inside his leather greatcoat, Max mined for his purse, tied at his hip, being cautious not to jingle the coin. He and his partner never drew attention to themselves. After encountering one too many cutthroats with a greedy taste for stolen coin, Max had come to accord with discretion.

Ah, to the devil! They always drew attention to themselves. Life wasn't worth the walk unless the world joined in.

But they did know when to play it quiet—when the law was about. Neither had caught sight of the king's guards since returning to Paris, hours earlier from the west.

Max drew out a silver *demi-écu* from the leather

pouch. The size of a sliced egg, it was old, issued fifty years ago during Louis XIV's reign. It was one of hundreds he and Rainier had "procured" earlier this evening, thanks to the forced kindness of strangers.

The carriage had brandished King Louis XV's coat of arms, and five heavy, metal coffers of gold and silver coin destined for Versailles.

The coachman had spied Rainier's and Max's silhouettes, sitting each upon a fine mount waiting alongside the road, pistols drawn and aimed for the coachman's forehead. Still, the lackwit had shouted a warning to the guards inside the coach.

Max hated when they made noise. It upset his partner.

Rainier had shot the coachman in the jaw—not a killing shot, but certainly it had taken the victim's voice. Max prided himself on never taking a life, yet he'd been forced to deliver a wounding shot on more than a few occasions. He absolved his guilt with a prayer to his father, who had been shot in the head by a highwayman when Max was six.

Pistols had fired from within the coach. Gunpowder sparks danced in the clear night.

Max had advanced, heeling his mount determinedly. The snow was deep, and the gelding kicked up a storm in their wake. Rare did a bullet connect when shot without aim and out of fear.

With a slash of his épée, he'd disconnected one pistol from a hand.

Rainier charged the opposite side of the coach, disarming the other guard.

They'd argued whether to tie up the guards and leave them alive, or to kill them. Rainier insisted leaving behind witnesses was a chance they could ill afford.

Max had won the argument only because Rainier had dropped his pistol in the deep snow and found no time to dig it out. They had only taken two of the five coffers. The weight burdened their horses as it was.

Now celebration was in order.

Max held the silver coin between the two of them, not caring who witnessed. Let them admire the shiny coin. The common man might rarely see such a sight.

He and Rainier were common. Both orphaned before they were eight, they were forced to live on and work the streets. They had come together when they were ten and, in a boisterous boys' pact, vowed they would take their fortunes by trick or by trade.

Trade had never been an option once trick had gotten into their blood.

"To us!" Max prompted. "The most successful highwaymen in all of France."

"And handsome, too." Rainier chuckled heartily and pinched the coin between his fingers.

"I do love the shiny stuff," Max said.

The two held it between them, above Max's empty tankard.

"So what is the plan?" Rainier prompted. "The usual split and regroup in a month?"

"Excellent strategy. Tonight was a large take. We'll need to lie low."

"I do believe I shall follow that wench home tonight." Rainier nodded toward the waitress who still wanted to catch the eye of either of them.

"You've no discerning bone when it comes to women." But then Max laughed. He was in the mood for a celebratory roll in the hay as well. "Am I to wager I'm to look elsewhere for my entertainment this night?"

"I stake claim to this watering hole. We'll meet—"

The coin flipped out of the men's fingers as a burn skinned the pad of Max's forefinger. He recoiled, slapping his stinging hand to his chest.

Time slowed. Both men watched the coin flip end over end in the air before them. No longer round, it was twisted from the lead ball that had pierced the thin disk.

"Morbleu." Rainier upset the tankards as he jumped up. He tugged a pistol from his hip holster, splashing beer onto his suede breeches.

With a sharp look, Max cautioned his partner not

to fire at the king's guard who stood in the tavern doorway. Instead, he nodded over Rainier's shoulder. Beyond the fieldstone hearth roasting half a savory sow, the kitchen reeked of onion and smoke.

Escape out the back was always Max's first choice. It provided less risk to civilians being accidentally injured from a stray musket ball or slash of the blade.

"To danger!" Rainier called as he kicked aside a chair and dashed around behind the hearth.

"To adventure!" Man finished the rallying cry that had become their motto.

Max dodged a man swinging a half-chewed pheasant leg and bumped into the wench with the needy eyes. "And to lust," he said as he gripped her shoulders to make sure she wouldn't stumble. "Another time," he added, then took off out the door behind Rainier.

Though their mounts were out front, they were not an option right now.

Instead, they beat a pace to outrun the devil on foot. Melting snow slickened the cobbles. The clop of horse hooves told Max the guards were behind them, and mounted, which would stunt their efforts to put distance between them.

"I told you we should have silenced those guards for good!"

Perhaps so, Max decided, but he'd rather run for his life than hang for taking the life of another.

Either way, if they were caught, they'd be hanged.

"We split up," Max hissed as he gained Rainier's side.

Ahead, the narrow alley they'd escaped into parted two opposite ways. "No." Rainier shoved Max to the right. "The aqueducts."

They clattered down the dark stairway into the subterranean tunnels snaking below the city. Rainier was a master of the network, having spent much of his childhood years living in them.

They paused when darkness enveloped so thoroughly Max couldn't see his own hand before his face. Above and behind, the fast gait of the mounted guards passed overhead.

"You see?" Rainier's chuckle echoed. Max managed to slap a palm over his mouth even in the dark.

"We cannot return to the surface," Max said. "They'll post a guard outside the tavern and at the entrance to the aqueduct."

"Then we go onward. There's a turn ahead, and then a long stretch that'll lead us under the palace."

"You think sneaking about beneath the palace with the royal guard on our asses, and the king's gold jingling in our pockets, is a wise decision?"

"No, but since when do we analyze our moves so much?"

True. He and Rainier lived a free and reckless life. Their motto—To Danger! To Adventure!—was to be lived.

So far their heads still remained atop their necks. A man couldn't ask for more than that.

Except the wench Max had developed a craving for.

Exhaling, Max counted his heartbeats to five before drawing in a breath in the confines of the Mustang. The familiar was his only hope. He'd not played his cards right. But he was not a man to cash in his chips when there were more hands to be played. Nor did he run when a re-advance was the best option.

It took less than five minutes before he spied the wolf escorting Aby to a black limo parked before the building. Man, that woman's legs could walk through his dreams any day.

If he had dreams.

He tapped the steering wheel to an imagined beat. What it must be like to have those gams wrapped about his waist as he plunged himself inside her. He imagined those long fingers gripping his shoulders, urging him to move faster and faster, and that soft red hair tickling his face, his chest.

On the other hand, he had sworn off familiars two and a half centuries earlier. They weren't the sort of female a man wanted to have a relationship with, let alone sex. Sex with a familiar served one purpose.

And that was why he'd slain every single familiar he could find.

He muttered what had become his mantra for this mission, "Find her, screw her, kill her. And don't forget it."

The man called Severo opened the back door for her. While Max expected the long-haired freak to lean in for a kiss, instead the wolf squeezed Aby's hand and closed the door after her. He spoke to the driver, then watched as the limo rolled away.

Max gave them a two-block head start, then put the Mustang on the limo's trail.

The limo dropped Aby off before her building. She shared a two-story double condo with Brenda Meyers, an elderly woman who had once modeled for *Vogue* in the 1950s. She had moved here a month ago, and on the second day, the elegant ex-model had knocked on Aby's door and presented her with still-warm brownies. Brenda was on vacation in the Bahamas now with a younger lover.

Aby looked forward to becoming friends with Brenda. As much as her job would allow.

Severo had owned this condo for years, and had

hired a construction team to "enhance" the place so Aby could use it as her office. The outer walls in the shared foyer were decorated with a pretty tile mural. The walls inside Aby's home were sound-proofed, and the wood floors warded as well. A good thing, or her neighbor might wonder if she were a sex-crazed lunatic.

She was not. But her job did require surrendering to climax. Over and over. Not a bad gig, until a girl considered that the results of such exquisite pleasure brought forth demons.

And unfulfilling relationships.

Heck, she didn't have relationships. She'd love to have sex with a man and not worry demons would send him screaming. Which was exactly why she'd told Max she was retired.

Because there was a big difference between job sex and relationship sex.

Damn, she'd been lucky. What if she'd said yes? Aby had no idea the man was *the* Highwayman. That was an important detail he'd neglected to reveal. Good thing Severo had figured him out.

She smoothed a finger over the tattoo on the inside of her left wrist. It was a month old and the tiny lettering still felt raised.

"The Highwayman," she whispered. "My enemy."

She'd be more careful about talking to strangers from now on.

Without bothering to flick on the lights, she crossed the room, slipping the dress sleeves from her shoulders. Moonlight crept across the hardwood floor, puddling near the head of her bed.

She'd been on her own for a month. That first day away from Severo's estate had been scary but exciting. Now, the scary part was diminishing, and the excitement growing.

Still, she couldn't quite get the independent woman thing right. A girl would think, after three lives, she'd have that mastered. Unfortunately, she didn't retain personal knowledge from life to life. The basics of survival, like eating, reading, as well as her sensory memory, she retained.

Yet, she liked to believe she took some things she'd learned from each life into her soul. Things like the desire for independence, a strong curiosity and a love for nature.

She was on her own now, trying to live life normally. Yet just when she'd thought it possible to touch normality, a freakin' demon slayer shows up begging her to bridge for him.

A handsome demon slayer.

Who wanted to kill her.

Although he had told Severo he'd no intent to harm her.

Could she trust him?

Chapter 3

Max observed the familiar's shadow move away from the second-floor window. She'd seen him. He'd parked across the street, and now leaned against the Mustang, arms crossed high on his chest.

"I've got all night, sweetheart. Hell, I've got all day, too. All week, all bleeding century."

His smirk didn't touch mirth. Immortality wasn't all it was cracked up to be. He had an ink-scribbled stack of sudoku books stuffed under the front seat to prove it. How pitiful was that?

The night was warm, and he should take off his coat, but it concealed his weapon. Immortal or not, he still had to be wary of the police. Imagine life in prison with his never-ending mortality?

He wouldn't close his eyes. He would stand outside the car, waiting, even as the sun rose.

If he did close his eyes, it would only pick at the open wound he'd worn for centuries. Normally when one closed his eyes, he intended to drift off to sleep. But it didn't work that way with Max. He'd tried. Thousands of times. Tens of thousands of times. He'd closed his eyes, quieted his mind, and…wound up focusing on some latent noise or a bastard demon he was tracking. He simply could not sleep.

He'd been knocked unconscious a few times and recalled the experience of lying stone-cold out on the ground had really rocked.

Now he glanced around him on the dark street. If he had to stay in this town longer than a day, he'd have to check in to a motel. Camping out in the Mustang wasn't comfortable, or cool. He'd passed a motel at the east end of the city that advertised a swimming pool. He loved a swimming pool, his one salvation.

A white Monte Carlo rolled by, its booming speakers vibrating the tarmac with the beat. Max nodded to the faces inside. They drove on.

No one wanted to mess with him. Especially not tonight when he was pissed at being turned down by a thin slip of a familiar who denied her very nature.

Retired? The chick was a familiar. They walked this earth for the purpose of bridging demons. A familiar who didn't bridge might as well go the lemming route and jump off a cliff.

A bad comparison. Aby was a living, breathing creature, who was as close to human as they came, save her ability to shift shapes and call forth demons. He shouldn't consider her as a mere tool for his use.

But it was easier that way.

Over the years he'd grown impatient. Two previous familiars had been unable to bridge the demon whose shadow he carried. They weren't powerful enough. So he'd slain them. One familiar fewer in this world meant hundreds less demons.

It was finding the familiar that proved the hard part. He didn't get invitations to have wild all-night sex with a beautiful woman anymore…

Paris—1758

After two hours of stumbling through the darkness and feeling along rough limestone walls that dripped noxious damp, the men emerged from the bowels of Paris. Moonlight glistened on Rainier's wet, brown hair, which he kept closely shaved. He shook his broad-shouldered frame like a dog.

"Must have passed below the sewers," Max commented as he tugged off a knee-high leather boot to dump out the cold, reeking water.

They'd landed in deep water halfway through their journey and had waded up to their waists. But Rainier had been sure of his path, and Max trusted him.

"Looks as though we've landed in the Tuileries." Rainier heeled off his boots and sat on the rock below a barren apple tree. Snow blanketed the gardens, and their boots sank in to their ankles with each step. "I wager the insipid boy king is looking out his window right now, wondering where his coin is."

"It'll be clinking between a fine wench's fingers soon enough," Max answered.

"You know it. But why must they be fine? Pretty never does appease you, Max. You always need that other something as well."

That other something. That certain glint in the woman's eye. A glint of intelligence and refinement that allowed Max to see the queen beneath even the tawdriest of wenches.

"You have your preferences, I have mine."

Rainier may not be as discerning, but he did have a knack for choosing the loud ones.

"I think the mounts are a loss. No doubt the guards will round them up. I really liked that one."

Rainier chuckled. "You've had the gelding but two days. Stole him from a bastard *vicomte.*"

"Yes, and for two days I loved that horse!"

Max slicked his fingers through his shoulder-length hair and shook out the wet. His fingertip still stung, but he had been lucky. The musket ball could have sheered off his trigger finger.

With a relieved mixture of laughter and a sigh, he declared, "I'm hungry. We've yet to eat."

"The brothel on rue du Rocher has soup and bread," Rainier suggested. "And a warm handful of bosom waiting to be suckled."

"Gentlemen!"

Alerted, Max spun to face the shadowed figure of a man, his hand going to his left hip, ready to draw blade. He would not draw the pistol tucked at the back of his waist unless sure of a threat.

It was late, but the city rarely slept. Always the streets were populated and wanderers were not unexpected in the royal garden's bare-branched straits.

"You two appear in desperate need of lodging and a warm fire." The man splayed his arms grandly as he approached.

Rainier drew out his pistol. He didn't cock it, but he did aim at the intruder.

"Oh, no need for weapons," the man reassured him.

Max decided he was about fifty. The lines

cracking his flesh must be from hard labor, he
deduced, taking in the man's twisted, arthritic
fingers. He wore dark breeches and a plain shirt
beneath a tattered black wool cape. No gloves,
which meant he wasn't well-off. Max was ever
aware for small hidden blades or pistols.

"We've our own designs for the evening," Max
said. "We thank you for your concern. Be off, old
man."

"I've no desire to disturb your evening repast."
The man turned away, but paused, and glanced
back. "You look to be discerning gentlemen who
know the value of coin."

Max narrowed a glance toward his partner, who
returned the suspicion. For as many times as they'd
avoided the trap of dangerous lures, they knew to
be cautious now.

Spreading his arms carefully, the man said, "I've
a business proposition for you."

Rainier's brow lifted. Leave it to Rainier to hear
the coin clink in any offer, no matter how vague.
"What sort of proposition? And who are you?"

"Just a poor old man who's desperate to satisfy
his young lover."

"If it's coin you're looking for, old man—" Max
dug into his coat pocket. It was easier to toss the
beggars a few coins than talk to them overmuch.
"Take this and be gone."

He tossed a gold ecu through the air, but Rainier caught and pocketed it. His partner gave Max the evil eye. "Man said he had business for us. Let's hear him out. What kind of satisfaction is your lover looking for?"

"The intimate kind," the old man said. "I should have known better when I took her to my bed. So young and beautiful. And I…well, you see I am not as hearty as the two of you."

"She went willingly to your bed?" Rainier asked, disbelief obvious in his tone.

"Oh, indeed."

"Then you're not so lacking as you believe," Max offered. What an odd conversation to have with a stranger. He kept any discussion regarding amorous liaisons strictly between himself and the amour he was liaisoning with. "Perhaps you should take the coin and buy her something fine. Women adore sparkly things."

"Useless pretties will not please my lover." The man tilted his head and his face gleamed in the moonlight. One eye winked, or perhaps it was a twitch. "Here is what I ask. I wish the two of you to go to her bed tonight and satisfy her. Completely. Over and over."

Rainier's brow rose clear to his hairline. Max recognized the lusty smirk. The man's mind had already been decided.

"I can do little to please her, you see," the man continued. "And she is insatiable. Irregularly so. She requires more than one man to be completely satisfied."

Now Max's brow lifted as high as his partner's.

"She's beautiful, I promise you. You will not regret it should you accept this offer."

"You want us to…" Max couldn't finish the question.

He raked fingers through his wet hair. This was a new one. Never in his years had he been propositioned in such a manner.

"What do we get out of it?"

Max chuffed at Rainier's question. "We're not interested. I'm sure she's beautiful, but we don't have relations with other men's wives."

Max avoided looking at what would be a castigating grimace from Rainier. Other men's wives were fair game—so long as they were dripping in diamonds, jewels, silver and gold in need of removal from their soft skin.

"We'll do it," Rainier said.

"He's drunk," Max shot out. "Pay no attention to him."

"I'd hate to leave a female wanting." Rainier backed into Max and hissed out the side of his mouth, "Why such a quandary?" To the old man he said, "You promise she's beautiful?"

"Stunning."

Rainier pocketed his pistol. "What does it pay?"

The old man tilted his head quizzically.

"Hell," Rainier said. "It should be a holiday making love to a beautiful woman, but if I have to share her—"

"Rainier," Max chided.

"It pays immortality," the old man replied.

Now the truth emerged. The man was touched, a lackwit spinning tales to whomever he could find.

"Not sure I can spend immortality," Max said, barely muffling his chuckle.

"Listen, old man." Rainier was determined not to lose this one. "Feed us and allow us to bathe and warm ourselves by the fire, and then we'll talk about this further."

Rainier looked to Max for approval.

He shrugged, but offered consent. He was tired and hungry, after all, and if the woman was beautiful…? Why the hell not. Pray the man wasn't an idiot, and there really was a warm bed with a wanting female waiting.

Wanting females. He knew the feeling of want. Too painfully.

Max wanted to get this horned monkey out of his system before it overwhelmed him and he became a demon himself. He didn't know if it could manifest within him, but he did know it was getting harder to shuck off the shadow after a dream walk.

And he needed to shadow, because it satisfied those aching needs that required fulfillment.

Every man had a few basic needs. When those needs went unmet, life wasn't worth the trip. Max clung to his sanity with clawed fingers that, at times, seemed greased. Dream walking allowed him to experience those unmet needs, albeit from a distance, as an inactive participant.

He'd take what he could get.

He was exhausted from settling for less than the tangible. Which was why he had to get this thing out of him. Now.

The cat flap set in the lower left corner of the building's door swung upward. A reddish-brown cat bobbed its head through and scampered to the curb. It sat, curling its tail about its feet, and stared across the street at Max.

"Thrill me," Max muttered.

He didn't recognize the breed. It was a lithe, lean feline with extremely short hair and a thin tail. Not that he was an expert, but he had read a few books on cats. What a man won't do when he has time to kill and a penchant for haunting city libraries during the early morning hours.

"Here, kitty, kitty," he called.

Thinking to whistle, he then remembered that

was for dogs. No need to alert the werewolf if it was lurking nearby.

The cat scampered across the street, looking both ways, then darted around the front of the Mustang. Max remained, not wanting to spook the critter.

The cat mounted the hood with a graceful landing. It padded a few steps, sniffing at the still-simmering engine. Wide green eyes beamed at Max from a narrow, small face.

"You decide to hear me out?"

No response, save to sit and wrap its tail about its feet. *Her* feet.

"I mean no disrespect," Max said, "but you've not heard my reasons for wanting you to work with me. You're the only familiar around who has the power to bridge the demon I'm hunting. I'm sorry for calling the wolf your pimp."

The cat hissed, revealing fangs.

"I said I'm sorry. Listen, let's talk inside the car."

He opened his door and got inside. The passenger window was already rolled down. Max watched as Aby sniffed at the hood, taking her time, then leaped out of sight to the roof. The soft pads of her feet tracked across the car. Then the cat landed in the passenger seat.

"Thanks. Uh…" He shrugged off his coat.

"Here's my coat. I'd prefer to hold a conversation with a woman, not a cat. Nothing against cats, I just don't speak the language."

He carefully arranged his coat on the seat before the feline so it formed a cove the cat could sneak inside. Which it did.

Max had seen all variety of shifters change shapes many times. It had ceased to amaze him, and now the process didn't even quicken his heartbeats.

The coat moved and the cat let out a mewl. Bones sounded as if they broke, but Max knew they were lengthening, reshaping and fitting into cartilage. The intense smell of musk filled the car, but as quickly dissipated.

Aby sat beside him, fully formed in female human shape. She tugged his coat over her shoulders and, knees bent to her chest, arranged the heavy leather duster over her legs. Only her head showed. She was naked beneath the bulk of his coat.

"Thank you," he said, and nothing more.

He'd work this one carefully, not press as he had in the gallery. But patience had never been his forte. Nor could he recall the last time he'd sat in the car with a naked woman. Knowing her skin touched his coat thrilled him unexpectedly.

"You comfortable?" he asked.

"Are you insane?"

"I gave you my coat."

"I mean you following me from the show, and then waiting out here. I have rights, you know. And I don't appreciate my privacy being intruded upon."

"Man's got a right to park on a public street."

"I don't like you," she said.

"I'm finding it difficult to warm to you, as well."

"Then leave."

"Can't. I have a demon to summon."

He shifted on the seat to face her, propping one wrist on the steering wheel. She looked so small and vulnerable tucked inside his big coat. "Maybe we should go inside so you can put on some clothes?"

"You're not going in my house. Talk. Quickly. I'm getting chilly."

"It's seventy degrees out, lady—okay."

As he turned to switch off the air-conditioning, Max sensed something. A presence. And the irrefutable scent of brimstone.

"Oh, hell, no."

Aby's nostrils flared. "What the—?"

A blue-eyed demon manifested above the Mustang. Its curled horns speared the air as it twisted its muscled neck and growled.

"Stay out of sight." Max swung out the car door. "Shift back, if you can. You can hide better that way."

Chapter 4

A lash of whip cut the demon's tail from its body, but the creature didn't flinch, instead renewing its attack on Max. It swung out an arm bulging with red, leathery muscle, its razor talons scraping the air.

Max dodged. Talons scraped his back, but didn't cut through his coat. Twisting his wrist and flicking the whip, he delivered another lash. The whip bit the air, cracking near the demon's face.

It stretched its maw into a gruesome grin and growled, "Missed."

Out the corner of his eye, Max saw that the familiar had indeed shifted shape. The cat had jumped to the Mustang roof. "Get out of here!"

The demon fixed its glowing blue eyes on the car. Instead of avoiding the feline, it lunged for it.

The cat meowed and sprang for the street. An obsidian demon claw sliced fur.

Drawing the whip around, Max eyed some loose gravel at the curb. He aimed and the frayed end on the whip flung the gravel toward the demon in a hyperspeed spray. The beast took the attack as if from a propulsion of bullets. It writhed and jerked as pebbles pierced its body.

Max searched for the cat. It was nowhere in sight.

Oozing sulfur smoke from its wounds, the demon growled and spun up into the air. Max appreciated when his opponents put space between them and him. His advantage came when he was allowed room to swing the whip and lash out.

The braided leather snapped, the binding sigils glowing, and severed a limb from the demon. The arm landed the tarmac, spilling out a yellow cloud of sulfur. The injury didn't slow the demon.

"She's not yours," the creature rasped.

"I know that. But why do you? Who are you?" Max dashed sideways to stand before the car, now aware Aby had crawled beneath the vehicle. "Who do you work for?"

"Not your concern."

"And your master wants the familiar?"

"Enough chatter, Highwayman."

A scythe of talon cut through his cotton shirt and opened the flesh on Max's shoulder. He took the cut, rolling over on the ground and coming to a stand. Whip swishing the air, he aimed for the demon.

Why a demon would be interested in a familiar was unknown to him. Familiars weren't the easiest to control. Using her as a means to allow more demons entry into this realm wasn't practical. Spells were required. Spells only performed by a witch—or a highwayman in the know.

A blur of russet fur scampered across the street. The demon lunged, catching the feline by the tail.

Aby twisted onto her back, hissing and baring tiny claws. One swipe pierced the demon's distorted black nose. The creature released the cat and relented, but did not retreat.

It paused long enough to allow Max the perfect swing. One lash sliced the razor-lined leather around the demon's neck. The binding sigils glowed brilliantly, sucking the essence from the creature and disabling it. The beast's blue eyes glowed madly. A tug pulled the razors through its demonic flesh, gristle and bone, and severed the head neatly.

The cat dodged to avoid the fallen head rocking

on the ground. The blue eyeballs melted and dripped from the skull over the red flesh.

A brimstone cloud rose from the demon's head. The body, still standing, began to quake, and it burst, exploding into a yellow mist that settled to a pile of demon dust. The head did the same.

Max did a periphery scan. Just because he saw no car headlights didn't mean someone in the nearby houses wasn't watching. He hated when things went public like this.

He rolled up the whip and hooked it at his hip.

The cat had already fled into the apartment building.

He stalked across the street, but a distant police siren stopped him halfway.

Max backtracked, turned and dashed to his car. Headlights flashing on, he pulled away from the curb and gained half a block before two patrol cars passed him by.

He watched in the rearview mirror as one patrol car stopped right where the demon had been slain. They'd find a pile of dust, which consisted of sulfur, charcoal and some unnamable substance from the demon realm. It was enough to make them curious. And if a neighbor had ID'd Max, getting himself away from the scene of the crime was the smartest course of action.

Talking to Aby would have to wait until

tomorrow. But he was concerned she'd been injured by the demon. The familiar couldn't die before he could use her for his purposes.

He had to figure out a way to see her.

Aby landed on the soft goose-down mattress with two paws, and followed with her rear paws. Safe in her home, she began to shift. Fur retracted through flesh and limbs stretched. It pulled at her muscles, but the shift was never painful, just uncomfortable. Shifting made her appreciate her human form all the more.

She was still shivering when her human limbs had completely formed. But it wasn't from the change.

The demon had had her by the tail. She could have been toast. Never had she had to fight for her safety against one of the dark denizens.

Tugging the bedsheet about her bare shoulders, Aby coiled forward and concentrated on her breathing. Relax. It was a fluke. It was because the Highwayman was out there. Demons must be attracted to that man for some reason.

And what of the Highwayman?

"He isn't so quick with the whip as legend tells. I almost lost a tail."

It wasn't as though she'd been counting on the Highwayman to protect her while she fled for the safety of her home. Stupid fear had pushed her across the street when she would have been better off to remain hidden under the car while the big boys battled.

She'd never seen a demon appear like that before. Out in the open. In a neighborhood. And so close to her home.

What would a demon want from her?

She couldn't conjure a demon without a witch. After her assistant, Jeremy, brought her to climax, a spell was required to complete the bridge to the demonic realm.

Had it been a demon she'd bridged here? Did it have a beef with her?

But that made little sense. Most demons enjoyed wreaking havoc in this realm, and would never purposely return to their own realm, nor would they go near anyone who could make that return happen.

Unless it wanted to bring forth some of its friends?

"No, this is irrational thinking. I should call Severo. He'll know what to do about this."

As soon as she stopped shaking she'd call him. If Severo knew she was in danger he'd insist she move back in with him. Now that she had some semblance of independence, she was going to do her best to keep it.

The flashing red lights from the patrol car drove

away. The police must have decided whatever it was, it wasn't worth further investigation.

Who could have called the cops? Mrs. Meyers was on vacation.

Hopefully, no one had witnessed the altercation, and it had merely been a cop out patrolling.

If Aby knew one thing, it was she existed in this mortal realm only because mortals did not believe in her. The day they found proof of her existence was the day she had to go into hiding.

Max slipped quietly into shadow outside the stucco wall at the rear of Aby's condo. The act of giving way to the demon within was at once exhilarating and also devastating. He was feeding the shadow. A shadow that fought for control, to wander, to peer into dreams and suck life.

Just a few minutes. Then he'd shift back.

The demon shadow was never able to take control, to win over Max's human form for once and for all—it wasn't that strong. Even two centuries had not increased the shadow's strength. Yet every night he allowed it rein, to stroke the night's depths and creep along the edges of dream. It felt so good. An escape from his wide-awake reality.

Once on the roof, he found the access door and slipped between a crack. Gliding around the tight edges, he insinuated his shadow form down the thickly painted cement stairs. Under another door, and out into dim light.

He transformed back to human shape in the shadows of a landing one story up from street level. To his left stood a door, and another to his right.

He glanced right. An old Christmas wreath hung on the door, six months past its prime.

To his left, the door was plain, save for the small cat door in the lower right corner.

He looked up and noticed the wall that stretched from Aby's door through the length of the condo was tiled in brilliant glass tiles. At first glance they formed a mosaic of colors.

But as he looked over the whole, patterns emerged. Among small squares of emerald, crimson and saffron glass, deep indigo tiles formed sigils and warding signs. In fact, he recognized one of them as a powerful demon bind.

"She's got some serious juju going on with those things."

He bent to inspect the cat door. It, too, was decorated with what looked like a black marker drawing of a warding symbol. "Clever."

It made sense. The woman dealt with demons. Best to keep uninvited guests out—like the one that had just attacked outside.

But what about the ones she bridged to this realm? These wards would keep demons out, but would they also keep in those already inside? There must be a release within her apartment.

He hoped Aby kept a tight leash on her subjects. But then, it likely wasn't her choice. The witch she worked with would have the say in what happened after the demon arrived.

"Ian Grim," Max muttered. "Christ. I wonder if she realizes what a bastard that witch is?"

It hadn't seemed apparent to her when he'd mentioned the witch at the charity ball. Could the werewolf have purposefully partnered her with the less-than-savory witch?

Max did not like that wolf.

Tracing a finger over the black symbol on the cat door, he retracted as the ward sizzled a path through his veins and sparked at his wrist. The demon shadow he carried within made crossing wards difficult. He could do it, but not without some hurt.

Standing and scruffing fingers through his hair, Max blew out a breath. He'd come this far, so he had to see it through. But he'd keep his nose high for the scent of brimstone. And if the familiar showed any sign of siccing her demonic cohorts on him, he'd head south in search of that New Orleans familiar she'd mentioned—after taking this one's head.

Knocking, he waited. He didn't hear anything on the other side of the door. She couldn't be sleeping already, only twenty minutes since the cops had driven away. Was she still in cat shape?

The slick little feline had certainly held her own when threatened by the demon. But he couldn't be sure the demon hadn't hurt her when it had nabbed her by the tail.

It's not like you to give a care about anyone.

Again he knocked. "Aby, it's me."

A chain slid against the door on the other side. It opened to reveal a disheveled sweet-faced redhead wrapped in a thick terry-cloth robe. Short spiky hair tufted this way and that on her head. She didn't smile, or hold the door open wider than six inches. Big green eyes mastered her face—and Max.

He leaned one palm against the door frame. *Strictly business, Max. You don't care.* "You okay?"

"How did you get in? The front door is the only entrance."

"I took the roof. Had to be careful the cops didn't see me. So you're fine? That's cool. We need to talk, Aby."

Her eyes lowered, then she looked up through her lashes. A devastating move. Max swallowed a sigh.

"I don't like you. You're my enemy."

"So says your werewolf."

"How many familiars have you killed this year?"

He wasn't going to answer that one. He did it to protect innocent mortals. He'd had the moral argument about killing one to rescue thousands many a time, and the familiar always lost the battle.

"Please leave."

"Can't." He shoved the toe of his boot between the door and the frame. "I have a demon to summon."

"And a familiar to murder?"

"I meant it when I said I've no intention to harm you." Tonight.

"You don't give up, do you?"

"Just a few minutes. I give you my word you'll be safe. I won't take out the one person in this world who can help me. Trust me. Please?"

"Trust?" She chirped out a chuckle.

But then she looked aside and the air about her, once tense and tainted with adrenaline, changed. It softened. Sensitive to the atmosphere, Max's flesh felt the whisper of her presence like a sigh.

She stepped back and held the door open. Seeing her barefoot and not all done up in makeup and sexy clothing, Max realized how tiny she was. How vulnerable. He wanted to wrap his arms about her and whisper that the world was a dangerous place, and he'd protect her.

But he didn't.

Max had given up on wide-eyed innocent

women decades ago. No, make that centuries. The only thing women were good for now was to draw him away from the shadow for a few hours and give him a teasing glimpse of the normal life he'd once had. Sex could be so bittersweet.

"Will you invite me inside?" he asked.

She tilted a curious moue at him. Definitely wide-eyed, but considering her profession, probably not so innocent. Reason number one to avoid getting too friendly with this one. If sex with mortals was bittersweet, sex with a familiar could be downright dangerous. But he was prepared.

Hell, he was impervious.

Realization softened her crooked grimace and she dashed her gaze along the threshold. "You can't enter of your own free will? What are you? A vampire?"

"Nope. But I still require an invitation." He nodded toward the tiled designs on the outer wall. "Your wards are powerful. It feels as though you've had them designed to keep out anything that isn't human."

"Even some humans. The sigils can determine intent and integrity."

"Fancy."

He didn't want anyone gauging his integrity. He'd never considered himself a saint, or even honorable. A man did what he had to do to survive.

"So you can't enter?" She propped a hand at her hip. "Maybe I prefer you right where you are."

"We need to talk, Aby."

"We just did, or we began. A nasty demon interrupted. I take it that's common on your watch?"

"You think the thing apported because of me? The demon was after you."

"Doubt it. You're the demon slayer. I'm sure you've an entire realm of enemies just waiting to take off your head."

"Arguing about who most deserves to be a demon snack will get us nowhere."

Her lashes fluttered and she rubbed her arms. Max could imagine rubbing his palms up her arms, stroking the silken skin, licking her to a frenzy— and bringing himself to the ultimate in frustration.

Yeah, well, it had to be done one way or another.

"I'm tired, and still not completely over what happened," she said. "I'd prefer not doing this right now. Besides, you rub me the wrong way, Highwayman. You want things I'm not willing to give. And you ask without integrity or gratitude."

"I offered to pay."

"Money means little to me. The services I offer are…elite. And personal."

"I realize that."

"And you've given me no reason to believe I'll be safe. Should I decide to accept the offer—which

I won't—I'd need to get to know you. To determine if you are trustworthy. And that's not going to happen tonight."

She pushed the door, and Max withdrew his foot. Yet she called through the warded door, "I eat breakfast every morning at the International down the street. If you're interested in holding a normal conversation that involves being cordial to each other and with no mention of demons, you can catch me around nine. Good night."

She closed the door on him, but then opened it again. "And thank you for saving me from that demon."

He nodded, gave her a smirk. "Tomorrow, then. As long as you're all right?"

"Nothing a good night's sleep won't fix."

"Sleep." He hitched up the corner of his mouth. "Now that's a goal I want to reach."

Chapter 5

Aby sashayed down the sidewalk, head held high and arms swinging. Confident strides slashed her legs in the pencil-tight skirt that emphasized her long gams. She embodied sensual grace.

Her spiked hair caught the sunlight and shimmered ruby. Its color was interesting, much redder than the russet fur she wore while in cat shape.

"Rubies," Max muttered, sorting through his memory. "Haven't taken any of those in a long time. But I sure do like them."

He banged the back of his head against the seat. His need to steal frustrated him more than his need for sex did. It wasn't what he wanted to do.

Somehow, when he'd taken on the demon shadow, it had fixed his penchant for theft into his very being. He couldn't shed the Highwayman if he tried. And he had a stash in the glove compartment to prove it.

Max had parked across the street from the restaurant. He realized it was a place where the business suits held meetings and power-shopping cosmopolitans met for lunch, so out of his comfort zone.

Sure, he'd hung with royalty and dined with dukes and viscounts in his lifetime. But he'd always considered himself the average Joe.

Make that Max.

Stepping from the Mustang, he slid off the heavy coat that had become a sort of safety shield. The leather fended off most demon talons, and, hell, it kept him warm on the nights he camped out behind the wheel.

He tucked the coat and whip in the trunk where he kept a packed duffel, a few books on demonology and engine mechanics, also specially made whips and knives, and his favorite SIG Sauer pistol loaded with salt rounds.

Vacillating on whether or not meeting the familiar was a good idea, he shrugged fingers through his hair. Why was he doing this? He didn't like it when people forced him to do something. He was always the one in control. Aby's request put him under her thumb.

"Screw it." He took off across the street, putting up a hand to stop a car that zoomed from around the corner and honked incessantly. "Keep your drama to yourself, buddy," he muttered, then quickened his steps to land on the curb.

The writing on the restaurant door listed the current wines and the white truffles that had arrived from Italy. Did the elite realize their favorite treats were snuffled up by sows? Max had to smile at that. He'd never tried them, and by the time he could afford to give them a taste, he'd lost all appetite for good.

He resigned himself to play along with whatever the familiar had in mind. If he were going to get this demon out of his system, he had to make nice.

Max strode inside and smiled charmingly at the hostess, whose pearl necklace shimmered in the sunlight.

"Another pitcher of cream, please," Aby directed the waiter as he set her rooibos tea on the table beside a plate with a cheese danish.

She'd seen the Highwayman park across the street. It was as if she'd suddenly garnered her own personal stalker. One who killed familiars professionally.

That made her nervous. Until she remembered she had invited him here.

Turning her wrist, Aby stroked the small tattooed words. My enemy.

The Highwayman wanted something from her. Would he follow her endlessly until he broke her down and she agreed? Could she bargain for her life by giving him what he wanted?

Lately, Ian Grim was the only witch she worked with. Much as she abhorred the witch's flirtations, he was trustworthy. And Severo approved of him.

Grim was booked this weekend for a minor demon bridging. Aby hadn't worked for weeks and was skeptical about this one. It would be her first since moving out of Severo's home. But the appointment was already written in her book with red pen. Jeremy would be by around midnight tomorrow to assist.

She had not bridged demons at Severo's home. Always, she'd gone to this condo for a bridging.

When she'd decided to move out, it made sense to simply make the office her home. Jeremy liked it because it was already soundproof and the tile wards had been put up on the outer walls years ago. Grim found it convenient as well.

Yet what had the Highwayman said about an urban legend? Ian Grim and some werewolf's wife? She had to ask Severo for more details next time she saw him. Legend or not, it was too interesting to let pass.

Aby sipped the tea and forked a luscious piece of danish into her mouth. Divine.

The waiter returned with cream, and he pointed to the setting across the small two-person table. "You're expecting a guest?"

"She is." The Highwayman slid into the opposite chair.

His sudden appearance put her straight on her chair. Max's manly scent crept through the atmosphere and tickled Aby under the chin. She tucked her hands under the table, where she threaded her fingers together. Right there, at the apex of her thighs, Aby was struck by a tingle far more thrilling than cheese danish could ever produce.

"Would you like to order, sir?" The waiter's repulsion at Max's presence was apparent in his flared nostrils.

"Water is fine."

Aby drew her hands up and fingered the silver fork. Warmth flushed her pores, opening her to take in sensations. She'd felt the same way last night when sitting next to him at the bar in that over-air-conditioned ballroom.

Most men put her off with their leering gazes and attempts to touch her. Maximilien Fitzroy, well, what did he do to her?

His hair was tousled, but she liked it, sort of a just-crawled-out-of-bed look. The thought of it made her imagine him naked, dragging himself from between the sheets, his hard pecs slick with perspiration after a night of lovemaking. Nice…and threatening.

She was threatened by a naked man? Not usually. A naked man meant business was in progress. But Max Fitzroy naked?

He quirked a brow. "What?"

She shuffled the lusty images from her mind, which still didn't chase away the warm flush tracing her neck. "You clean up nicely, Highwayman. Where's the whip?"

"In the trunk. And don't flatter me." He shuffled fingers through his hair and from his forehead. "I could use a shower something fierce."

She couldn't smell anything unappealing, and her senses were keener than a human's senses.

"You don't live around here?" she asked, then answered her own question. "I suppose not. I've heard you travel all over. Slaying familiars."

"But mostly demons."

Uh-uh. Damn her curious nature.

"How do you live? Do you travel from town to town in your car? Stay in motels?"

"Hotels and motels are my home. I haven't

checked in yet, wasn't sure how long I'd be staying."

"I see." She speared a forkful of danish to have something to look at instead of his piercing gaze. "You were expecting me to refuse? Or haven't you taken a moment to actually converse with a familiar before?"

"Something like that. So about the job—"

"We're not going to talk business, Highwayman. Remember? I invited you to breakfast to get to know you better."

His wince made her bite away a grin. If he wanted her to trust him, he was going to have to play by her rules. Knowing she held the upper hand lifted her courage measurably.

"So tell me things, Max. Can I call you Max? You've been around a while?"

"I told you, two hundred fifty years."

"Right. Where are you from?"

"Originally? France."

"France? The entire country?" She bit into the danish. The man was no conversationalist. She suspected if she were going to learn anything about him, it would have to be wrenched out.

"Blois."

"Ah. Didn't one of Dumas's musketeers live in Blois?"

"The Comte de la Fère. Not sure if the real man

actually lived there, but the character returned there after serving the musketeers. You're familiar with France?"

"Never been out of the States. But I like Dumas. Adventure stories are a favorite pastime of mine. I can't imagine what it must be like to live such adventures. I believe Dumas based a lot of his stories on his own life."

"He had a way of enhancing the truth and making details larger than life. I knew him."

"Really? How fascinating. Have you known many celebrities?"

He took a swig of water the waiter had dropped off. A shrug was all he offered.

He was burning to get what he wanted, she could tell. But the fact that he'd come this far and was going along with her game gave him points. And he was cute, so that helped, despite him being a killer.

"So what are you, Max? Immortal?"

"Yes."

"Not human? Because my wards…"

"Human, but infected with…" He looked aside, scanning the dining room, seeing dozens of round tables draped in white linens, with shining silverware and fresh-cut white roses. It was early; the place wouldn't be packed with business lunchers for another hour. "This isn't a conversation I want to have in public."

"I agree. We'll stick to the nonparanormal stuff. Though, I've never liked that term, *paranormal*."

"Because it's a mortal term. You're normal, and mortals are the strange ones, yes?"

She answered with a smiling, "Yes."

She took another bite of danish, then tilted the fork toward him. "Want some?"

"Even if I did want a taste, I couldn't."

"Why?"

"Aby, for two hundred fifty years I haven't been able to eat, sleep or, well, other things."

"Really? I can't imagine."

"Now can you understand my urgent need to get this demon off my back?"

"Maybe. I don't understand how you can watch me eat. Doesn't it make you curious? Hungry? Would you get sick if you did eat? What do you mean by 'other things'?"

"Yes to being sick from it. No to hunger. As for curiosity, you tell me." He propped his elbows on the table. His deep blue eyes looked tired, perhaps even lost. "What does that danish taste like?"

She examined the bite speared upon the silver fork. "You never ate a pastry before you were unable?"

"When I was growing up, pastries were a luxury, only available to the aristocrats. I've never had one."

"That's so incredible."

Turning her fork, she displayed the soft, oozing cheese on the flaky slivers of pastry. "It's sweet and decadent." She took another bite. "Rich, like velvet and fine parchment."

"Parchment? Doesn't sound like something I want to eat."

"Melt-in-your-mouth-flaky stuff. Trust me, Max, you want to taste this." She popped the rest of the wedge into her mouth. "You're missing something wonderful."

He leaned forward, hands tucked under the table, and whispered, "If I knew you better, I'd kiss you so I could taste it. That's the only way I can taste food."

Aby sat back, bits of danish still lying on her tongue. A kiss? The suggestion startled her. And excited her.

But she knew better.

"Kisses are so personal."

"That they are."

He sat back, drawing with him the sensual energy that had seemed to coil about her shoulders in a welcoming hug. As his heat receded, goose bumps arose on her flesh.

"Sorry," he offered. "That was forward. So, can I ask you some questions?"

"Give it a try."

"Are you really retired?"

She sighed.

"Right, not discussing business. Let's try this one. That man who's standing outside the front window, talking to another man—should I be leaving quickly?"

Aby spied Severo outside, talking to a client whose face she recognized but whose name she'd forgotten. She'd forgotten, too, that today was one of her and Severo's usual twice-a-week meetings.

"He usually doesn't come inside. This is a vegetarian restaurant and he says if they don't serve red meat, then he doesn't want to know. But maybe you should leave."

"Tell me something first. Is he your boyfriend?"

"No."

"Why doesn't that come out of your mouth like you mean it? Never mind. I'm being too personal again." He stood and sucked down another swig of water. "Can we have the uncomfortable conversation later at your house?"

She was all for continuing the conversation. Sharing time with this intriguing man. Finding out what other things he'd skillfully avoided telling her about.

But alone together at her home? Aby's reply came out before her mind could weigh the cons against the benefits. "Sure."

"Will I get past the wards?"

"We'll see."

"What about the werewolf?"

"He won't be there. Promise."

That seemed to appease him.

Aby watched him swagger toward the back door, and really, it was a swagger. He walked like a man who didn't care, a man relaxed within his skin.

She dug in her purse for a twenty, left it for the waiter, then walked out the front.

Severo greeted her with a kiss on the cheek. Aby slid into his embrace as if slipping on a beloved sweater. He smelled masculine and safe, like meadows and dirt. She had developed an intense connection to him, and when she was away from him for more than a few days, she usually found herself teary-eyed at his absence.

"How was breakfast?"

"Delicious, as usual." Today's came with the added bonus of a handsome and mysterious man to savor. "What's up with you today?"

"I'm going out of town for the weekend. Wanted to touch base with you and see if you'll be all right."

"Sev, I'm a big girl. You know I'll be fine." Would she be? Of course. A weekend was but two days.

"I worry about you."

"You shouldn't. How will I learn to fly if you're still tugging on the reins?"

"You wound me, sweetness."

"Sorry." She turned in his embrace and put her head upon his shoulder. It felt so right here in his embrace, so safe. But not exciting like the way she felt with Max. "I'll be fine."

Unless the demon that had attacked last night really was after her. She didn't want to worry Severo, and she did need some distance between them. She could do this independence thing. Heck, she could go for an adventure like those in Dumas's stories.

"Give me a call on Saturday if you like."

"I will. You haven't heard more from that highwayman?"

She tucked her head against the warm fibers of his shirt. "No."

He tilted up her chin. Severo's gaze never failed to touch her core, reading her mind even before she formed the thoughts herself. "Why are you lying, Aby?"

He knew her so well. His deep brown eyes sought her truths, and Aby found she could never look at him and keep a lie for long.

He turned her wrist so the tattooed words were right before her eyes. "I had you do this for a purpose. This is your life, Aby. There are few things of great import, but avoiding that man is one of them."

"I know, I know!"

"And what does it say on the bottom line there?" He tapped her wrist.

Tiny words read: My enemy: the Highwayman.

"I did see him again." She spoke quickly to stifle Severo's huffing anger. "But I didn't talk to him long. He won't bother me. He understands now that I'm…retired."

"You told him you were retired? Why the lie? Why not tell him you're not interested?"

Severo would never understand her need to retire, to just…be. To discover herself and maybe find romance, a real relationship with a man who could love her without needing to bring demons to this world. It could happen. She'd never give up hope.

"Maybe if he thinks I'm retired he won't feel compelled to kill me."

"I looked into his eyes, Aby." His grip on her intensified. "That man is a murderer. Hell, I won't leave if he's still in town."

"I'm sure he's gone by now."

"I can't smell him. I couldn't get a scent off him. So strange."

Severo could scent a candy bar in the middle of the Sahara desert. His wolf senses were very acute.

"He's gone, Sev. Go and do whatever you have to do, and don't worry about me. I have the appointment with Grim this weekend, and I think I'll go paint shopping next week. I want to redo the bathroom. I'm going to be fine."

He cupped her hand and kissed the knuckles. "Very well. But I leave town with great reluctance. Something's up with you. I don't know what it is, but I'm crushed you won't tell me about it."

"I'm trying on independence and liking it." She stroked a hand over his beard-stubbled cheek and through his long brown hair. "Love you."

"Love you, too." He kissed her at the corner of her mouth, where he usually did, but this time it felt intrusive, almost as if he was trying to claim her.

Why, she wondered, did it suddenly bother her?

Chapter 6

This time when Aby opened the door, she stepped aside, as if to allow him entry. Max took that as a good sign.

He conjured his best you-can-trust-me smile.

Aby took a few moments to ascertain said trustworthiness, drawing her gaze from his smile to his shoulders and then down to his cowboy boots. It felt awkward. He was accustomed to a blatant dressing-down from women, but never before like this. This was personal.

Of course, what did he expect from this woman? Her job did involve sex. And lots of it. She must be comfortable with her sexuality and men.

What the hell am I getting myself into?

Could he accomplish task number two, then deliberately move onto number three?

"What's the magic word?" she asked, green eyes gleaming.

"Abracadabra?"

"In some magics, yes. But not for entrance into my home, Highwayman."

"All right, let's try 'please.'"

She beamed. "You're very talented. Got that one on the second try. I grant you permission to cross into my home."

He stepped forward across the threshold, yet felt the wards resist. The magical protections sought the shadow within him. They tugged at his flesh, as if the exodermis were being shifted over his musculature.

"That hurt, didn't it?"

Hell, yes, it hurt like a mother. He managed a gruff affirmative noise.

"So what is it that keeps you out of my home?" she asked, gesturing him to sit on the Victorian-style sofa heaped with an assortment of crazy-colored pillows. "Have you a curse? Picked up some bad mojo over the centuries?"

Max shook his head as she offered him a glass of some pink stuff, and seated himself on the sofa. He shoved aside the pillows, scattering some on the floor. All this girlie stuff made him uncomfortable.

"The shadow of a deprivation demon lives inside me."

He noticed the elaborate scratching post-cum-adventure climber up against the wall. It took up half the wall. Hmm...

"That's right, you mentioned no sleep or food. I'd definitely call that deprived." She sat on the opposite end of the sofa, tucked among the shaggy pillows as she sipped the pink drink. It smelled sugary yet tart. "How'd that happen?"

He leaned forward, resting his elbows on his knees in a deliberate position that made it harder to look at her. She wore a flimsy blue shirt designed to draw attention to her nipples poking out eagerly. Hip-hugging white pants stopped mid-calf to reveal slender calves and bare feet. She looked summery and sexy.

And that red hair emphasized her shapely jaw and drew all eyes to her long neck. Heaven help him.

He was a man, not a machine.

Max shoved a hand in his coat pocket and fingered the strand of pearls as if it were a rosary. A focus away from the more alluring jewel that sat next to him.

"You want the whole sordid story?" he asked her.

"I need it," she said. "I won't agree to anything until I know you up, down, backward and forward.

You think you can get me by myself to bridge the demon? That's going to require trust on my part. I don't let any man work with me."

"You don't?"

"No, I've an assistant who's worked with me for years. For lives, in fact. Jeremy Stokes. I never do a job without him."

"Interesting."

Lives? The man had worked with Aby during a life previous to the one she now lived? He wondered how that worked, since familiars didn't retain memory from one life to the next.

"So this Jeremy, he…" How to ask? He was curious but he didn't want to offend her when he needed her to trust him. "You two…"

"Jeremy and I have sex until I'm sated. That's how it works for a familiar. We have to be relaxed and completely open."

"Yes, I…I know."

Yet it had been so long. The intangible mockery of satiation he experienced during dream walking was nothing compared to the real thing. Or so he recalled.

"And since you're wondering, I'll give you the whole setup. The witch waits in a room on the first floor. When I'm ready, Jeremy gives the witch a call, and he comes in to perform the summoning. It's all very businesslike. It's not sexy, as you might believe."

"But having sex until you're sated. That isn't even a little sexy?"

"It's satisfying, but, no, not sexy. I look at sex differently than most. I'm uncomfortable talking about it, if you must know."

"I apologize. It's none of my concern."

Unless she agreed to help him. Then he'd have to explain how he viewed sex, which was also completely different than anyone else. There wasn't a man alive who'd trade positions with him. Not for all the money in the world.

His fingers worked fastidiously at the pearls. Still, it was difficult to focus when the soft hiss of fabric across Aby's bare legs tempted his tormented desires.

"What's with that thing?" He nodded toward the huge pet climber against the wall. It was carpeted and featured climbing poles, hiding nooks and dangly toys.

"It's mine."

"Yours? So, no pets?"

"No, Highwayman, no pets. Severo gave it to me after I refused a plant for my moving-in gift. Much as I adore nature, I have no earthly idea what to do with a plant. I'm not big on, well…taking care of things."

"You're used to being taken care of."

"Yes, I am. So talk to me, Max. Who are you? What is inside you? And why now, after so long, do you suddenly need to chase this demon out of you?"

"It's not a complete demon, just its shadow. It…tries to control me whenever I give it rein."

"Then why do so?"

"Because I need the release. The shadow stalks dreams, Aby. What physical pleasures I can't enjoy in my life? I can experience vicariously through the dream walk."

He expected to find horror in her gaze. But then he presumed one didn't hang with a werewolf and summon demons without learning all about the paranormal realm.

"So if someone dreams about eating?" she prompted.

"I can taste it, but it's an intangible taste. Never fulfilling."

"That's so sad. How did you get the shadow in you?"

"It all started on a cold winter's night in seventeen fifty-eight."

"I love a good tale."

"Yeah?"

He'd not repeated this story for ages. But now, with little time to spare as he raced against the madness of deprivation, he decided it was time to dredge out the details once again.

"I used to ride the high roads with my partner,

Rainier Deloche. We were young, arrogant and thought the world owed us whatever we could rip from its fists."

"You were mortal?"

"Yes. Until we agreed to a ridiculous bargain."

"Which was?"

"A stranger wagered my partner and I that together we couldn't bring a gorgeous woman to complete and utter satiation by having sex with her all night long."

"I'm guessing the two of you took that as some kind of challenge to your manhood?"

"You bet we did."

Paris—1758

The woman was indeed beautiful, as the old man had promised. Max gazed into her soft blue eyes, quite sure he was falling in love. Or rather, stumbling into love, for the whole situation still felt awkward.

Delicate curls of palest hair framed her small but intense eyes. A pursed mouth so red he thought it would taste of springtime berries beckoned.

"Nice," Rainier whispered. He removed his sodden frock coat and dropped it to the floor without regard. The rank odor from the aqueduct still clung to it. "Your husband tell you what we're here for?"

"Husband?" The woman sat upon an overwide

trundle bed, highly uncommon for the underclass that lived on the left bank of the Seine. "Yes, of course, my husband. He's brought me two handsome men to ensure my night is blissful. You both are up to the challenge?"

The challenge, Max thought with a smirk.

Was she one of those women who couldn't climax no matter the gyrations and positioning a man used? He'd met a few of those in his lifetime. Wasn't his responsibility to make sure they came. Sex was for pleasure, and he was here to get what he could.

"Are *you* up for the challenge?" Rainier tugged free the string at the top of his shirt and shucked the loose Holland white over his head. He was lean and his muscles taut. The hard life did that to a man, as Max's own body could attest.

Max tugged at the jabot wrapped snugly around his neck, fumbling with the knot, not quite at ease. It wasn't as though he and Rainier had never shared close quarters while making love to two different women. Taverns and brothels left little for privacy, nor did they require it.

But they'd never before *shared* a woman.

"Shall we take turns?" he asked, and felt an utter lackwit for asking. "I mean, how would you like to do this, madame?"

She crooked a finger at them. Rainier crawled

onto the bed, always eager when invited. Max, wanting to know the flavor of that rosebud mouth, joined him.

He kissed the woman and spread a hand over her soft, lush hair. Her moan stoked his desire, and he gave little notice as Rainier moved to stroke her belly and lick at her breasts. They'd find a rhythm. One way or another.

Hours passed and the log in the hearth had been reduced to embers. The woman had climaxed many times, as had Rainier and Max. Each time she came, she cried out softly, as if a lost, mewling kitten.

As if holding back.

Now, sprawled in the chair before the fire, naked, his limbs stretched out, Max could barely summon his legs to move him onto the bed. He was sated. And he suspected Rainier was, too, because currently, the man couldn't find the fast rhythm the woman insisted he achieve.

If she'd stop holding back and simply succumb to the intensity of climax, perhaps she would tire, too.

The old man had been right. This woman was impossible to sate. But their very manhood depended on accomplishing the task set to them.

Hell, Max didn't require payment now. He just wanted the bragging rights.

Not that either he or Rainier would brag about this one. Because truthfully, they should have sent this woman to oblivion hours ago. And it wasn't as though she couldn't come. She came easily, and for a long time, yet so softly. But then after each climax, cheeks blushed and sweat beading her breasts, she'd merely sigh and ask for more.

More?

Max tilted his head toward the door, wondering how soon before morning. This was definitely the celebration swive he'd been thinking about. Only, if he had to rise and attend the woman one more time, he felt sure he'd collapse.

Maybe they were going about this all wrong. Both he and Rainier had climaxed many times. If they wanted the woman to achieve satiation, surely they had to stop concentrating on their own pleasure and focus solely on hers.

He nodded, inwardly chiding himself for not realizing this earlier.

Soft, moaning chirps clued Max she was going to climax again. Rainier gave it his all. Cheers to the fellow for his efforts. At least it allowed Max a short rest.

The woman, her voice hoarse, gave it up.

Rainier rolled to his stomach and dropped an arm over the bed's edge. Exhausted. There was possibly something to having too much of a good time. Hell, this might put Max off sex for a week.

Maybe.

Probably not.

"Yes," the woman moaned. "Ready!"

Now that was a different plead.

Max lifted his head as the door swung open and the old man swept inside. A black wool cape covered his head, shoulders and torso. He wielded a book and lifted a hand high as he mounted the end of the bed and leaned over the woman.

Rainier was half-asleep and lolled there, unmindful of the strange turn in events.

"I invocate and conjure you," the old man began, but then his language changed. Must be Latin, for Max had heard the intonations in church before, although he didn't understand the language.

Damn, he was too tired. He swung a look at the heap of clothing on the floor. The effort of dressing seemed monumental.

With an exhausted slur, he asked, "What are you doing?"

The old man continued, oblivious of him and Rainier.

On the bed, the woman's back arched, her shoulders pressing deep into the rumpled sheets. Her fingers clenched the feather mattress and then—

Well, then it got strange.

Some kind of yellow dust exploded out from every pore on the woman's body. It stank worse than the aqueducts. It formed above her, seeming to cloud and then take a shape.

Max's jaw dropped. This was not normal. Not that making love to a woman all night long in tandem was any closer to normal, but still, this was…wrong.

He eyed his clothing. Rainier remained oblivious.

The old man jumped from the bed and shouted grandly, "I commandeth thee!"

The woman collapsed.

The yellow cloud coalesced to something like a human shape, yet not like at all. Arms jutted out and legs formed—legs ending in hooves not feet. Horns coiled at the side of the black head.

Rainier sat up, saw the figment and scrambled over to Max. "What the hell?"

Both men stared with gaping mouths as the thing lunged toward them.

Steeling himself for impact, he watched as it instead dispersed into a yellow cloud. The foul-smelling dust permeated Max's body. It moved through him, squeezing through his rib bones and crushing his heart as if solid and possessed of fingers. It put him stiffly upon the chair, his arms and legs slashing out.

It was as if whatever had gotten inside struggled to become mired in his organs and ribs. As it pummeled him from the inside out, he shouted in agony and clawed the chair arm.

And then, it exited behind him, sucking at his insides till he thought surely his organs would be lying on the floor around him.

He was aware the same thing happened to Rainier for the man's arms outstretched and his grimace tightened as he fought the inner torment.

Max gulped air and dropped to the floor on hands and knees, unsure if he'd been wounded or if part of him had been ripped out through his back.

Rainier stumbled and collided with the fieldstone wall.

The yellow cloud swept from the room with the old man in pursuit.

"What happened?" Bile rose in Max's throat. His legs shook, as did his hands.

Foremost, he needed to get out of here.

He gripped his breeches and pulled them on. Not bothering with his shirt, he tucked it in the front at his waistband and flung his greatcoat over his shoulders. Stuffing his feet into his floppy leather boots, he wobbled, catching himself against the door.

Rainier followed suit. "That was not part of the bargain. What was that thing?"

"I don't know." Max glanced toward the bed, but the woman wasn't there. Instead, a white cat sat coiled on the wrinkled bedclothes.

"Where'd she go?" Rainier searched the room, his head dodging frantically. "I don't remember that cat being in here. Damn, my chest. Did it feel like that thing moved through you?"

"Yes."

"What *was* that thing?"

"I don't think we want to know. Let's get the hell out of here."

Rainier followed Max from the inn, and into the bright morning light. It had snowed while they'd been slaking their lusts. The ground was thick with white flakes.

"Split up," Max muttered, still not sure what he'd just witnessed and unwilling to think on it right now. He switched to survival mode, which meant securing a safe hiding place. "Regroup in a week at Notre Dame."

"Sure. If whatever the hell went through us doesn't kill us first."

Max shoved a hand in his coat pocket. It was bare of coin. Had the old man robbed him? No, likely the gold had spilled out onto the floor. He had no desire to reclaim it. Yet at the bottom of the pocket, he found the damaged silver *demi-écu* the musket ball had gone through.

"A week, then. Take care, Deloche."

But Rainier was already hoofing it down the cobbled street.

Chapter 7

"You had no idea what happened to you?" Aby asked.

Max took out the damaged silver coin he'd carried for centuries and tossed it in the air, catching it smartly. Unfortunately, the coin had never put off his desire to acquire more valuables.

He tucked it away without showing Aby.

She snuggled closer to him, curling her hands over the back of the couch and propping her chin on it. She smelled like cherry lemonade and she looked better than any sparkly gemstone Max had ever tucked into his pocket.

Sitting so close to her—a familiar—brought up

all sorts of strange feelings. Memories that mirrored his tale.

He hadn't known what the woman had been that night he and Rainier had made love with her. But since learning her truth, he'd stalked familiars as if they carried the plague and he was the cleansing fire.

"I'd never encountered the paranormal before then," he said. "You can imagine what a trip it was to see a demon emerge from the woman's chest like that."

"It doesn't hurt," she commented, her stare fixed on his mouth.

Max looked aside, uncomfortable with her attention. Was this wrong? Perhaps he shouldn't be making friends with the familiar he required to wrangle the demon.

And when that task was complete? He intended to kill her so she could not bring another demon into this realm.

Their relationship should remain business, as she'd already said it should.

Yet, everything about Aby attracted him. Her green eyes, her eager openness. The slither of satin across her skin. The admittance she didn't know how to take care of a plant. Hell, she was like him, walking this world, focused on one goal. The rest of the surrounding world? Forget trying to fit in.

He leaned forward to wrest his eyes from her, but

her scent infused him. She smelled great. Her kiss would taste like cherry lemonade. He liked to know the taste of things. It was small reward for a life without sustenance.

The sustenance Aby offered with her sensual body would serve as an anchor. Women always did. They pulled him away from the shadow, the madness, and secured him in the real, if only for the few hours he shared with them.

"What kind of demon was it? Or is it? The one inside you."

"I didn't know it was a demon then. I didn't find out until a week later why I hadn't been able to eat or sleep for days…"

Paris—1758

Notre Dame loomed before Maximilien. He'd been inside the cathedral only once, when he was a boy and had raced inside to escape pursuit from a nasty duke. He knew what the rich did when they caught young orphan boys. The boys were never seen again.

That night he'd hidden in the cathedral until darkness had frightened him out into the nave where a few candles burned. He'd wandered across the dais, counting stone tiles with each step. How could a mortal man create something so wondrous?

He wanted to create buildings such as this when he grew up. It would be a fine occupation for a man.

A priest had interrupted his study of the night-darkened windows. Max scrambled from his grip as the old man had tried to wrangle him, and escaped again.

As he looked back now, the priest would not have harmed him. But he had never taken chances. Only lately had he and Rainier been pushing their luck. They'd become sloppy, careless. And, yes, greedy.

"Should have taken up building after all," he muttered.

He trundled across the bridge toward the ancient stone cathedral, drawn to the holy. Perhaps connection with sacred grounds would lift him from the misery that had consumed him since that night with the insatiable woman.

Since then, he hadn't been able to keep food down. Wine and beer was all he could temper, yet in small amounts. Oddly, he didn't feel hungry, only he kept attempting to eat because he thought he should. Man could not survive without food, and yet, he did.

And his nights had been restless. Certainly he'd gotten less than six hours of sleep in the se'nnight since he'd last seen Rainier. How was that possible? He sat awake at night in the small room he'd rented over an inn, listening to lovers couple and rats skitter overhead in the rafters.

How surreal it was to have the world intrude on his brain like that. There was nothing to do but listen when the sleep would not come.

Twilight hugged the cathedral in an eerie gray clasp. Congregants milled on the tiled parvis before the cathedral's massive doors. Vespers must have ended.

Max ducked his head and tugged the coat collar to his ears. He wore a mask when riding the high roads, and his need for caution had returned.

He brushed past a pair of chattering females and spied a petite woman with hair white as the moon.

Dashing to the familiar female, he gripped her by the shoulder. "Are you well?"

She tugged roughly from him, but did not run away. Perhaps her husband was close by. Shouldn't matter if she talked to Max now after all they'd been through. He knew her intimately.

"What happened that night?" he asked. "I need to understand."

She looked like a moondrop, blue eyes lost in her pale complexion. Small and thin, she didn't wear fine clothing; in fact, her skirts were shabby and she wore but wooden sabots.

With a sigh, she led him away from the crowd near a mound of snow pushed from the parvis.

"I did not think to ever see you again." She

scanned the crowd, then whispered, "Have you been well since then?"

"Well?" With a smirk, Max scanned the river's opposite bank. It was hard to look her in the eye. He knew this woman's body in ways perhaps her husband did not. But he did want answers.

"Depends on how you define well. Food makes me sick. And while I haven't slept more than a few hours, I'm not tired. Mayhap I've gone beyond exhaustion. I don't know if you'd call that well."

"The summoning did not go as planned."

"Summoning? There was a—a thing in that room. And it touched me. I cannot know for sure, but I believe it—it entered me somehow."

"It moved through you." Head bowed, she toed a wet stone. "We hadn't anticipated that would happen."

"But you expected something to appear out of you?"

She took him by the arm and led him toward the cool shadows near the church.

"I'll say this once, and then I'm walking away from you and you will not pursue me. Ever. Do you understand?"

"Sure."

If it would get him answers, he'd agree. This woman obviously didn't know it wasn't wise to ask a thief to promise anything.

"What moved through you was a demon."

"A demon? You jest."

"I am not taken to jesting."

"I am not taken to believing lies."

"But you would lie with a complete stranger to master a challenge to your manhood."

He huffed out a breath.

"Now listen," she admonished, "and do not interrupt. It was a demon. I am a familiar. I am a bridge for demons to this realm. I need to be sexually sated to do so. We hadn't anticipated Gandras would move through you and your partner. I'm sorry for that. The demon dissipated soon after—we were unable to control it. It's gone from this realm."

"You wanted to control a demon? What kind of black magic—?"

To speak of it put up the bile in Max's throat. This could not be. And he was an unknowing participant in the occult ritual?

"We thought the demon a loss, but had no idea it had actually entered the two of you. I'm going to guess the demon's shadow must have been left behind, inside you. Which has its benefits and disadvantages."

"Not eating being a disadvantage?"

"Perhaps, but a benefit is immortality. Are you not pleased?"

"Immortality? A demon shadow?"

She was touched. Max had actually had sex with an insane woman, and his partner had joined in. Why hadn't he listened to his instincts that night when the old man had talked of immortality?

"It is your new truth," she said. With a lift onto her tiptoes, she then kissed him on the cheek. "Accept it."

When she turned to walk away, Max caught her by the sleeve. She tugged but he held firm, though he could feel the stitches at her shoulders give way. He didn't know what to say. A demon had moved through him and now he was immortal?

"Where's Rainier?" he asked.

"I don't know where your friend is. But if you see him, you'll want to give him the same information I gave you. Release me."

And he did, because nothing made sense right now. And to hold on to insanity felt wrong, like insects crawling up his arm and he could not shake them away.

Max wandered to the bridge and looked down into the Seine. Chunks of frozen snow floated by like miniature icebergs. He waited for an hour. Rainier didn't show. Nor did he show the next day or the next.

"Immortal," Max said on the fourth day as he waited one last time for his partner in decadence and debauchery. "Impossible."

* * *

Aby gazed out the patio door. She'd listened intently as Max related his tale. Initially he'd come off as a sex-crazed jerk. Two guys and one woman?

What was it with men and their need to prove their manhood? Many times she'd witnessed Severo puffing out his chest and shoulders as he moved before her to fend off another man's approach. The display was silly.

"It's a deprivation demon," Max said from the couch. "Gandras is the name I was given, but I've never found it in lore or mythology. I'm sure once loosed it would create havoc. Trapped inside me, and only half the demon it should be, it can but dream walk."

"Dream walk?"

"I—*it*—likes to peer into people's dreams. When I shadow."

"That's interesting. And since you can't dream you allow it?"

"Yes." He hung his head. "Sometimes I like it. I need it, Aby. I've been denied the basic pleasures of life. Man can't remain sane without them."

"You said you could taste things in your dreams. It must be wondrous to see the dreams of others."

"At times. I like it when children dream of flying. They soar so high," he said on a whisper of wonder.

Aby hugged her arms across her chest. The reverence in his tone touched her. He wasn't the murderous slayer Severo had warned her about. This man suffered, and he was trying to make his way in the world.

"I won't tell you about the nightmares."

"It must be difficult," she said. "But can you stop looking at the dreams if they are bad?"

"The shadow doesn't discern between good and evil. It likes to observe them all."

"And what of the sexy dreams?"

His teasing wink struck her deeply. "Those are the ones I like to experience the most."

"A voyeur, eh?"

"Aby." He sighed and still could not meet her eye.

"What?"

"Never mind. It's just the sleep and food I'm deprived. I figure it's some kind of mortal sin thing. I was once gluttonous, and ate without care and wasted much. I lived for adventure and danger, not bothering for rest, hence the sleep."

The man's eyes tracked to the cat climber. Why did that disturb him so much? He'd seen her in cat shape once already.

"So now you know the whole bloody tale. I was in the wrong place at the wrong time. But now I'm in the right place. And I've done what you've asked.

You're getting to know all my dark secrets. So I need an answer."

Max got up and crossed to the kitchen counter. "Either tell me you'll do the job and I'll book an appointment, or whatever it is you do, or tell me you're not interested, and I'll be on my way."

"If I refused to do the job, would you kill me?"

He bowed his head. The passing seconds were far too long for Aby's comfort. "You would!"

"Aby."

"I need to know, Max. Why should I trust you?"

"You shouldn't, all right? You know what the wolf told you. That's the way it has to be. Except—"

He ended his heated confession by stalking into the kitchen and turning on the faucet. Cupping his hands under the water, he then splashed his face.

Clasping a hand to her chest, Aby swallowed a scream. The wolf had told her the Highwayman killed familiars—and Max hadn't denied that. Rather, he'd implied it was so.

Where was the phone? Could she call for help before he reached her?

"Except." He slammed a fist on the faucet, shutting off the water. "I'm not going to kill you because you're too precious. You're like a jewel I want to steal from that damned wolf and keep for myself."

"What kind of lie is that? I'm not stupid, Max."

"It's not a lie." He shook his head, dispersing water. "At least I don't think it is."

"Please leave," she said.

"Not until we work things out. Far as I know, Gandras wasn't able to maintain corporeality on this realm without its shadow. It must have dissipated soon after the summoning. I have the summoning spell in my brain. I just need a conduit."

"And you never thought to summon it to get the shadow from you until recently?"

He cocked his head. The look he stabbed her with could have frozen water. "I've thought of it every day since. I've tried many a time with witches, wizards, magicians."

"But never with the use of a familiar?"

"They've always been enemies."

Aby turned her wrist inward and tucked it against her stomach. She'd had the truth tattooed on her wrist, and still, she'd thought to mistrust it. Fool.

"I'm not sorry for the things I've done, Aby, but I do know they could have been handled differently."

"How so? Perhaps you would have said sorry before killing all those familiars?"

"Listen, I know there's nothing I can say that will make me honorable or halfway likeable in your mind. And, yeah, I think I can actually get beyond the need to kill another familiar if you'll agree to help me. I mean, hell, if you do help me, then your reward should be life."

"Magnanimous of you."

He clutched a fist near his head, but then released it. Frustration hummed from his being. Aby felt the heaviness of it.

"I've tolerated this curse for so long," he said, walking over to her. "But I'm tired of it, Aby. I want to be mortal. I want to sleep. I want to eat. I want to…" He fisted the air. "I don't want to be a slave to the shadow, because if I forget about it one night the next day my mind will be chaos. And if centuries of witches, warlocks and soothsayers weren't able to dredge this bastard out of me, then it's time I gave familiars a try. Do you…do you think it possible?"

Aby didn't know for sure if it was possible. Obviously this was one tough demon. "Maybe."

On the other hand, it had originally been summoned with the assistance of a familiar, so there was no reason why that couldn't happen again.

She had mastered her bridging techniques and was considered one of the best familiars in the country. There weren't a lot of familiars around, so she figured the ranking wasn't so hard to come by. Also, her Abyssinian breed placed her top of the charts. She'd like to see a Persian go an all-nighter and then not freak out over the sudden appearance of a demon. Ha!

Normally she left the conjuring details to the witches. She couldn't summon a demon on her own; that required a spell. She was just the catalyst. But any demon could be contacted if you had its name. And if Max wanted to do this on his own…

"You know the summoning spell?"

"I've studied it for decades. I'm prepared."

"Why don't you want to involve another?" she asked.

"You mean bridging the demon via the spell, or the having sex part?"

"Both. I work with Jeremy. I'm not sure I can do it with a stranger. You're asking quite a lot, Max."

"I know. But trust me, I don't want to do this to get into your pants. Aby, this is very personal for me."

"I'm beginning to understand that. But…" It would be personal for her, too.

Despite his penchant for killing familiars, she was beginning to warm to Max, to notice things about him. Like the way his hair was always tousled and that made her want to run her fingers through it. Or the dimple in his left cheek that wasn't obvious and only peeked out on occasion.

He was sexy. And she could entirely imagine having sex with him. Real sex.

But then, Aby wasn't sure what real sex was.

And why did she keep overlooking the part where he wanted to kill her?

"So what life are you on?" he asked softly. He pointed to her hand, loosely fisted at her thigh. "Can I take a look?"

Aby tugged down her sleeve and wrapped her fingers about her left wrist.

"Are you right-handed?" he asked.

"Yes."

"Let me see the left."

He knew the past was imprinted on a person's less dominant hand. Hell, what was wrong with showing him? They already knew exactly what they were to each other.

Opening her palm, she displayed it for him.

Max leaned in and drew his finger along the curved lifelines that arced at the base of her thumb. That he knew how to read a familiar's lives impressed her. Of course, he would know everything about her species.

Breathing in the scent of him, Aby closed her eyes. Danger had never smelled so seductive.

"One, two, three," he said as he traced the lines. "Three lives behind you."

"Very good. I'm on my fourth."

The warmth of his touch made her so aware he was a man. A man who could touch her, do things to her, kiss her.

Seeming to realize the awkward silence, Max let go of her hand. "Do you remember anything from your past lives?"

"Nope. I came to this life sometime during my late teens, or so that's what Severo guesses. Eleven years into this one, and determined to make it the longest ever by avoiding the big bads as much as possible. Thus the retirement."

"Demons being the big bads? I would think it's something you're accustomed to."

"One never gets accustomed to bridging demons into this realm. Or all the sex."

Now she was telling him entirely too much. Yet she felt comfortable talking to him, as if he understood her, and he wasn't going to impose rules on her, as Severo did, or try to flirt, as Ian did. His distance made him dangerously attractive.

"Can I look at the tattoo?"

She flashed her gaze to his.

"I saw it this morning at the restaurant, but didn't want to stare. If it's personal…"

"It's something Severo had me do before moving." She stroked her wrist, unsure. "You know we can't recall our previous lives from one life to the next."

"So it's important information?"

"Yes." Aby twisted her wrist, then held it out, displaying it for him. Yes, she wanted him to look.

She needed him to know how much he asked her to sacrifice.

Max took her hand gently and swiveled to stand close to her to read the small text. *"I am: Aby,"* he read. "You don't remember your name from life to life?"

She shook her head.

"That's gotta bite." He read the next line. A group of letters and ten numbers. "Bank account? Maybe the werewolf isn't so stupid after all. This is good info to have. Next line. *I trust: Severo.* I'm guessing the numbers are a password?"

"To get into his home. Don't ever let him know I showed you this."

"I won't. There's Jeremy's name. You also trust Jeremy Stokes." He paused, then read the last line. *"My enemy: The Highwayman."*

He turned a condemning look on her. Finally, he nodded. "The wolf looks out for you."

"He loves me." Aby tucked her arm to her chest.

"It's good to know who you can trust and who you can't."

"I might be able to trust you."

"Yeah? According to the tattoo, you should be a hell of a lot more fearful of me."

"This is Severo's thinking. He once said something to me about keeping your enemies close."

Max chuckled. "I don't think he had this

scenario in mind. Bet the wolf would pop his talons if he knew I was in your home."

Aby shrugged.

"Thought so," Max said. "You and a wolf. You say he's not your boyfriend?"

"He's not."

"Have you asked him what he considers himself to be to you?"

"What do you mean by that?"

"Just that he's pretty cozy with you."

"Severo and I are good friends."

"Right, and that *friend* thinks it's okay for you to work with Grim, and he's got his name tattooed on your wrist."

She also had Max's moniker tattooed on her wrist, Aby thought, but he didn't seem to put merit in that.

"He bothers you so much that it makes a girl wonder why?" Aby looked over her shoulder at him. "Do you like me, Max?"

"You're a—"

"Familiar? Why, yes, I am. Good of you to notice. So you hate us all, no matter what?"

"You're nice enough."

Ugh. Did the guy not have a charming bone in his body?

"I do like you, Aby. More than I should."

Now that was better. "I like you, too."

"So have I earned your trust?"

He hadn't done anything to earn her trust, except saving her from a crazed demon. And coming to breakfast to talk.

"Do you think you'll still be immortal when the shadow is gone?"

"I hope not."

"Why?"

"I want to sleep. I want to eat a cheese pastry and taste it. I want to…to dream."

Aby could understand the desperation of wanting to escape a fate life had stuck you with. How many times had she wondered what it would be like to be normal? Too many to count.

"Here I thought you were some he-man highwayman who protected the innocent from the big bads. You're not so tough."

"Would you like me better if I forced you to bridge the demon for me?"

She shook her head, but didn't say anything. She'd like it very much if he simply touched her. And kissed her. And put his body close to hers so she could feel his warmth.

Outside the sky was bright white with high sun. Max observed the flight of a robin across the yard. "What's your usual asking price?"

"Two thousand."

"I said I'd give you ten."

"How's a guy who spends his nights fighting

demons and days driving a muscle car make money? You still rob people?"

"Fifteen thousand, Aby. I'll be respectful, and we'll take precautions to ensure your safety."

She didn't want to have business sex with this guy. But she did want to help him. It wasn't fair what had happened to him. He'd had no choice in what he was now.

"Aby, I've lived my life by trick or trade. I avoid trade and mostly utilize trick. You can't trust me. You shouldn't trust me."

Pacing before the double glass doors, she shrugged her fingers through her hair. "I'm out of my element here, not working with Jeremy."

"So that means you'll do this? Aby, you don't know how much that would mean to me."

"I think I do. It would give you back your dreams. Your love for life. You've lost it, haven't you? Life is simply slaying demons from one town to the next. You don't have meaning."

"A guy tends to get into a rut after a couple hundred years. But I'd do anything to make it right. Will you help me become mortal, Aby?"

"I can give you the life you want?"

He nodded.

"Then yes. I will." Because this would be an adventure she could have. "With two requests."

"Name them."

"Promise you won't kill me."

"Promise." He said it so quickly, and with surety, Aby was inclined to believe him. She wanted to believe him.

She would believe him.

"What else?"

There was only one way to seal a deal. "Kiss me, Max."

Instead of stepping away, as she expected, he curled his fingers about hers. "A kiss?"

"We'll be doing a lot more than that when it comes to bridging Gandras. Please, Max?"

He didn't nod so much as dip his head close to hers, and Aby knew it was going to happen. Her heart shuddered against her ribs as the clean scent of him wrapped about her. She sighed and closed her eyes just as his mouth found hers.

The tenderest touch warmed her lips for a brief moment, then he pulled away. Their eyes met. Before Aby could decide if it had been a good or bad kiss, he pressed his lips to hers again. Longer this time.

The glide of his hand along her back tilted her slightly forward and deeper into the kiss. Melting. Connecting. Falling into wonder.

And when he parted from her, their breaths meshed.

The Highwayman held her, searching her eyes.

Aby could but grasp his shoulders to stand without stumbling. With a half smile, Max nodded, satisfied with his work.

Aby touched her lower lip. It was still warm. He was still there. Could she keep him there?

"That was awesome," she said. "My first kiss."

"What?"

Chapter 8

He couldn't have heard her right.

"Your first kiss?" Max swallowed all kinds of oaths.

But then, maybe he was looking at this wrong.

"From me, right? I mean, you've had plenty of kisses before this one."

Aby smiled sweetly, silent in her bright-eyed innocence. A newly emerging innocence that reached out and slapped Max across the face. Ha, it said, fooled you good, Highwayman.

"No." He shrugged a hand through his hair. "Not your— Really?"

Aby nodded. "And it was more than I imagined it could be."

He bent before her, meeting her eyes. They were green. Green had never let him down. Green meant good memories, only good things.

Her lips pursed and he wanted to kiss her again. She tasted sweet and new, like things he'd refused for fear of frustration. But he was too stunned.

Actually, he felt as if he'd done something wrong, like steal a neighbor's mail, or a woman's virginity?

"Are you telling me you've never been kissed before by *anyone?*"

"Well, Severo has kissed me on the cheek, the forehead and the hand. Other guys have done the cheek thing. But, yes, you're the first man who's ever kissed me for real."

What about all the sex she'd had? "Don't you…? I mean, when you and whatshisname…?"

"Jeremy."

"The two of you don't kiss when you summon a demon?"

"Never. Kisses are too personal, Max. Jeremy respects me. He understands what we do together is a job." She clasped her hands beneath her chin. Her eyes absolutely twinkled. "Kiss me again."

"Again?" Max swallowed. He gripped his chest. Mercy.

How in hell did a woman who had lived four lifetimes manage to go without a kiss? It astounded him.

"The first for this life, right?"

She shrugged. "I think it's the first for all of them."

Max gulped audibly.

If he'd known it was her first, he would have tried to make it…well, more spectacular. How to do that? He wasn't into romance and all that gazing-adoringly-into-one's-eyes stuff.

She'd blindsided him. He felt as if he'd been gut-punched by a vicious demon.

He wasn't beyond retreating from an uncomfortable situation.

"I should go." He walked toward the door.

Aby followed closely. "What's wrong, Max?"

"I need to figure some things out." He stepped over the threshold. The wards were not so strong leaving, but they still zinged at his energy like pins pricking his flesh.

"We didn't set an appointment!"

Max disregarded her urgency and rushed through the doorway. An appointment—to summon his demon, to have sex with Aby.

Sex with Aby… No, he wanted to make love with Aby. And the thought freaked him out.

Outside, he kicked a stone into the street. His spur skidded on the cement. "Damn it!"

Find the familiar. Have sex with her. Then kill her. Those were the rules he had made. The line he'd drawn in the sand.

And today he'd scuffed a heel through that line.

He found a motel a mile south of Aby's condo. Max paid housekeeping to launder his clothes and to stay out of his room. He didn't need the maid snooping through his stuff.

Once a year he returned to his home base in Milan. There he owned a small country estate bordering a neighboring olive grove. It provided a retreat, quiet to recharge, and an opportunity to research the occult and paranormal in his extensive library.

After dropping his things in the motel room, Max stopped into the local library and looked up his bank account information online. Credit cards were in order, automatically paid each month from his account. The amount in his savings was ample. He didn't need to work to pay for travel expenses, thanks to a shrewd financial advisor who invested in Apple, Amazon and Google. Just because he didn't "get" technology didn't mean he didn't understand the earnings value of its stock.

He had no patience for computers, and so the library visit was brief. Max preferred the feel of paper, of old books and real money.

He barely made it to the post office before it closed. Slipping the pearl necklace he'd nicked from the hostess at the International in a plain brown padded envelope, Max addressed it to Ginnie in Paris, for services rendered. She liked the sparkly stuff as much as he did, and, unlike him, she had a use for it.

The sun had set, but he used the overhead light in the car as he flipped through a book he kept tucked at the bottom of the trunk. *Cat Breeds and Their Care*. The Abyssinian was a breed he'd not before encountered.

"One of the world's oldest recognized breeds," he muttered as he read. "An elegant feline. Muscular body, beautiful arched neck, with large ears and almond-shaped eyes."

Aby's ears hadn't seemed overly large to him. But her body? Nice.

"Focus, Max. Drag yourself back behind the line. This is serious."

Right. He'd never faltered before.

He read more. "One of the most intelligent animals in creation. Hmm… People-oriented. This cat wants to know what you're doing, and wants to help. Yikes. That's Aby to a *T*."

"Abys—" that was what breeders called them "—are good at training people to do what they want them to do. This breed gets along well with dogs."

Max set the book aside. "That explains the wolf."

He glanced across the street to the condo. He had parked a house down the street from Aby's. If a demon was after her, he wasn't about to step down from his post.

There was someone inside her second-floor apartment. He'd seen two men enter earlier when the streetlights had flickered on. That had been two hours ago. He recalled she'd said she had a job this weekend. Must be why they were in there.

The thought made him uncomfortable. He was watching her place, while she was likely inside having sex with a man. Voyeur, much?

Hell, wasn't like he didn't do it all the time when dream walking.

"I wonder if she's kissing him. Oh, hell, Max, get it together!"

Tuning the radio up a few notches didn't chase away the guilt over that kiss. It seemed impossible to get his head around the idea of such a gorgeous woman never being kissed.

"She's just a familiar," he muttered tersely. "Don't forget it. There's nothing you want from her beyond a demon summons."

But he wasn't prepared to leave her unprotected. Not until he'd gotten what he wanted from her.

And what did he want? Sex. He was the man

who would pay her to have sex with him to serve his own selfish desire.

She could never imagine how frustrating having sex with her would be. He'd bring her to climax, over and over, while the tension built in his body and he got right to the brink, only to hover there—then drop.

Yeah, that was the third blow he'd been served by the demon shadow—inability to climax. He may have opened up to Aby with the story of how he'd gotten the shadow, but no way was he going to reveal that devastating bane to her.

Over the centuries he'd tried to climax with many women. If there was a trick to setting him off, he'd yet to find it. The women had either apologized for his inability to get off or they didn't say a thing, content in their own pleasure.

The humiliation should have stopped him long ago. Hell, he had once considered the monastery. But just because a man avoided sex didn't put it out of his mind. In fact, it probably made him think of it all the more.

Dream walking served as a faux climax. If he didn't have that, he would have gone mad long ago.

It was a bane a familiar could never relate to, or understand.

As a rule, Max usually didn't get involved with paranormals. He preferred his women human. Uncomplicated and unaware. So he'd put up with the remarks about being unable to get off. The closeness of skin on skin was almost enough to appease his ache.

Almost didn't cut it.

He'd once approached an *über*-sensual faery with hopes she might break the curse. Hours later, however, she'd flown from his bed, defeated.

Someone had once told him the sacrifices he made should be worth it to know he was able to save thousands from demonic attack.

Yeah? Maybe so.

Max twisted the silver ring on his thumb. "You were always right, Rebecca." The fleur-de-lis design, worn through the centuries, still glinted brightly.

Knowing a trip down memory lane would shove him into a melancholy, Max swiped a hand over his face. He beat a fist on the steering wheel and raised the volume on the radio.

Another hour passed, and a man sauntered out from Aby's building, barefoot and buttoning up his shirt. He sat on the top step and dug out a cigarette from his shirt pocket.

Compelled for no other reason than he wanted to make sure Aby was all right, Max stepped out and crossed the street. He drew his gaze up the front of the condo to the second floor. The window was dark; no interior light glimmered within.

The man on the step acknowledged Max's approach with a nod. "Hey, man. Kinda late for a walk, eh?"

The cigarette smelled like cloves, a favorite with vampires. But he didn't seem like a longtooth. The man wore a rumpled black shirt and loose jeans. His blond hair stuck up on one side and his gaunt cheeks were flushed. He looked obviously pleased with himself, in a daze, as if stoned.

Max remembered the name tattooed on Aby's wrist. "You must be Jeremy Stokes." Listed under *I trust.*

She had Max's moniker on her wrist, too, though he wasn't sure how to feel about that. *My enemy.* It was the truth, and yet, it didn't feel right. How could someone so petite and gorgeous have enemies?

So you've forgotten the dead familiars in your wake?

The man focused enough to reply.

"That would be me. How'd you know?"

"Aby mentioned you."

"Cool." Jeremy patted the cement stoop. "Sit a spell, dude. She's busy right now. Are you one of Aby's clients? Haven't met you before."

"I'm a new client. She didn't mention me?"

He sat on the step and refused the offered ciga-rette. The smoke made him want to gag. He didn't do nicotine. Hell, it couldn't kill him if he had a six-pack-a-day habit.

"Nah, but we don't talk much." Jeremy offered a hand to shake.

He was neither vampire nor demonic, Max decided. Vampires reeked of blood, and humans possessed by demons appeared normal but their veins tended to bulge and there was always the blue glint mirrored in their eyes if you looked at them from the right angle. Jeremy possessed none of these, nor did Max smell brimstone.

"She told me you're her assistant," Max said, wanting to know more. Yet, did he really want to go there? "Is the witch summoning the demon right now?"

"Yep, he's up there. Won't be long. I do my part," Jeremy said, "then I get the hell out of there before the big bads come through, you know? 'Cept tonight I forgot my shoes. Now I gotta wait around until after the fireworks."

"I thought you were the fireworks?"

A self-satisfied smirk narrowed the man's eyes. "You know it, man." He took a deep drag then flicked the glowing cigarette into the street. "It's an exhausting job. There aren't many guys who can do what I do."

Max studied the red embers as they slowly burned out. "Wouldn't think making love to a beautiful woman for hours on end would be so trying."

"There is a certain amount of stamina required. Because, dude, it's all about the girl, you know? Her satisfaction. I gotta hold back my climax or risk exhausting myself before her. Then we'd be at it all night. We've got it down to an art form, though. One, two hours tops. Tonight, though, it was short thanks to my discovering the A spot."

The A spot? Max really didn't want to know. "You were up there less than an hour."

"You keeping watch on the place?"

"Maybe."

Jeremy nodded and gave him the satisfied grin again. "Forty-five minutes. That's my best time. We've got the moves down pat so I can bring her to satiation like that." He snapped his fingers. "I am the master."

"All right then."

"Like to see you try to get a woman off so quickly and reduce her to purring slush. Just isn't possible."

It was, if the woman was human and required only an orgasm or two. The familiar's sexual threshold was not at all like that of the average mortal woman.

Jeremy touched the gold cross at his neck. "God, I love the woman."

"Like romance love?"

"Nah. Aby is the sweetest, most adorable woman on this planet. I love her like a friend, not as a girl-friend. That would be weird. I mean, how could you separate the job from the relationship part? I'm not into nonhumans anyway. Besides, Severo is keen on me, and I want to keep it that way. I know how he'd feel if I tried to move in on his woman."

"I thought Severo was Aby's friend?"

"Yeah, well, that's what they like to tell people." Jeremy reached into his shirt pocket and dug out a white disk and handed it to Max. "Here, you might want to suck on one of these when you go up."

Almost ready to take it, Max retracted at the last second. "The Host? Where'd you get that?"

"Stole it from the Catholic church down the street. Dude, it's not wise to go anywhere near a familiar without some protection, know what I mean? I have all my clothes warded. Even had my dick warded."

"Seriously?"

"You ever see a demon? They're not pretty. And I like my head exactly where it is, on my neck. Same goes with the other head, know what I mean? So, yeah, I ward everything. That tattoo hurt like hell, let me tell you."

So there were a few wonders Max had yet to discover in this tired, old world.

"So many things can go wrong with a demon summoning," Jeremy said absently. He dug out another grit. "Dude's gotta be careful, you know?"

"Yeah."

Max wished he'd known Jeremy two hundred and fifty years ago. He'd have taken his advice about the tattoo. Now it was too late. Max couldn't ward his body, because that would lock the shadow in permanently.

The door opened behind them and a nondescript man in a trench coat shuffled past Jeremy down the steps. He carried a titanium case, secured with four padlocks. Great for keeping demons contained.

Max looked aside. He wasn't sure who would recognize him, and keeping his cover was always paramount.

"Thanks, Stokes," the witch muttered, and quickly made his way down the sidewalk.

"Cool, man. See you next time." Out the side of his mouth he said, "Grim's not much of a talker, which is fine with me. Witches creep me out."

"That was Ian Grim?"

"Uh-huh."

Max's fingers clenched. The witch was already too far to reach with the whip. Max had no reason to take his life; he just liked to imagine.

"I'll see if Aby will see you, man."

Five minutes later Jeremy reappeared on the

front step and reported she wasn't in the condo. He tugged on his shoes.

"She's probably in meow mode right now. She usually shifts after a job. Could be out scampering around. You should come back later."

Aby rubbed her whiskers against the rear tire on Max's car. It wasn't warm, so it must have been parked here a while. Resisting the urge to pee on it, she scampered down the sidewalk.

Looking both ways, she crossed the street and scooted past Max, who sat on the front step, and into the cat door. When the big door didn't open immediately, she looked back and meowed. The man took that as the invitation she'd intended and walked inside.

"You must have snuck out the back," he said. "I hope you don't mind," he continued as he followed her four-legged journey up the stairs. "I know it's late. I didn't realize you were working. But you did want to get to know me better. If you want me to leave, I will."

She entered her home through another cat door, which left Max outside the locked door.

Shifting immediately, Aby yawned. She should have taken time following the bridging for a nap, but the urge for a quick run to stretch the odd kinks that always formed in her muscles after a job had called.

Now she could fall asleep merely by looking at the sheets, so she avoided the bed and retrieved her fuzzy white bathrobe from the bathroom. Shifting didn't maintain clothing, so she was always naked when she shifted back.

Come to think of it, she was usually naked before the shift, too.

She opened the front door. "Ten minutes," she said as Max entered. "Then this kitty needs some rest."

"I could come back in the morning."

"You've obviously been waiting for some time."

"Just watching."

"Get a good show?"

"Not like that. I'm sorry, this feels awkward."

"You're telling me." She tucked the robe tighter and sighed. "Come and sit. I can't refuse a handsome man a few minutes. Especially one who is such a good kisser." She glanced over her shoulder. "So did you talk to Jeremy?"

"He's quite the character." He sat on the couch and Aby sat in the middle this time, real close. "The dude smokes."

"Yep."

"I'm surprised you'd let a man who smokes make love to you."

"It's a habit he can't kick. Mortals, eh?"

"So he's never kissed you?"

"Like I said last night, you were my first. So what was with you anyway? You escaped faster than Jeremy does after a job. It's like kissing me freaked you out."

"It did."

Aby bristled. That was not what she wanted to hear.

"I mean, you come off as very…"

"Very what?"

"Sensual and attractive and confident about yourself and your body."

"I am."

"And yet, you hadn't kissed a man. Do you know how many ways that freaked me out?"

"Are you afraid of me, Max? One familiar does you wrong, and you intend to hold it against all of us? You promised you wouldn't harm me, that I could trust you."

He chuckled and turned to face her. Anticipation sparkled giddily in her stomach. Max moved closer, so their faces were but a breath away. He smelled like cheap hotel soap and a little like Jeremy's clove cigarettes.

She closed her eyes and waited.

And waited.

Aby popped open one eye. "What's wrong?"

"Nothing's wrong." He lifted her wrist to display the tattoo. "Everything's wrong."

"This means nothing, Max."

"It's your guide through the world. You should respect it."

"So you do regret kissing me?"

"No. And I could kiss you again. But I want it to be right, you know? I've never been under so much pressure before."

"I'm sorry, maybe I shouldn't have—"

And then he drew her into an embrace, silencing her lips with his own.

Aby took the delicious moment into her soul. He kissed with his lips closed and with just the right pressure. It tingled at her mouth and down her neck and to her breasts. A sigh echoed in her body.

What a wonder, to kiss a man. To make contact, flesh to flesh, face to face. The act was intimate. Far more intimate than sex, where two bodies joined in a frenzy of sweat and exertion. This was quiet, delicious.

His thumb stroked her jaw. Aby murmured against his mouth, and he touched her lower lip with his tongue.

She pushed away from the kiss, regretting it even as she did so. Her heart beat frantically. "I'm not sure about tongues."

"Seriously?"

"I don't know. It just seems so strange, you putting your tongue in my mouth."

Hell, Jeremy put his tongue all over her body, and inside it to bring her to climax. But again, this was personal.

"Maybe it's time for you to get some sleep."

"You think I'm a little girl," she said.

"No, I don't want to step over any boundaries you've set. You're a hard woman to figure, Aby."

She knew what he meant. It was because her profession involved having sex—a lot of sex—to bring into this realm the creatures he sought to destroy.

"You're so innocent," he said. "I never imagined."

"Is there anything wrong with innocence? It doesn't make me ignorant of things."

"You're certainly not ignorant."

"Let's try once more," she urged softly. This time she caressed his face with both palms. "I want to learn your kiss, Max. Slowly."

"Aby," he whispered. An ache tainted the utterance. "Aby."

She came to him and their mouths joined. Max's throaty groan sounded in her being. The sound of his pleasure.

It thrilled her to know she could do this to a man.

She let her fingers roam through his hair, slide behind the curve of his ear. There, at the edge of his jaw, stubble roughened his flesh. She liked the feel of it, found it to be masculine. His lips, however, were firm but soft. He lingered at the mouth, as if branding her with his heat, and only when she thought surely she'd die of pleasure, did he part her lips slightly so his breath tangled with hers.

"Aby," he whispered upon her lips. "You kiss well for someone so new to it."

When she opened her eyes to meet his, the intensity there dazzled her. He looked at nothing else, focused so solely on her, she could see herself in his eyes. Surrender imminent, she snuggled closer to him. His strong hands eased down her back. The terry robe was too thick, and she wanted his hands upon her flesh.

Daring to dash out her tongue, she traced the firm curve of his upper lip. The smell of him, so clean, challenged her to find some part of him not so clean, more mysterious. He opened his mouth and allowed her to touch the soft, wet inside at her own pace.

His fingers traced up her neck and through her hair, gripping the short strands, pressing a little. He wanted more.

She needed more.

When her tongue touched his, he slid it over hers. The texture thrilled her and she let him inside her mouth. There he tickled and traced her tongue.

Why she'd ever ignored kissing was beyond her. Too personal? Hell, yes. But just right with Max. He wasn't too rough. He followed her lead. And he tasted like power and strength and comfort. She loved every bit of his mouth, his tongue, his sexy white teeth grazing her lips.

"You like this, Aby?"

"Better than anything—"

Max's entire body stiffened. He clenched a hand near his hip where he kept the whip.

"What is it?" She followed his gaze, twisting her head to look over her shoulder.

A dark shadow glided before the patio door.

"Smells like a demon to me."

Chapter 9

Fingers pressed against the glass patio door, Aby sucked in her lower lip. The Highwayman wielded the long leather whip against the demon as if it were merely an extension of his arm.

The demon, a thin, gangly thing with prehistoric fangs, hadn't a chance against Max's prowess. It charged and slashed, and tossed Max against the high wood fence. Max merely shook it off, and then sliced off the demon's head.

Before meeting Max, Aby had never witnessed a demon being slain. She was only there for their birth into this realm, though she never paid much attention to that, either. Soon as the demon had moved through her body, she shifted and made a mad dash under the bed. Demons weren't keen on cats, and she wasn't about to take chances.

Watching the demon fall disturbed her. Could it have been one she'd bridged here? Ian Grim wouldn't unleash his demons willy-nilly like this.

Why was it here? Was it really after her, as Max suspected? It made little sense.

Aby had always thought demons should revere familiars. The familiar was their link to this realm, after all. There were few wizards talented enough to bring a demon here without a conduit, even fewer demons that could bridge on their own.

The Highwayman rolled up the whip and placed it at his hip. He shook his head, tossing the long bangs from his eyes. His broad shoulders thrust back as he scanned the skies.

Aby traced her lips with a fingertip. If Maximilien Fitzroy was supposed to be her enemy then why couldn't she take her eyes from him, or stop imagining him in her bed?

He rushed into the house and pulled Aby to his chest. Cupping her head, he held her there, feeling her frantic heartbeat against his body. It wasn't fair a fragile woman like her had to face the big bads.

Why couldn't they pick on someone their own size? Like him?

She shivered against him. Max surfaced from the
adrenaline high and for the first time he really felt
Aby against him, warm and delicate. She clung to
him.

He clung to her.

When had he become so needy? So eager to
draw another body to his and give it comfort?

*This has nothing to do with your lack of sexual
fulfillment.*

*You want to possess her. To steal her. To tuck her
away like those jewels you take, and then forget
about her.*

Right. And that disturbed him more.

He stepped from the embrace and paced away.
"You're not safe, Aby. Maybe I should find a way
to stick around, on lookout, you know."

"I don't need a bodyguard."

Her obstinate remark pricked at his concern.

"So a tiny thing like you thinks she can take
care of herself?" She stood with her hands defiantly
on her hips. "The wards and sigils will protect for
the most part, but they're not foolproof. What if a
demon gets in one night while you're sleeping?"

He saw the move coming—and let it happen.

Aby brought up a roundhouse kick, connecting
low behind his knee. Wincing, he went down. A
punch to his jaw had him blinking. She packed a
hell of a right hook.

He landed on his back, arms sprawled. It hadn't hurt that much, but a little acting could prove a point.

Aby bent over him and gripped his collar. "Still think I can't protect myself?"

Silly kitty cat. "You've got the moves, I'll say that much."

Gripping her wrists, he used surprise and lifted her as he stood. Wrists held high, he twisted them and brought her arms down before her stomach, her back to his chest.

"Demons will laugh at your ineffectual kicks, Aby," he hissed into her ear. "You can't punch out a demon. They're likely to bite off your fist."

"Let go of me!"

He released her, and she shot away from him toward the bed, which sat in the middle of the living room. Strange place for a bed. But what about this woman was not strange?

"I'm trying to show you what it's like," he said calmly.

"Then all I need do is lure the demon closer."

She crooked a suggestive finger at him, while she climbed upon the bed. Her smile worried him.

"You're playing with fire, Aby."

"Just humor me, Highwayman. Come on. A little closer."

He stopped before the bed, the skewed black

comforter skimming his knees. Aby gripped him by the shoulders. What was she trying to prove? He didn't want to do this with her, on the bed.

And then he did. So he dropped to the bed.

"Gotcha," Aby declared sweetly.

She sprang up and gave the bed a shove. Max started when it rolled easily across the floor. The bed was on wheels? Bleeding cowboys!

Not wanting to take the ride, he stepped off and onto a curious design. He squatted to study the ten-foot-by-ten-foot circle. The sigil was worked into the parquet floor with a darker maple wood.

"Well, well. Thrill me."

"A binding ward to hold the demon in place." Aby walked the circumference of the sigil. It was as wide as the bed and easily concealed beneath it. "I wouldn't be a very smart familiar if I didn't keep them locked to one spot after bridging them."

"Why the wheels?"

"I don't like to sleep with my head away from the wall." She gave the bed a kick and it butted up against the brick wall. "Just depends on what I've got going on, for the position of the bed."

When she wasn't bridging a demon, but entertaining a lover, what position did she put the bed in? Or did she release the wheel locks and let it ride all across the floor? Hell, that was a ride he'd be willing to take.

Max swiped a hand over his face. Stick to business. "You're in danger, Aby. I still don't like leaving you alone."

"I'm a big girl." She made a walking gesture with her fingers, and nodded toward the door. "Time for you to leave."

"All right. I don't like it, but I won't stay where I'm not wanted."

"You're wanted, Max."

Oh, yeah?

Tugging her into his arms, Max kissed her. Deeply, so she would remember he'd marked her. Lingering, so his heat would remain long after he'd left. Soulfully, because he felt the connection on an inner level he couldn't explain.

Aby's small breasts hugged below his pecs. Her narrow hips pressed to his. The duster coat impeded their closeness, and he was thankful, for he tried desperately not to have her feel his erection. There was nothing she could do for it, anyway.

She purred into his mouth, like a lazy cat sprawled in the sun. The sound hummed through his bones and fixed itself in him more securely than he imagined his kiss stayed with her.

"I like kissing you, Max. Is that so wrong?"

He sighed and reached for her hand. Drawing it up, he turned her tattooed wrist toward her. "You tell me."

He stepped away from her wanting arms, and found it was harder than expected. It was better if she kept him his enemy. But for whom, he hadn't yet decided.

She tried to sleep. But sitting at the end of the bed, her legs dangling over the edge to toe the demon ward set into the floor, Aby could only think of Max.

The notion of the Highwayman was such a romantic one. A man who had lived for centuries and had once traveled the high roads as a thief and gentleman robber. She found it appealing—the image of him slipping precious jewels from the necks of women in big pouffed dresses and sumptuous décolletage.

Aby could imagine rolling along in a carriage, her heart racing to discover the unexpected arrival of a deep-voiced intruder. A hand wielding a pistol would plunge in through the carriage door. The wide cuffs of his coat would brush her knee. She would press her fingers to her breasts rising and falling rapidly, exposed to the nipple by the risqué fashions.

And he would notice. Those dark, sad eyes would take her in. He'd lick his lips and grant her that sexy smirk, and the dimple in his left cheek would wink at her.

She didn't wear fancy jewels. All she had to offer was her body…

"What idiotic story are you writing yourself into?" she chided herself aloud.

Standing and pacing the ward, Aby rubbed the back of her neck.

She'd never done that before, daydream about a man.

She couldn't deny there had been times she'd fantasized about Severo, though never sexually. Yes, there had been a few touches, but it had never gone far. It didn't feel right to think of him that way. He was a mentor, a companion and the best friend she had.

She needed a girlfriend. Someone she could chatter to about her lusty thoughts of Max. Severo didn't have many female friends, so she'd never had the opportunity to form those kinds of friendships.

"A couple days and he'll want to have sex with me. To summon the deprivation demon."

The idea should not disturb her. After all, it was her job and the sex was great. But it was so impersonal.

Aby had often wondered what real sex would be like. Sex that didn't result in a demon. Slow, lazy and lingering sex. Sex between two people who cared about one another.

"Can I do this with him?"

It could never be impersonal with Max. There was no way she could get naked with him without feeling…everything. Emotionally. Physically. In her heart. In her very soul.

Would it be easy for him? Would he come in, have sex with her, then breeze out after the demon shadow had been exorcised? Men were experts at hiding their feelings, at taking without considering what emotional remnants lay in their wake.

"He doesn't think of me as a potential relationship." That was why he didn't require a witch.

Sighing, she sat on a stool before the kitchen counter, but couldn't summon an appetite. Not even her favorite late-night apple-and-almond-butter sandwich appealed.

The man carried a demon's shadow within him, so all they had to do was summon this demon and reunite it with its shadow. Max could then slay the demon and be off to whatever adventures next waited.

Without killing her. He had promised, and she would hold him to it.

Something Max had said simmered up to Aby's brain. It was his story about how he'd gotten the shadow. He hadn't been alone.

He and his partner had been in the room when the demon came through. So that meant… His partner must carry half the demon's shadow as well.

Why hadn't that occurred to her as soon as he'd told the story?

"We can't do this. It's impossible."

Chapter 10

Aby entered the motel and checked the reception desk. No one sat behind the Formica counter. She didn't have Max's room number, but it didn't matter. She could sniff him out.

He was still abnormally clean, but now she had the taste of him in her mouth, and the impression of his heat clung to her flesh. Finding him would merely require her to follow the beats of her hungry heart.

She'd considered not coming here for about two seconds. What she'd realized was important for him to know. Sure, it was nearing three in the morning, but the dude didn't sleep, so he should welcome a visit at any time.

The atrium housed a large indoor pool and was dark save for the lights at the base of huge plastic palm trees. Aby wandered by the glass doors, intent on scoping out the rooms.

A reflection from the pool caught her attention. There was something floating in the still waters. A man.

Quietly opening the door, she slipped off her heels and padded around one side of the pool. Chlorine pricked at her sinuses. Puddles of water pooled on the green and blue patchwork of tiles. Water rippled, glittering with the ambient light.

He floated on his back, arms spread out and eyes closed, like a dead body—only this one had an incredible musculature and wasn't livid. Black swim trunks conformed to his thighs and hips.

Aby snuck to the water's edge. She didn't like large bodies of water. The idea of her head going under made her shiver. Once, she had fallen into Severo's pool and hadn't used the patio for the rest of that summer.

"How'd you find me?"

She started at Max's deep voice. He still floated. If he hadn't spoken she wouldn't have known he was aware of her.

"I saw your car out in the lot. You dare to park it in this neighborhood?"

"It's warded."

"Against demons, but what about human hood-lums?"

"Hoodlums? Do people still use that word?"

"Apparently so. Is this pool open now?"

"Nope." A swish of his fingers redirected his wavering path and his body turned slowly. His head floated closer to the edge where she knelt.

"You have an in with the owners?"

"A crisp hundred-dollar bill speaks volumes. I was meditating."

She felt no desire to leave. In fact, seeing him in the water was like spying a perfect leaf floating by. She wanted to grab it, hold it close and marvel over it.

"You do this often?"

"Float? Whenever I get a chance. It's the closest I'll ever get to sleep without drowning. Drowning's better though, because then you die."

That he placed death so highly disturbed her. Immortality apparently wasn't all everyone thought it was cracked up to be.

"Can you drown?" she wondered.

"Probably not. I've been sliced from shoulder to gut, dragged behind a runaway horse, stabbed in the kidney and had more body parts mangled than you can imagine. Still here."

A swish of his fingers sent him gliding. Aby marveled that he needn't kick or flap his arms much to move about the water's surface. If she jumped in she'd sink to the bottom. It was an irrational fear, but she utilized better-safe-than-sorry thinking around water.

"I thought you wanted the demon released so you could be mortal? That won't happen with you dead."

"I don't want death, Aby. Sometimes…it's like a fantasy. With death I'd close my eyes. I'd sleep."

"It would be a very long sleep."

"A man needs sleep to stay sane."

She thought him completely sane. Fighting demons and protecting others, like her, was as far from madness as she could imagine.

"Want to join me?"

Goodness, did that offer appeal. She'd love to join him in another hug, a kiss, even. But on dry land. "Wouldn't want to interrupt your meditation. I'm not keen on swimming pools anyway."

"Is that a cat thing?" He righted suddenly, standing so his shoulders were level with the water's surface. Water dripped down his face and neck. His hair, darker when wet, slicked across his forehead.

"It is a cat thing. Though I do love to soak in a nice hot bath."

"So next time I do a bubble bath you'll be interested?"

She laughed. "I can't see you doing bubbles."

His was an easy smile. Aby wanted to trace it, but he was too far out to reach. *Come closer, and let me lick the water from your mouth.*

Seeming to sense her secret desires, Max floated forward and hooked his elbows on the pool's stone edge, bringing his face but inches from hers.

He didn't say anything, but the way he was examining her, from the inside out, made Aby look away from his intense gaze. No man had ever looked at her so straight on, and without a word.

What was that about? He'd left her feeling as though they could be nothing more than business associates. One minute he was kissing her, the next he was pulling away.

Was it because he thought he should comply when she asked for a kiss? What did they call that? A mercy kiss. She hoped not. That would be such a lie.

She felt compelled to stand and walk away. Instead, she turned her gaze to his. Maybe she could see deep into him, too. Did she want to know what lived inside Maximilien Fitzroy?

His narrowed eyes did not waver from hers. And there, she thought to see a distant pain, or perhaps a pain so close it could only survive by burying itself deep within Max's being.

"What'd you see?" he asked, resting his chin on a fist. "Demons?"

She shook her head. "Something private, I think."

He smirked. "You know more about me than any person on this planet, Aby."

"Does that bother you?"

Water droplets slid down his nose and dropped onto Aby's toes. "Not as much as it should."

With a lunge, he levered himself up to kiss her on the forehead. Beads of chlorinated water dripped onto her cheeks. And then he plunged backward and did a somersault that kicked up more water.

Aby stepped back. A flick of her finger wiped away the water from her cheek. There were times her fur ruffled, even when she was in human form.

"What did you come for?" he asked as he resumed floating.

"It's about the summoning. It won't work."

"'Course it will. I've got the spell right here." He tapped his forehead. "Or are you having second thoughts?"

"Not at all. I'm in for the adventure." And the close contact with him. "Fifteen thousand, right?"

"Yep. In cash."

"Cash is always good. But, Max, you said you and your partner were in the room with the familiar when the demon was summoned."

"Yep, Rainier Deloche, the old rascal."

"So what makes you believe he doesn't carry the demon's shadow within him as well?"

"I'm sure he does. If he's still alive."

"Then it won't work. You each carry one half. The two of you must be present if you wish the demon to retrieve its complete shadow and leave your bodies. Without both halves there cannot be a whole."

Max stood, the water sloshing about his hips. Water slicked down his steel-hard abs. He flicked his head to shake off the moisture. He hadn't considered what she suggested?

"You've had over two centuries to think about this. It never occurred to you that you might need your partner present?"

"No. I've never thought about the half thing. Feels pretty whole when I shadow. What makes you think we each have a half?"

"Intuition."

"Intuition is not fact."

"It's better than fact, it's instinct. That's how I survive. It's the only way it'll work. I'm sure of it."

"Christ." The Highwayman slapped the water, sending it off in splatters around him.

Skittering sideways to avoid the splash, Aby slipped. Her wet toes losing footing on the slick tiles, she wavered. Her body swayed forward.

Screaming, Aby landed in the water.

Her face went under. Arms scrambling to grasp something solid to keep from sinking deeper, Aby choked on water. It spilled down her throat, muffling her cries. Chlorine burned in her nose. She couldn't breathe.

She was going to die. Again. And she would never remember the sexy Highwayman.

Something grabbed her—Max's strong hands— and pushed. Her body skimmed through the water until her face surfaced and she gasped. She slid her arms around his broad shoulders, digging her fingers into his flesh.

"You okay?" he asked.

She sputtered.

"It was only four feet there. You don't swim?"

"I…" She shivered against his solid chest. Her tears mixed with the pool water. She was thankful he could not see her cry. "I hate water." She choked and spit out a mouthful. "Get me out of here."

He lifted her easily to set her upon the edge. Shivering and gasping, Aby scrambled away from the pool until her back hit a lounge chair.

Max heaved himself out from the pool. Dripping water from his body, he leaned over her, and she cringed.

"I hate water," she said again.

"Aby, it was just a little spill."

It wasn't his fault. But she was too upset to explain. "T-towel?"

He grabbed a towel, and shuffled it over her hair then wrapped it about her shoulders. He

squatted before her, their knees touching. He
hadn't wiped the water from his skin, and it glistened in the light beaming indirectly from beneath
the palm trees.

"Sorry, Aby. I think it was my fault. I scared you.
Damn, I can be an idiot sometimes."

No argument there. Aby snuffled and hugged
the towel.

"You need to get some dry clothes."

Her loose blouse clung to her body and the skirt
twisted about her legs. She clung to the towel as if
it were a life vest.

"I'll be fine. I—I want to go home. But…" She
shivered, her musculature reacting to the chill and
scare. "It won't work. The summoning. Trust me
on this one, Max. You need your partner to make
this happen."

"But I haven't seen Rainier since the night we
took on the demon shadow."

"Never? You haven't stumbled across him?
Looked for him?"

"I've looked, and wondered. If I'm ever near a
phone booth I'll pull out the book and scan for
Rainier Deloche, but I'm sure he's changed his
name."

"You didn't."

"It's easy enough to keep it when you're off the
grid. I missed the social security number thing. I

don't exist. Which means Rainier also doesn't exist. He's impossible to track."

"Isn't there a paranormal detective you could hire to find the guy?" She sneezed delicately. "I would think, if the two of you share the demon's shadow, you'd have some kind of connection."

He shook his head. "Never felt it."

"Have you ever tried?"

"Listen, Aby, Rainier may be dead for all I know. Are you sure we can't try this without him?"

"Yes."

Didn't he realize all she wanted to do was pull him against her and warm her shivers with his body? The man was half-naked, dripping with water like some Atlantean god raised from the depths. She wanted to dive into his clean scent and lose herself in the splashes.

"Kiss me, Max." The words spilled out before she thought them through.

He straightened, planting his palms on the lounge chair.

"I like your kisses," she tried. "I need them." To get warm. To know he cared.

"This can't happen between us, Aby."

There was no warmth in that reply. "But I thought it already was."

"That was a mistake I made. I should have never encouraged you. I know I'm starting to sound like a broken record, but we have to keep this business."

"Max, I—"

"I think you should leave."

Blinking at the cruel swiftness of his refusal, Aby found the sense to nod and stand. Tugging the towel about her like a cape, she grabbed her high heels. Shivers wracked her body.

She would not beg for anything from a man. Not even kindness.

"Then I suppose we won't be seeing each other again. Because I won't expel the energy to bridge a demon for you when you've but half the means to do so. Nice meeting you, Highwayman."

She couldn't walk from the pool atrium fast enough. By the time the air brushed through Aby's wet hair, she was crying and walking swiftly away from the one thing she'd always wanted.

A relationship with a real man.

"Hell."

Max fisted the wet towel into a thick twist. He'd played it wrong with Aby. The hurt in her eyes had slapped bars around his hopes of freedom.

He hadn't meant to be cruel to her. It was a defensive reaction, to push away the one thing that had made him feel in years. Because the last time a woman had appealed to him so much, he'd fallen in love.

And he'd had to watch her die.

Max had vowed to never again have a romantic relationship. He wasn't meant to take responsibility, to care for a woman and put down roots. Women were anchors. And anchors tended to dredge up detritus best left buried.

Demons stalked the world. He had to constantly work the high roads. It was who he was. He wasn't a boyfriend, or a lover. He was a hunter. He could not be tied to one place or person.

But he couldn't let Aby run out of here thinking he hated her. He had to stay on her good side if he were to ever get this demon off his back.

He'd follow her. She wasn't being careful, and with demons after her, for reasons unknown to Max, Aby needed protection.

Rarely did she get lost. Aby possessed a sort of homing instinct. Severo had said she followed electromagnetic fields. He called them ley lines. She didn't know about that. She just had a good sense of direction.

She scrambled across the street and toward the all-night grocery store. The air was strange with imminent rain. She hated water!

Her skirt had dried a bit in the breeze. Her short

hair always dried quickly. But still shivering, she thought a building would be the place to warm up. She entered through the sliding doors.

The air-conditioning swept from above like an Arctic wind. "Bother."

Turning to retreat, she saw the sky suddenly crackle and lightning flash. Rain plundered the parking lot.

"This is not my best day," she muttered.

"You're tellin' me."

Aby turned to the store clerk who'd spoken. An elderly black woman with braided hair and soft brown lipstick. She propped a hand at her hip and gave Aby the once-over. "You fall in the pond out back, or what?"

"A pool." She clasped her arms over her breasts. "It's raining."

"I can see that. You brought it with you, girl."

Aby followed the clerk to her checkout lane. "No, I didn't. I can't make it rain."

There were no others in the store. It was small and the aisles were low. Aby could see everything from here. She'd never been in a grocery store before. There were so many things!

The clerk leaned against the register. "I wasn't being literal. Where'd you come from? Planet of the bimbos?"

"I resent that."

"Sorry." The woman rubbed her hand along Aby's shivering arm. "I've had a long day—two six-hour shifts without a break because someone called in sick. No need to take it out on a skinny little thing like you. There's sweaters in aisle nine. Clearance for five bucks. You should go get yourself one and warm up."

"Thanks."

Making a beeline for aisle nine, Aby smirked at her late-night adventure. Soaking wet, browsing the grocery store shelves. She didn't do stuff like this.

So this was an adventure, she wondered wryly as she eyed the stack of zip-up sweaters. Amazing—food and clothing in the same store?

She grabbed the pink one and tried it on. It fell to her knees and the shoulders landed above her elbows. Shuffling her arm, she worked the sleeves up to expose both hands.

"Are there only extra larges left?" she shouted over her shoulder.

"Mm-hmm," came the reply. "Take it or leave it, girlfriend."

Being called *girlfriend* gave Aby a tickle, though she knew the woman could probably care less and wasn't about to take her under wing as a potential friend.

As she glanced around, her spirits lifted. While

she lived at Severo's estate, he had all the groceries delivered, and his chef, Heloise, prepared their meals. Since she'd been on her own, a delivery truck brought Aby her groceries, mostly prepared meals that simply needed heating in the oven. Who had time to learn to cook when their death could be just around the corner?

Wrapping the sweater across her chest, she wandered toward the back of the store where she eyed the wax cartons of milk. Low-fat, two-percent, one-percent, whole and…

"Cream. Mmm, yummy. You don't need it, Aby," she said aloud. "You just crave it. You are not going to walk home in the rain with a big jug of milk. Not even a small carton of cream."

Fine. Tracking to the front of the store, she admired the rows of colorful products. How did the bees get the honey in those funny bear-shaped bottles? Why didn't they put all the red juice together, rather than sorting it all out amongst the colors? What the heck was a kumquat?

"I'll have to come back here. This really is an adventure."

"What's that, girlfriend?"

"This store is amazing. There are so many things. And clothes in the same store as food?" She hugged the sweater to her wet body.

Aby filed down the row of carts to the front

window and ducked to look below a huge sign that advertised peaches for forty-nine cents. The downpour still bulleted the parking lot.

"You got a ride home?"

"I live a couple blocks up the street."

"Then you'll have to make a run for it. But not in those high heels. Better go barefoot."

Aby sucked in her lower lip. "Yeah, I suppose."

She was the one who had wanted adventure. But after a near-drowning did she really want to go out there?

"That'll be five dollars."

"Huh?"

The clerk rubbed her fingers together, expectantly.

"Oh, sorry." She dug through her purse for a five. At the sight of her cell phone she wondered if she could call for a cab. For a few blocks away? "Maybe it'll let up."

"You have a good evening, girlfriend."

"You, too, girlfriend." She waved and went out the doors.

The rain was cold, but not as cold as the pool had been. Aby shivered under the awning. The sweater took on spatters and jeweled with water beads.

"I should have stayed home." She took a step out into the rain, and leaped back under the safety of the awning. "But I had to go. He needed to know. Jerk."

But he had rescued her.

And then told her to leave.

"Men are maddening. I don't need him."

She wanted him. But *need* and *want* were two different things.

Shoes hooked on two fingers, she made a dash for it across the parking lot. The sweater soaked up the water and weighted her shoulders. She stepped in a puddle and water splashed her leg.

"Oh!"

When a black Mustang pulled to the curb, Aby could but stand there, her shoulders hunched against the wicked weather. Shivers renewed, her teeth chattered.

"Aby?"

"What is this, my unlucky night?" She thrust out her shoes and marched before the car. "I hate this stuff. I've never had to walk in the rain before. When I lived at Severo's he had a driver. All I had to do was say, 'Driver, take me somewhere,' and he would. Easy as that. No need to walk in the rain."

He stepped in front of her. "Get inside the car, Aby."

The Highwayman offered his hand, but Aby kept on pacing.

"I wanted adventure!" she shouted. "What do I get? Nearly drowned the first time around, and if that didn't work, then why not try again?"

"Aby."

With the sound of her name she was swept from her feet and cradled in Max's arms. He drew his nose across her cheek, and Aby thought he was smelling her, or maybe savoring her. The touch surprised her. He slid across the passenger seat, tucking her onto his lap, and pulled the door shut.

"It's all right, Aby. I'm sorry."

She pounded his chest with ineffectual fists. "You told me to go away. Now you come find me? What do you want? I don't know anymore, so please, just tell me!"

"I'm sorry about what happened by the pool. The things I say…sometimes they don't come out right. There is something more between us than two people coming to a business arrangement."

So he felt it, too?

The confession worked wonders to her sodden soul.

He coaxed her head forward and she dropped it to his shoulder. "I'm getting your car all wet."

"The seats are leather. They'll dry."

"And you?"

"I dry, too. I should have never sent you off like that, Aby. Especially not after you fell. You needed comfort not distance. Forgive me?"

Burying her face against his shoulder, she hugged him. "I don't want you to be my enemy."

"I don't have to be."

"But Severo is smart." She stroked her tattooed wrist. "He had me do this for a reason. He's never wrong."

Gripped in a fierce hug, Aby ceased her blabbering. It was like no hug she'd ever had before. Wet, sloppy and perfect. She drew up her knees and snuggled into him. He kissed the crown of her head.

The rain relentlessly pattered the hood of the car. Water streaked the windows, entrancing the gleam from a streetlight.

And she suddenly knew everything she wanted could *never* be hers. Max was too distant. He didn't have a home. What made her believe he could drop the important mission he'd dedicated his life to and just fool around with her?

Turning on his lap, putting her back to his chest, Aby twisted to look out the windshield. She tucked Max's hand around her waist and held him as fiercely as he held her.

"Why is it when you really want something," she whispered, "life steps in and says, 'Sorry, not for you'?"

A soft chuckle sounded near her ear.

"It's not funny, Max."

"I know it's not. But that's exactly how I feel right now."

"Really?" She twisted to study his dark gaze. "You…want me?"

He nodded. "But life is saying no. It's shaking an admonishing finger at me and warning me to keep back."

"Oh." Laying her head aside his neck, she toyed with the metal button on the leather strap at his shoulder. She liked sitting like this—surrounded by man. A man as confused about life as she was.

"Know what I do when someone says I can't have something?" he whispered.

Meeting his gaze again, she found the answer. "You steal it?"

"That I do."

His kiss was urgent, not about to allow any naysayers to part them. A kiss to slay her demons. A kiss to bring him new ones.

He slipped his hands over her wet hair. Aby traced across the wet leather jacket as she straddled him.

She was ready to unzip the sweater and press her breasts to the warmth inside his coat, when a fist banged on the driver's window.

Chapter 11

Alerted by the intense scent of brimstone, Max swung a look over his shoulder.

Three demons stalked outside in the rain.

"What the hell is with all the demons following you?" He shoved Aby off his lap. "Stay inside. It's warded. You'll be safe. No shifting this time. Promise?"

"Promise."

Max got out and unhooked the whip from his hip belt and released the ten-foot length of braided leather with a smart crack across the tarmac.

"You the Highwayman?" one of the three demons asked.

"The one and only."

"Then Severo wants your ass."

"Wolf boy, eh?"

So that's who was behind the demon attacks. Didn't surprise him one bit.

"Let's do this," Max muttered, and stepped up to meet the first demon that lunged with glinting talons.

While the whip snapped the air and caught bits of demon limb here and there, the three did not relent. They went at Max as a team, and had him on the ground and on his back more often than standing.

Max was able to take one out before the leader slashed his face with a nasty talon.

Aby moaned. Her fingers clutched the door handle, but she knew better than to go out there. There was nothing she could do to help Max. As he'd said, the demons would laugh at her silly kicks and punches.

A splatter of blood traced the window. Max's blood, because demons bled black tarlike substance smelling of sulfur.

The Highwayman dropped near the front tire. The one remaining demon lunged for the window. Exposing razor teeth, it growled at her, then misted off into the night.

Counting to five as she scanned the sky for signs the demon would return, Aby didn't make it to four. She scrambled out into the rain and knelt over Max. He groaned and pushed himself against the front tire.

"Get in the car, Aby."

"They're gone," she said. "Are you going to live?"

"Unfortunately, yes. Just got my pride beat out of me, is all."

"It was three against one."

"Yeah, but I had the fancy weapon. Never been taken down so easily like that before. Those bastards packed a punch. I don't like it when I lose a fight in front of my girl."

His girl? He couldn't be aware of what he just said. Maybe she should ask him to repeat it?

No. She'd take what she could get without giving him a chance to renege. *His girl.*

Aby's mirth quickly vanished. He bled everywhere. On his hands, the side of his neck, from his nose. But most prominent was the gash at his hairline.

"Do you heal like werewolves do?" Severo, if ever wounded, would heal within minutes.

"Nope. Broken bones and cuts take as long to heal as if I were mortal."

"Then you're coming home with me. I happen to be talented with a needle and thread."

* * *

He was a mess. The fight with the demons had drenched him in muddy water, all of which he'd tracked onto the white rug before the bathroom vanity.

Max sat on the toilet seat in the stark white bathroom, wincing at the thread tugging through his flesh. Aby wielded the needle like a charm. She attributed the skill to her third life, as she'd cheerfully explained while gathering medical supplies, spent in a foster home with a crafty matron who had sewn clothes, bedding, even curtains. She knew that snippet from the past, thanks to Jeremy, who had met her during her last lifetime.

There seemed to be only men in her life, he realized then. That disturbed Max for reasons he couldn't put a finger on.

"Almost done," she said. "Sorry I didn't have anything but green thread. Your hair will cover it, though. You sure you don't have any broken bones?"

"Why? You know how to set bones, too?" He resisted putting his palm on her hip. She stood between his legs, bent over him, her tongue sticking out the corner of her mouth. "Nothing broken. Promise you won't tie that thread in a pretty bow?"

"Promise."

Now he did touch. He couldn't stop himself.

The slender curve of her hip was the perfect place to press his thumb and curl his fingers around back. He felt as if he was touching something he shouldn't, and any second he'd get a swat of admonishment. He liked the dangerous aspect of their proximity.

For a moment they held each other's stare.

What was that touch for? she seemed to ask.

I'm not really sure, he silently beamed at her. *But I like it.*

Aby was the first to clear her throat and start fiddling with her supplies.

"Green's my favorite color," he said of the slender skirt she wore.

"Really? Good pick. I like it, too. It's one of few colors I recognize."

"That's right, cats don't see red well."

"Mostly green, blues and sometimes yellow. Good thing your eyes are blue."

They appeared blue to her because of the demon shadow within. Max's eyes were really gray.

He slid his hand up, pushing up the wet shirt to expose her skin. Soft, pale and warm.

This time her look said, *I dare you,* followed with a sweet, *pretty please?*

What the hell was he doing? That demon must have whacked him hard because he wasn't thinking straight.

In proof, Max leaned forward, and kissed her on the soft patch of exposed skin. Then he pressed his cheek aside her stomach and held her, arms wrapped about her hips.

"You saved my life, Highwayman. Again."

He'd do it again if he had to. But he shouldn't have had to do it once if he'd been on the ball. Way to protect the girl, Highwayman.

And yet, he'd learned something incredible while fighting those demonic bastards.

He drew away and she tapped his forehead. Still a few stitches remaining. "They were after me."

"What makes you think so?"

"Because the leader, the ugly one, said Severo wanted my ass."

"Severo?" She tugged the needle and Max winced. "But… Severo sent them? Do you think the one the other night…? Oh, gods. But why?"

"He's looking out for you. I can understand that. I am the man who kills your kind. But doesn't the wolf realize you could become collateral damage? Ouch."

"Sorry. Just have to snip off the end. There. You're good as you can get. Let me dab it with some alcohol."

Max gritted his teeth as she went over his bruised face with an alcohol-soaked cotton ball, not because it stung, but because the heat of her touched him, enveloped him. He wanted to lean forward and bury his face against her breasts, and close his eyes.

He wanted to find silence. Peace. Dreams.

Thinking about dreams, he'd need to shadow, and soon. It always aided the healing process if he could surrender to the shadow following any kind of injury.

"Would you mind if I took a shower?"

"I was hoping you'd ask. I haven't seen so much mud."

"I'll try to clean up your floor, too."

"Don't worry about it. I have a mop. While you're at it, I need to call a certain werewolf and tell him to back off."

"No, Aby." He clasped her hand, so delicate in his. She was so…perfect. "Let the wolfman protect you. It's his right. I can deal with a few demons. I just don't want you getting hurt."

"Exactly. Which is why I'm going to call him. If you toss out your clothes, I'll put them through a wash and dry."

"That's okay." He paid the maids at the hotel to do that. The last thing he needed was to walk around in Aby's place with a towel about his waist. Mixed signals, anyone?

Yes, on both their parts.

Severo wasn't answering his phone. Of course, it was nearly four in the morning. Aby left a message to call her when he got back in town.

Lying across the bed, she tucked her head against her arm and listened to the shower beat a syncopated rhythm with the rain.

The Highwayman was naked in her home. Heat infused her at the mere thought.

Aby yawned, and with visions of soap-slickened abs, she drifted to sleep.

Exiting the steamy bathroom half an hour later, Max found Aby lying on the bed, which had been moved up against the wall.

"Sleeping?"

Drawn toward her peaceful slumber, he stopped at the end of the bed to admire her. He stood long minutes, watching, trying to match his breath with her languorous ones. Wondering—for the umpteenth time—what it must be like to sleep.

And also, would she flinch out of sleep if he touched her there, where her breasts rose and fell with each soft breath?

Max drew his fingers away from her skin. He had no right.

But then, she did want to get to know him better. Wasn't turnabout fair play?

Just a peek was all he wanted.

"It won't hurt," he muttered, with a grin. "Promise."

The pull to shadow always manifested as a

dark desire he would not resist. Clenching his fists at the tug to his soul, Max surrendered to the shadow. It melted over him, claiming, cracking away his humanity. He could be a solid man-shape as the shadow, or a mere blot upon the floor. The shadow chose.

Tonight, he hovered in solid form at the end of Aby's bed. Adorned in darkness and raiments of night, the shadow devoured the peaceful quiet. Opening its maw, it breathed the silence.

Before it lay a sleeping being. It did not discern age or sex. The energy was strong. So strong, it drew the shadow forward.

It glided, dark night-robes of insubstantial shadow slipping across the rumpled white sheets. A hand spread out, its long taloned fingers splayed as it positioned over the sleeping entity's head. There, where dreams dazzled and reviled. Dreams so delicious and wicked and cruel. It fed upon emotion ensnared by sleep. As the eyelids fluttered with movement beneath, the shadow hitched a ride.

This one smiled in sleep, a cozy slumber. Flickers of another being manifested in the shadow's preternatural experience. Larger. Stronger. Shaped differently than the dreamer but of the same species. The being pressed its mouth over the sleeper's mouth.

A kiss. The shadow knew the ways of mortal sleepers.

Freedom. Green. So clean. Scampering over grass. Not this time, but from time long ago. The images were not in the sleeper's mind, though.

The shadow marveled at the strange connection to the other being's dreams. The sleeper was not the one it observed. That being was…itself.

Curious. It had never blended with the dreamer before. It must know this one.

Another look.

Flashes of skin. Fingers dragging along flesh. Groaning bodies. Sweat glistening. Mouths kissing and moving along skin and curves and there, to a hard nipple.

The dreaming being arched her back. The other, dark and intent—him—slipped his fingers between her legs. In exquisite surrender the dreamer cried out.

He, the shadow as human shape, entered the dreamer, hilting himself inside her. He moaned, riding the tremulous promise of orgasm.

They fed one another until they could take no more. Until exquisite release overwhelmed both of them. The shadow experienced the climax with a surprising shudder. Its entire form trembled. And it felt the intensity of orgasm.

What was this? The sensation of climax felt so

real as if it had shaken the shadow's very being. It
made it gasp and its form trembled.

Bleeding cowboys.

That thought hadn't been the shadow's but the
other—itself. It had little control. The nonshadow
form would soon take over.

Delicately sinister, the ravishing tremors flickered away.

The shadow relented. Night receded from the
white bedclothes. With it, the shadow extracted a
minute chord of soul from the sleeper. It was a different sort. Not human.

Seeking the night, it turned and floated across the
room toward the tall window it could easily
permeate.

Aby sat up. Something was in the room.

"Max?"

She'd forgotten he was taking a shower. No
sound came from the bathroom. The room had
darkened considerably. She'd been so tired she
must have drifted off.

She slid a hand down her stomach and realized
she was moist between her legs. Dreams of the
Highwayman had caused that.

The crystal crackle of glass alerted her, and she
snapped a look to the patio door. A dark figure in
glossy black clothing flashed her a blue-eyed stare.

Then it turned to the door and became shadow, melting through the glass without damaging it.

"Max?"

No one answered. That thing—that creature— had been a demon. Nothing else had eyes that glowy color.

How had it gotten past her wards? Where was Max?

Scanning the room, she made sure no other shadowy things were about, then scrambled into the bathroom.

It was dark and empty, with only a wet towel caked with mud hanging on the rack. Max was gone. So, she wondered, what was that thing?

Tiptoeing out to the bed, she spread a hand over the sheets. Could that have been his shadow form?

It was the only explanation. No matter what the thing was, or how many wards she might have against it, if it had entered her home as Max, it had been given permission to be here.

With a shudder, she settled onto the bed and tucked her knees to her chest. There were some things in this realm she couldn't comprehend. And that scared the crap out of her.

Max released the shadow outside the condo. Gasping, he clung to the stucco wall, palms skinning against the rough surface.

"What the hell?"

He felt out of breath, as if he'd just climaxed. Max struggled with what he'd experienced.

"Impossible. I've never…" He panted.

Never had he climaxed during a dream walk before. As a shadow he could watch lovers and feel the moment of pleasure in the dream. But he could never recall that pleasure or retain the feeling after dropping the shadow.

Besides, he couldn't climax. Hadn't since 1758. Yet now…?

He slid a hand over his erection. Breaths still coming rapidly, he wanted to believe, but wasn't that stupid. He'd felt Aby's hands on him. Her hot wetness. He'd listened to her cries of satisfaction. He'd felt himself slip inside her. And then…

He slid a hand inside his jeans and felt a sticky wetness. Had he really—

Too good to imagine. But he'd felt it. It was real.

Max's smile didn't last long as the realization hit. He'd finally found the one woman who could give him all the pleasures he'd been deprived.

And she was on his kill list.

Chapter 12

Sometime in the early morning hours, Max decided to walk down the street to the café he'd noticed earlier, for hot coffee and cinnamon rolls. The smell satisfied him. Getting to watch Aby eat would, too.

Just getting to see her again would rock his world. She'd dreamed about him. Them. Making love. God, if he could dream, he'd dream the same.

During any dream walk through a sexual fantasy he experienced some form of satisfaction. He felt looser, relaxed, as if he had climaxed. Yet the inability to viscerally recall that pleasure did not cease to torment.

Until Aby.

He'd felt it all. He'd ridden the feeling even after shucking the shadow. He'd actually climaxed.

Bounding up the stairs in the foyer, he wanted to shout to the world. She did it! I did it! Aren't you happy for me?

He had to tell her. To let her in on his darkest secret. After she accepted that he'd walked in her dreams without permission, she'd be happy for him. Because she would understand. She had to. Aby chose to understand him, even knowing that he was in it to kill her.

"Not anymore. Never." He couldn't kill the one woman who could give him pleasure.

And if she could also help him exorcise the demon? Man, he'd owe her the world.

Tracing his fingers along the tiled wall as he approached her door, he sensed the energy in the sigils hum through his fingertips. She was smart to have done this. He suspected, though, the werewolf might have something to do with it.

What was that man to her?

Even as he tried to put the wolf out of his brain, his hackles rose as he landed at Aby's door and sensed the presence inside. He couldn't smell them, or see through doors, but something about werewolves always made Max's skin prickle.

He hesitated. It was presumptuous of him to

think Aby would like another visit from him so soon. But he'd taken a piece of her into him last night. She had given him something he'd pined for over centuries. He could no more stay away than he could resist shadowing.

Aby had begun to sublimate his needs as much as the shadow.

He finally knocked. The door opened before he could rap a third time.

The werewolf actually snarled at him. "You?" He looked over the brown bag and coffee cup Max held. "Who the hell are you?"

"I was just thinking the same thing about you."

Max strode inside, tightening his jaw to prevent showing the wince as the wards tugged at him.

The wolf hissed against his neck as he passed closely. He thought of drawing out the whip, but the look on Aby's face immediately told him she hadn't expected the wolf to be here.

"He can enter without permission? I thought I told you to stay away from him?"

"Sev, he's a friend."

"The Highwayman is your friend? Aby, what the hell has he done to you? This man kills familiars."

"I wouldn't harm a hair on Aby's head," Max interjected. And he meant it, too. He set down the bag and cup on the counter. "She's different."

"Different?" Severo smirked, then looked to Aby. "You said he wants to hire you without Jeremy's assistance. Doesn't sound like a friend to me. You have no friends, Aby."

"Exactly!" She flashed Max an apologetic look.

Had he walked into a domestic squabble? Joy. But he wasn't about to stand down from the sneering wolf. Not when he felt on top of the world.

"It's business between Aby and me," he offered.

That wasn't true anymore.

He knew wolves marked their mates and could scent when they'd gone astray. If Aby's claim were true, they were just friends. But did the wolf consider her marked and his own?

She stepped before the wolf. "Severo and I are just friends. And you are always welcome here, Max. Did you bring coffee for me?"

"And cinnamon rolls. Hope you like them."

"He's become your friend so quickly? A slayer?"

"Actually I prefer hunter," Max tossed out. "I hunt all sorts—demons, vampires, ghosts." Sparkly things. "Werewolves."

"Is that supposed to be your means to threat?"

Severo stepped close to Max as Aby had gone to retrieve a plate from the cupboard. He sniffed the air, sneering at Max. "I don't like you, Fitzroy. Of all the familiars in the States, why Aby? You could have easily sought help far from here."

"I heard she was the best of the remaining few."

"You'd like that, wouldn't you?"

"Look, I don't mean to step between you love-birds. I simply want to—"

Severo reared back at mention of lovebirds. The man glanced to Aby, then looked to the floor.

Why the vicious need to protect on the werewolf's part? Werewolves usually only protected their own, meaning their mates. And most male wolves preferred to mate with a female werewolf. For all their differences, the two of them shouldn't even be in the same room.

"Severo isn't staying long." Aby offered Max water and he refused. She drank it herself, tossing the whole glass back in one swallow, and then set the crystal glass on the counter. "I told him about the demons attacking you and putting me in harm's way."

"That was not my intention," Severo replied. "I couldn't stand aside and allow someone who kills your kind to stalk you, could I?"

"I don't begrudge you the need to protect Aby," Max said. "I'd be surprised if you had not."

"For all the good it did. You're still here." The wolf growled.

Just try it, Max wanted to say.

Aby rubbed a palm up her arm. A pale-green jersey dress caressed her figure and stopped above her knees.

The woman was his now. Kind of. He'd shadowed her. He'd tasted her soul. She dreamed about him. He'd climaxed—for real. And— All that meant nothing, actually. Not unless he could tell her about it.

"Boys. Will the two of you climb down from your high horses and chill?"

A lift of his chin put the wolf's eyes above Max's. The aggression in the air pummeled. But Aby's presence softened Max's stance and he stepped back.

"I consider you both friends, and I won't be happy if either of you goes at the other."

"Did you tell him about the presence here last night?" the werewolf asked slyly.

"Presence?"

"It was something dark," Aby said. "I felt like…like it was hovering over my bed. It appeared after you had gone. I didn't notice you slip out."

Max swallowed and tilted his head. He really hated having to make this confession in front of the wolf. "That was me. I shadow after an injury. Helps the healing process."

"I kind of thought so." Aby's worried gaze went liquid with unreleased tears.

Could she know what she had done for him? No. The dreamers were never aware of the shadow's intrusion, though, as Aby had, they could sense a presence.

"Your shadow form?" The wolf had no problem showing disgust.

"He has a demon shadow inside him," Aby explained. "It needs to be let out nightly."

"To fight the madness," Max added, loving the sour reaction on the wolf's face. But he wasn't proud he'd let Aby see that part of him. "I'm sorry. It came on too quickly. It would never harm a soul. It merely peers into their dreams."

She'd loved it when he'd licked her nipples in her dreams and when he'd slid inside her...

The blush rosing Aby's cheeks caught his attention. She looked aside, but the wolf caught her reaction, too.

"This is too much," the werewolf said. "Aby, will you use reason?"

"It doesn't matter what happened last night, Severo. There are more important things to worry about. I realized something about the demon Max wants to summon."

Max caught Severo's renewed interest. It was sharp, so much so, it might cut if the man breathed on him.

"What about it?" Severo asked.

"He thinks to summon a deprivation demon and exorcise the shadow he carries in him."

Severo tilted his head, sucked in his cheek loudly. "You're half demon?"

"Completely human, save the demon shadow that resides within me. Scared?"

The wolf held his stance, authoritative and menacing.

"Max thought to summon the demon alone, but his former partner needs to be present, because he's got half the shadow in him, too."

"A partner?"

"Yes, partner in crime. We used to rob from the rich and give to ourselves." Hell, he didn't need to impress the wolf. "That's why they call me the Highwayman."

"I wonder if we should involve Grim to help us with this?" Aby said.

Max shook his head. "That witch is not welcome around me. You two might believe he's fine, but he's an asshole."

"Whether or not the legend is true," Severo said, "I've trusted the man for years. And if you don't agree to include the witch, then you might as well march right out of here now, slayer."

"It doesn't bother you what he did to the werewolf's wife?" Max replied.

"What is this legend you two talk about?" Aby wondered aloud.

Severo put an arm around her waist. "It's nothing, sweet. Just fable."

"The legend," Max said, "claims that centuries

ago a vampire fell in love with a vampiress and wished to marry her. He had an enemy, a werewolf, who decided he was going to win the vampiress's heart to piss off the vampire—and did so. In retaliation, the vampire lord hired a witch to bespell the werewolf's wife. He then locked her in a glass coffin and buried her beneath the streets of Paris. Legend says the spell keeps her alive, yet motionless. She cannot escape, but is always aware. Of course, after centuries, she has gone mad."

"As I've said, it is legend," Severo reiterated.

"It's not legend." Max found Aby's gaze. "I saw the glass coffin. Ian Grim had it specially made."

"Be that as it may…" The wolf put himself between Aby and Max. "She's already told you she doesn't want to work with you. Take a hint, buddy."

"I changed my mind," Aby said. She stepped around from behind the wolf. "He's a kind man, Severo. He just wants to be mortal. If I can help him, I want to."

"Which means we need to find Deloche," Max said.

"We?" Severo put an arm around Aby's shoulder. "I don't know who you're carrying around in your pocket, but we doesn't pertain to me or Aby."

"I need Aby's help."

And if he could fit her in his pocket he would.

"Not going to happen." He stepped up to Max. Severo was six inches shorter than Max but he made up for height in fierceness. "She's not yours to do with as you please."

"Nor am I yours." Aby stomped the floor, and both men turned to look at her. "You two are acting like wild dogs. Yes, Severo, you are. I'm not a female to be fought over within the pack. Step back. And, Max, take your hand off that whip. I will not have you two going at it in front of me."

"Then maybe we should take it outside?" Severo offered.

"Sev, please! Where do you think you'll find your partner, Max?" Aby asked.

"Don't know. I suppose I should start in Paris."

"Then I'll go with you."

The wolf beat the countertop with a fist. "Absolutely not! You need to give this some consideration, Aby. And if the Highwayman has any respect at all for you he will allow it."

"The wolf's right," Max contended. "Think about it for a day. I need time to track Deloche anyway, see if I can pick up his trail."

"You can use my computer." She gestured up the stairs.

"Thanks." Max shrugged off his coat and tossed it over the back of the sofa. "Don't mind if I do."

The wolf's gaze stabbed through Max's heart.

He smirked after his back was to the twosome.
Let the dog whine. He wasn't about to step down
now that he understood Aby was not Severo's.

She was his. Or she would be. As soon as he
could tell her she was his salvation.

Chapter 13

As Max tromped up the stairs to power up the computer in the little loft room overlooking the living room, Aby tugged Severo toward the door and out into the foyer. He leaned over her, pushing her against the wall, putting himself in the dominant position, which was normal for him.

She didn't mind. She loved Severo. Yet his anger sometimes frightened her.

"What does he mean to you?" Severo asked. "I can see something in your eyes when you look at him. You've known him for but a few days, Aby." He gripped her wrist. "Does this mean nothing to you? I did not make you suffer the pain of a tattoo for no reason."

"He's not the enemy right now."

"Right now? But after he gets what he wants from you? Aby, please don't be foolish."

This was the first time a rival for Severo's affections had stepped forward. And this rival could give her things she'd never ask of her friend.

"I like him. He's nice and respectful." Truthful to a fault, but at least he wasn't trying to hide anything from her. Max told it like it was, even if it wasn't very pretty. "And he's sexy."

The werewolf reared back, his eyes flitting from hers. "You crush me with such words."

"You knew this is what would eventually happen after I moved out from your place. I'm spreading my wings, Sev. Meeting new people."

"A new person who wants to use you for his own devious means. Aby, I don't trust the man. And why not do this the usual way, with Jeremy?"

"Jeremy isn't necessary. Max knows the summoning ritual."

"But he'll have to make love to you."

"It's not making love, it's having sex. There's a big difference."

"You think to know so much?"

Aby looked aside from Severo's piercing insinuation. Had he purposefully secluded her to keep her innocent of such things as relationships and kisses and falling in love? Why? That was not kindness but cruelty, and Severo had never been spiteful toward her. That she'd known, anyway. Had he sicced the demons on Max? She could have been collateral damage.

And, yes, Max would have to have sex with her. She looked forward to it. But how to tell that to a man who had been a mentor and friend for over a decade?

"Maybe this is a test between the two of us," she said. "To see if we can live apart. I don't want to make you angry, Sev, but I do want to be successful on my own. You've done so much for me. Taken care of me. Seen to my safety. My finances. Loved me."

"I will always love you. That's why it makes me angry to see you falling for the first handsome face that shows you the tiniest bit of attention. Do you see what he did in there? He stepped before you, as if to protect you from me. Me. He is claiming you, Aby. I don't like that."

Claiming her? Nothing wrong with that. In fact, it stirred giddy warmth in her belly.

Had he done it last night when he'd looked into her dreams? What had he seen?

"Severo, do you…" They'd discussed this once before. Or rather, talked around it. "Do you consider me yours?"

He faced the stairway, his broad back to her. He never did look at her when he was uncomfortable. The wolf was a loner. He'd left his pack after taking Aby in, relinquishing his principal status to another werewolf. He'd secluded himself from the world, as most wolves did. Yet, those other wolves had the pack for companionship.

Severo had no one now that she had moved out.

"Aby," he said softly. The side of his face visible, he gazed at the floor. "You know how I feel about you."

"Am I yours?" she insisted.

"No. Regrettably." He glanced over a shoulder.

Drawn to his weary stance, Aby hugged him, tucking her head against his arm. "I love you. I will never stop. You will find your mate someday."

Severo pressed his forehead to hers. His sigh warmed her cheek. She smoothed her hands over his long hair and spread it over his shoulder, then clasped her hands around behind his neck.

"Let me do this," she said. "Let me go on this adventure with Max, please?"

"An adventure? You're chasing demons, Aby."

"Not really. We're looking for Max's partner. Then, we'll summon a demon under controlled circumstances. It'll be safe, as you've always taught me. You know I'm smart around demons. Please, Sev, I've never been out of the state."

"Then drive across state lines to Wisconsin if that's what's pulling at you. But Paris? That's a long flight with a man I consider your enemy."

"I don't consider him that."

He sighed. "Has he kissed you?"

Now she pushed him away. But he moved in on her, suffocating her need for distance.

"He has," he said decisively.

"I don't think you need to know all the details of my personal life. Sev, we're not like that, you and I."

"Because the issue of you dating has never come up until now."

"You're acting more like a parent than a friend."

He had been prepared to make her his life mate. She had once been ready for that, too. But briefly. She couldn't love him romantically when she'd grown up living side by side with him as a friend and family member. Heck, when she was in cat shape, she pranced around with his wolf.

"Please." She met Severo's eyes. She'd always felt safe here, comforted. Now she sensed the distance, a falling away that might never again be bridged. "Trust me?"

"I do trust you—"

"Don't finish that sentence. You don't have to trust Max. I promise I'll call. I've always wanted to see Paris."

He stroked her cheek. Always, his emotions showed in his eyes. "I could have taken you there."

"We'll go together some day."

"Every day you exist here, in your own home, making your own new world and friends, you step farther away from me."

"You'll always be here, Sev." She pulled his hand to place over her heart. He touched her tentatively, not allowing his fingers to conform beneath her breast. "Promise."

The door opened, and Aby pulled down Severo's hand, though she sensed his resistance. The wolf thrust his shoulders square and lifted his chin.

"I've found a witch who does psychic imprints and mapping for people," Max said. "She'll see me right away."

"You want me to come along?" Aby asked him. She followed Max's gaze from her to Severo.

"If you like."

"Give me two minutes."

After Aby had disappeared into the bathroom, the wolf gripped Max by the coat collar and shoved him hard against the door frame. Max expected the move, and allowed it. The wards jittered in his nerves, warning, but not powerful enough to put him back after Aby's invitation.

"I don't like you, slayer."

"Haven't developed much love for you either, wolf."

"I have your scent in my nose. You know what that means? I can find you anywhere, any time."

"Good to know. Is that how it is with Aby? She's in you? You're not about to let her break free on her own, much as she desires to? Where's the leash, man? She's nothing more than a pet to you."

Slammed hard again, Max winced as the door frame collided with his spine. Still, he smiled through it.

"You think you know so much? You know nothing." The werewolf seethed. "Harm one hair on her head and I'll rip out your intestines and use them to strangle you."

"Sounds like a day at the park." Max changed his demeanor to a more respectful, softer tone. "I mean Aby no harm."

"When did you have such a radical change of heart about familiars?"

When he'd dream walked into Aby's thoughts and she had rescued him from centuries of frustration.

"Listen, wolf, I get that she means the world to you. And believe me, I'll protect her with my life, if it should come to that."

"If it comes to that, you've already failed."

"You're right."

The failures from his past flashed in his mind. There had been two women. One, he'd loved dearly. Both, he'd failed.

"How many familiars have you killed?" the wolf asked.

Max bowed his head. Yes, how many? He didn't keep a tally. Nor did he look in their eyes before severing their heads from their bodies. "Enough."

"Do their deaths really make a difference in the amount of demons running rampant in this realm?"

"I believe they do. Ninety percent of demons here in this realm have been bridged by familiars."

"Aby isn't safe with you."

"She will be."

Severo sighed and stepped outside the doorway. And Max understood perhaps Aby was the wolf's failure.

Ian Grim sensed the wolf's presence and looked up from his laboratory table. There were no weapons at hand. He didn't need one, but it was always best—

His shoulder hit the steel lab table a nanosecond before his nose crunched under a fist. Against the table, Ian snorted the ground ginger root he'd been preparing for a spell. It burned his bleeding nostrils.

"What in hell?" Severo growled. He held Ian firm with a hand to the back of his neck. "I asked you to sic the demons on the Highwayman, not Aby!"

"I did!"

"They went after her."

Shoved down the table, Ian's face cleared a heavy mortar and two glass vials with a crash. His body followed, slumping on the floor in a sprawl. His face burned with pain, exacerbated by the ginger powder.

The wolf shoved a boot against his chest.

"You're off the job, Grim. I don't know why I trusted you'd have the skills for this in the first place. And you won't be using Aby to bridge demons any longer. She's off-limits to you. You understand?"

Ian nodded. Bastard. It wasn't as though he could control the demons once set loose on the target. If Severo had wanted to keep the familiar safe he should have insured she was not in a position of harm.

So, the Highwayman and the familiar were hanging out together?

Ian bet that rubbed the werewolf the wrong way. Heh. His work was done here.

The wolf stomped out of his lab.

Ian touched his nose. "We're not finished yet, wolf. Someday you'll regret treating me this way."

The witch barely breathed.

Max leaned forward, across the round table

spread with a purple star-dotted scarf to inspect the woman's bowed face. She was pushing a hundred, surely. He'd never seen so many wrinkles on a person. It made him nostalgic for his mortality.

Beside him, Aby sat on the other of the two wobbly stools provided. They'd been escorted in without fanfare and told to remain quiet while the witch prepared to connect with the spirits.

He hadn't told her about the dream walk. Not yet. He wanted the time to be right. It was too personal not to tender carefully to her.

Max took Aby's hand and gave it a squeeze. Then he realized what he'd done. He didn't want to drop her hand right away and make her think he didn't want to touch her, so he held it in his own.

Aby looked at him and absolutely beamed.

Bowing his head to hide a shy smile, Max returned his gaze to the concentrating witch.

"You shouldn't repress your desires," the witch said, her eyes still closed.

"And you should concentrate on the business at hand," he retaliated.

A glance to Aby found her smiling. He needed to get this done with before the witch had them married. "His name is Rainier Deloche," he said to usher her along.

"Yes, and he was your partner in the eighteenth century. I didn't forget a thing you told me, young man. I'm not dead yet." She assumed a quiet state, drawing in a breath through her nose. The gold loops at her ears tugged at the lobes. "I can't sense him around you, which I might be able to do if he were a spirit."

"So he's still alive?" Aby questioned.

"Possibly. I'm not getting a read on this man at all." The witch opened her eyes directly on Max. "You're too clean."

He'd spent centuries killing and tracking dark denizens. A demon shadow resided within him. How could he possibly be clean?

"It's because he doesn't eat or sleep," Aby offered. "His scent is pure."

The witch nodded, accepting that explanation. Max had never heard that said of him before. He was the furthest thing from pure.

"You can't get a read on me, but what of Rainier?"

"Not feeling it today. Sorry, Highwayman." The witch flickered her gaze at Aby. "She, on the other hand, provides interesting diversion."

"Is it the demons?" Max prompted.

"She's a familiar," the witch berated, "one would expect demons. But there is a darker force close to her."

He still held Aby's hand and now her fingers curled tighter.

"A werewolf?" he asked.

The witch cocked open an eyelid. "It's someone close to her. Someone she trusts."

"Severo?" Aby spit out. "I trust him completely. He would never harm me."

"What is this Severo?" the witch asked. "Sounds like a bad case of influenza."

"He's my friend. A werewolf."

"Perhaps. The forces are dark though. I'm sensing a witch. You'd best keep an eye over your shoulder." The witch slumped in her chair, her body deflating as if she'd run a mile in a minute. "That is all. Two hundred dollars."

"That's it?" Max stood. "You didn't tell us anything."

"Just pay her, Max." The trace of Aby's hand along his arm annoyed him, and he jerked away from the touch.

He tugged out a roll of bills and counted out ten twenties and dropped them on the table.

The witch snatched the cash and chuckled. "Stay close, the two of you. One will protect the other."

Max waved her off with a gesture and marched toward the door. Aby beat him to the Mustang.

"That was a waste of two hundred dollars." He held the door open for her and closed it after she got in. Rapping his knuckles on the hood as he went around and slid inside, he then beat the steering wheel. "One will protect the other? What a bunch of mumbo-jumbo bullshit."

"I kind of liked her."

"Aby, please, she's a huckster."

"She was a real witch."

"Decades ago. Now she's just dealing out nonsense to pay her rent."

He fired up the Mustang and it rumbled to a lion's purr. Max spun out, his anger peeling rubber on the asphalt.

A dark influence? What if it was him? He was as dark as they came.

Bleeding cowboys.

Aby fastened the seat belt across her lap. "What do you think she meant about someone in my life being a danger?"

"A guess. If it's not the wolf, who could it be? It's not like you have a lot of friends."

"How would you know?"

"I— Sorry, Aby. I'm being an ass."

"You said it, not me. She said it could be a witch."

"Ian Grim," Max decided. But probably not. It was him. He sensed it.

"Yes. He's been not so nice lately."

"Not so nice?" He flicked a glance at her. "How so?"

"Just…flirtatious. I don't like it coming from

Grim. He's not bad-looking, but I work with him, you know?"

"If I had the sway over you that the werewolf does, I'd tell you to keep as far from that witch as possible."

"Severo has no sway over me."

"You just keep thinking that."

"I'm going with you, against Sev's will. Come on, Highwayman, give me some credit. I'm a big girl. I do what I want, when I want."

She tugged down the visor and inspected the mirror, then pushed it up.

"What did he say to you while I was upstairs on the computer?"

"I don't think that's any of your business. We have a complicated relationship. He found me after I'd come to my fourth life. When I first shift to human form in my new life, everything is so confusing."

"I know a little about familiars, but I can never figure how they age. Do you shift to the same age as when you died?"

"I don't think so. I mean, I usually can't recall how old I was when I did die. Severo guessed I was in my late teens when he found me."

"You don't revert to an infant."

"No. We are a mysterious breed. Unless we die and remain with the same person for all our nine lives, I don't know how anyone would be able to know for sure what goes on in our life spans."

"There's got to be someone who knows."

"I'm sure there is." Continuing her curiosity, Aby opened the glove compartment and strands of diamonds and pearls spilled out. "Hey, look here."

"What are you doing? That's my—" Stash. A side of him he'd never wanted her to see.

Max pulled the Mustang over abruptly and put it in Park. He leaned across, trying to gather the stash as Aby picked up a diamond necklace and dangled it before her.

"You still steal?"

"I have to." He snagged some pearl strands from the floor and shoved them in the compartment.

"You have to?"

If he didn't explain now, the curious kitten would never stop asking.

"So you're a kleptomaniac?"

"No. It's just…" He shoved the jewels into the slot. "I get distracted by sparkly things like a damned magpie. I think it's part of the demon curse."

"That's so cute."

"It's not cute, Aby. I steal. I don't want to, but I do."

Her flinch hurt in his chest. He shouldn't yell at her. Yes, he was definitely the dark influence in her life. God, he couldn't tell her about the dream walk. It would freak her out too much.

"What do you do with all this?" she asked cautiously.

"I save it, or sell some or give some away. Bleeding cowboys, do we have to talk about this?"

"You shouldn't be embarrassed if you're compelled to do it because of something inside you. Max, it's okay."

"It'll be okay when this conversation is over."

"Fine." She dangled the diamond strand over the glove compartment, seeming reluctant to return it to the dark cubby. It sparkled like her smile.

Dark and light. The Highwayman and the familiar. It was so wrong. He was a fool to think they could have something beyond a business relationship. It had been a fluke, the dream walk. It had to be.

The glint of diamond flashed in his eye.

"You want that one?" he asked, nodding to the strand she still held.

"I've never had jewels before. But it came from some other woman's neck. It could have been an anniversary gift or—"

"If you don't want it, fine. I thought it would look pretty sitting around your neck. 'Course, it wouldn't be as gorgeous as you."

She exhaled softly. "You think I'm gorgeous?" The diamonds trickled across her fingers as she studied the necklace.

"Aby, you put those diamonds to shame."

The compliment, whispered in a deep tone, brought a smile to her lips. Apparently no man had ever told her she was pretty. The wolf had certainly fumbled the ball on that one.

"Do you remember who you took this from?" she asked.

"Nope."

"Hmm, it's not like you have control over it… All right." She handed him the necklace and moved across the seat on her knees. "Will you put it on me?"

She smelled so good. Sweet, light and like things he could never have, yet desperately wanted. Max let the long diamond strand spill over her hair. It landed over her neck and twinkled down to rest atop her breasts.

The kiss sparkled more brightly than any jewel. She bracketed his face with her small hands and kissed him deeply. She had learned to French kiss masterfully. His little kitty cat was as sensual and daring as she put herself out there to be.

Max whispered against her mouth, "I like you, Aby."

She settled onto her side. "I could be your girl."

"You could."

Neither said another word as he pulled away the Mustang from the curb.

* * *

When Aby mentioned she was hungry, Max detoured into a drive-thru to pick up a Chinese salad and pink lemonade. Now at home, she emptied the plastic food container onto a plate.

Max paced her living room, checking corners and windows, making sure there was no means for a demon to slip in on a cloud of sulfur.

It gave her confidence to know he was so concerned about protecting her. She'd always felt loved and protected. But the feeling, coming from a new man, was a wondrous high.

She stroked the diamonds twinkling against her skin. These meant more to her than the condo Severo had given her, and the bank account he kept financed in her name. They were a token of Max's like, and that rocked her world.

"Now that we know it was Severo who sicced the demons on you, I don't understand why you think I might still be in danger."

"The wolf call off his witch yet?"

"I'm not sure."

"Then I want to be safe, not sorry."

Spearing a slice of cabbage glossy with oil and vinegar, she then spun off the stool and walked over to Max. She waggled the fork, displaying her prize. "Want a taste?"

She slid the salad over her tongue and pulled out

the clean fork. It was sweet and crunchy, with a bite of vinegar.

When he bent to kiss her, a giddy thrill sparked in her breast. It beat the thrill of owning diamonds, hands down. When he parted her lips with a nudge of his tongue, she complied.

The intrusion was not an intrusion at all. Rather, it stirred and surprised. The touch of his tongue against hers lifted her desire as if goose bumps were popping all over.

Aby shivered and clutched at his shirt. He slipped an arm across her back, holding her to him. Her breasts snuggled his chest. The heat of him invaded her everywhere.

He ended the kiss with a lick of her lower lip and a quick press of his mouth over hers. "Do you have any idea how long it's been since I've tasted something so amazing?"

"I can guess. But it was only Chinese salad."

"I'm not talking about the food, Aby."

He lifted her and she instinctively wrapped her legs about his hips. Setting her on the stool at the kitchen counter, Max crushed her body against his and took the kiss deeper, lingering, lazing his tongue along hers, and then dashing it across her teeth in teasing flicks.

Stoic, sensual, tormented Max. The Highwayman who had to taste food from her mouth and could never sleep.

"So you don't dream?" she asked when she could.

"Nope."

She wanted to give him what he desired—as slowly, carefully and attentively as he kissed her.

A rumbly moan accompanied his kisses. His hand slid down her back, easing along the base of her spine. He pulled her closer, as if trying to fit her to him with no spaces in between.

"Want to tell me one of yours?" he asked against her mouth.

"My dreams?" She tightened her legs about his hips. "Didn't your shadow look into my dreams last night?"

"Er… It did."

"It wouldn't hurt me?"

"Never. The shadow is darkness. Insubstantial. You couldn't touch it if you tried."

Slanting his mouth over hers, he glided his tongue inside and tickled across her teeth. "You were dreaming about us."

If he had seen her dream of them making love…

"I saw things," he said. "We were intimate in your dream."

Aby pushed away from the kiss. Releasing her leg-hold on him, she leaned back. She wouldn't look, but she had felt it—his erection—which meant he was ready to make love, to have sex. To have her.

Like he'd taken her in her dream.

He leaned in, kissing the corner of her mouth. "Did I do something wrong? I didn't go into your dreams on purpose, Aby."

"It's not that."

"I don't want to offend you."

"Mmm… Your kisses are incredible."

"I want more," he murmured. His warm fingers spread across her neck and slid lower. He stroked her hard nipple. "Aby, I can't fight this anymore. I had every intention to remain detached, not become involved with you, just keep things business."

"I'm glad you've had a change of heart. But I think we're going too fast," she said breathlessly.

"We weren't moving too quickly in your dreams."

"Max, I'm embarrassed you saw that."

"Don't be. If I could dream, I'd dream the same thing."

"You would?" It was all she'd hoped for. So why couldn't she grab it now? "This is going to sound weird, but I feel sort of like a virgin with you."

After her words he stood straight, separating himself completely from her. She felt the sudden loss of his touch at her breasts and at her mouth. How could she explain how she felt without offending him?

"I have sex all the time," she tried. "And you

know that's just a job. So now, with us, I want it to
be different. And it already is different. Just now,
when we were closer than close, and I could feel
your..." She sighed. "I want it to be right, Max.
And not just another job."

"It'll never be like that, Aby, I promise."

A kiss set her heart racing. The caress of his
fingers along her jaw dazzled her shivering soul. "I
can do slow," he said.

"Oh, Max."

Chapter 14

Max rapped on Aby's front door and she called for him to enter. He walked inside and collided with a large suitcase. A pink suitcase, of all things.

Aby rushed from the bed to the closet then the bathroom, where she shoved things into a small tote.

"I figured I should only bring along one bag," she said, "but can you imagine how hard it was to pack? I've never been to Paris before! It's so cosmopolitan. It's like a dream. Do you think I'll look like a tourist?"

She stopped briefly, her arms spread out to display her attire. A sleek black dress stopped below her thighs with a froth of white ruffles. It drew Max's eye down her long legs to the black heels that said so many nasty things to him he wondered if she could hear his answering thoughts.

"You look great, Aby." The sparkle of diamonds at her neck pleased him. "The Parisians won't be able to keep their eyes off you."

She made a giddy little jump, then scurried over to stuff the tote into the suitcase.

The woman made Max recall what it was like to be innocent, to have so few cares. To take joy in discovery. It had been so long, probably since before he was six. Before his father had been murdered by a highwayman. That same day Max's innocence had been stolen as well.

God, he wanted to know that feeling again. Or just touch it.

He had touched it. In Aby's kiss. It was the strangest discovery to find from a woman who had sex as a business.

Yet in her dreams he'd found salvation.

He most definitely could not reveal that to her now. She was so trusting of him, so innocent. And he was fouling it all with his deception.

But was it really deception if he didn't know how to tell her what she had done for him?

"I've never flown before so I researched on the Internet," she said. "I have moisturizer to keep my skin from drying out. I've got change to buy lots of water. I didn't wear nylons in case we crash and the fire burns the nylon to my legs—"

"Aby, if we crash, I think burnt nylons will be the least of your worries."

She did another little excited jump. "This is going to be so cool. I'm stepping out of my boundaries. I'm going to fly!"

This was not a vacation trip. It involved tracking a demon. It was dangerous. And he wasn't sure if Aby was a friend or something more.

Scratch that. He knew she was something more. A something more that demanded they take things so slowly he wasn't sure his frustrations wouldn't manifest in derelict behavior.

He wanted this woman.

He would have her.

But only for business.

And yet, she held the key to his pleasure.

How the hell did that screw with his brain?

"I don't know if this is going to work."

Aby stopped what she was doing, which was apparently fluffing her hair to look just right. Her hands fell to her sides, her smile fell from her face. "What do you mean?"

"This is not a pleasure trip, Aby."

"I know that. Am I too excited? I am. I'm sorry. I let myself get carried away. I've never been out from under Severo's grasp like this before."

"So he's had some kind of control over you all your life?"

"It's not like it sounds. And we were never lovers, because I know that's where your dirty mind is going."

"My mind isn't dirty." Not at this second. And really, she was the one who'd been having the sex dreams. "It's just concerned. Can you do this, Aby?"

"Can you?" She stepped to him and her heels put her at his height. He loved the soft, natural pink of her lips. "This is something new for you, too. You don't like to share yourself. Flying across the ocean and having me by your side—a woman you can't make up your mind about, someone you want, but life tells you to stay away from… What does that do to you, Max?"

"It freaks the hell out of me."

She was a threat. But not on the have-to-fight-for-your-life scale of threats. Aby resided on the smaller, but more intense, what-does-she-mean-to-you? scale.

"Aby, truth is…I like you. I've told you that."

He liked the way her beaming smile glittered in her eyes. She bubbled. Max had never known someone so effervescent.

"But I'm concerned about us together on this trip."

She fluttered her lashes. "You think we might fall in love?"

He chuffed. "I don't do love, Aby."

"Oh." She gave a little pout, but smiled quickly enough. "I'm cool with that. Slow and easy. That's what I'm about. Well, maybe not easy. Just cool and—"

He kissed her to rescue her from a tangle of words. The lithe shape of her, the sinuous warmth of her stretching along his hard contours ratcheted up his lust.

Slow and cool. Right.

He stepped back and shoved his hands in the front pockets of his jeans. "Love isn't in the cards. Never has been, never will."

He grimaced at the lie. He had loved Rebecca. Intensely.

But he hadn't been able to save her. He'd failed Rebecca.

"What's wrong with love?" she asked in all innocence. "I love Severo."

"Do you love him romantically? Do you think about kissing him, about having sex with him?"

"No. But you? Yes. I dream about your kisses. Well, you know what I dream about."

He swallowed. Now was not the time to reveal he'd climaxed while walking through her dreams.

"Like I said, I don't think this will work—me and you. And I don't want to piss off your werewolf. Maybe I should locate Rainier myself, bring him back here, and then you can do the bridging."

A pout had never worked so devastatingly upon his heart. For a woman who was innocent in the whole love-and-emotion department, Aby could work him like a puppet.

And when she leaned in to kiss him, Max knew pushing her away would damage her far worse than another innocent kiss might chink his armor.

A simple kiss was all she asked. And he complied. But the press of her lips upon his mouth stirred him so quickly, he deepened the kiss and held her tight.

Was it because of her strangely innocent sexuality that he was attracted to her? Talk about the Madonna and the whore. But Aby was reversed in such a manner that he didn't know how to take her.

"How can you leave me here alone, when if I come along with you there will be more kisses?" she asked. "Don't you like kissing me, Max?"

"Your kisses, I can honestly say, I love."

And he kissed her again, pulling her close, his hand spreading across her back. The way she moved into him was so automatic, as if they had been made for one another. And maybe they were.

In two centuries he'd never met a woman who had dreamed about him so viscerally.

"There could be more than kisses," she repeated.

He skated his partly open lips across her collarbone, yet their contact was only building his frustration. A man shouldn't complain about getting to touch and kiss a woman like Aby.

So he wouldn't.

A moan, deep and throaty, came from him, not her. He was letting this woman get to him in a way that he'd not allowed a woman to breach his defenses since Rebecca.

The wet skim of her tongue to his lip surprised him. He broke the kiss and searched her eyes. Dazzle and redirect was how the magicians did it. She'd dazzled and now she was switching the game to the redirect.

"More please," she whispered eagerly.

So he took his time, tracing the underside of her lip with his tongue and allowing her to re-create his actions. It was exquisite, this teaching and in turn, learning how willing he was to surrender control, to follow Aby's signals.

Or was it merely the power of her sparkle that distracted him as if he were a damned magpie?

When she undid the top two buttons on his shirt and the flat of her palm seared his flesh, he sucked in a breath.

"You like that?" she murmured against his mouth.

"I feel your touch all the way to my toes." A roaring need coursed through his system. A need that could never be met—at least not in Aby's waking hours.

This was going to be a long trip.

"We should go. The flight leaves in little over an hour, and we've got to check in, even if it is a private jet."

"A private jet?" she said, picking up her suitcase. "Really?"

"I've a few contacts. I'd hate for your first flight to be in coach in those cattle cars they call an airplane. Hand me that pink monstrosity, and let's head out."

The jet was luxurious, and owned by a philanthropist friend. That's all Max would tell her. Didn't matter. Aby enjoyed the whole experience. She could even find the fun in her ears popping as the plane increased altitude.

The interior was done in butter-soft russet leather that Max had commented was the same color as her hair. The chairs and couch were plush and a sound system displayed flashing red and green lights, waiting the touch of a button.

When Max returned from talking to the pilot, he

announced they had seven hours to get to know each other. And Aby knew exactly how she intended to do that.

He'd finally shucked off the huge dark coat and hung the whip near the door. He offered her bottled water and sat on the couch opposite her.

Aby sipped the cool water and twisted on the cap. Then she slinked across the aisle to sit beside Max. As if drawn to him, she couldn't resist his warmth, and his stoic need to somehow keep distance between them.

She'd change his mind about that.

A kiss was met with no resistance. He tasted delicious, clean like the spring water he'd sipped. He touched her, gently, yet holding on as if no one else could have her. He was reluctant, and she knew it was because she had requested they go slow. That was fine. It would keep him respectful.

The more she thought about it, she knew this was a bold step. Taking off to another country with a man she hardly knew. Though he was legend, she couldn't be sure the demon shadow he carried wouldn't suddenly rise up and make Max evil. If he was so desperate to be rid of it, it must be because he thought that would happen, too.

No, he just wanted to be normal, to eat and sleep.

Aby would exercise caution. But curiosity was both her boon and bane.

She wondered if he ever truly relaxed. And what about his sleepless, dreamless nights?

"Don't people go insane if they can't dream?" she blurted.

He laughed at her sudden question. Stroking a thumb over her lips, he asked, "Is that all you can think about me? Worried I might freak out on you?"

"No, but I thought a dreamless mind was a mad mind. I've seen TV shows. Do the dreams your shadow sees act as your own?"

"I witness them but I never feel them, not in real life. Only in the dream. Like if you pinched me now it would hurt. In the dream, I'd just know it hurts."

"So you don't experience the high of sex in a sex dream?"

"Aby, this conversation is treading a line I can't cross right now. Can you be okay with that?"

There were many things about Max Fitzroy she didn't know yet.

Aby sighed. "Yes, I can. But I'll have you know we cats are curious."

He toggled the diamond necklace. "I did notice that."

"So, you go to Paris often?"

"Haven't been there for over a century. I like America. And since I've been here, I've found plenty of demons to keep me busy. The States absolutely reek of them. Not to say the Americans have a market on evil. It's everywhere."

"I know. Heck, I live in Minnesota, but I've seen some bad stuff."

He hooked his boots on the opposite couch and leaned back. The move tightened his black button-up shirt across hard abs. Aby toyed with the next button.

"When you were a real highwayman," she asked, "did you ever say 'Stand and deliver'?"

He chuckled. "All the time. We Frenchmen borrowed it from the English."

"I had a dream about you robbing my carriage."

"Did you now?"

She slid the necklace across her lower lip. "You wanted my jewels, but I didn't have any."

He nodded appreciatively. "So what did you offer instead?"

A blush heated her neck. "The dream ended too quickly for me to find out. What made you start riding the high roads? You said you were orphaned?"

"My father was killed by a highwayman when I was six. We were well off. But then it was just my mother and I, and my mother fell in with a bad man who stole all our money. He killed her one night. I escaped to live on the streets."

"Max, I'm so sorry."

He shrugged. "I'm still here. Good, bad or otherwise."

"So you chose to do what the man who killed your father did."

"Aby, there wasn't much opportunity for a kid in those days. If I didn't get enslaved by the lechers then I had to steal to survive."

"I understand. But still it makes me sad to think of that lonely, orphaned boy."

"I got by. Rainier and I hooked up a few years after that. We looked out for one another and we mastered the fine art of theft."

"You're doing good things now."

"You didn't have that opinion when I first met you."

"I didn't know you then."

"Come here, kitty cat." He patted his lap and Aby snuggled to him. "I'm not sure you know what you're doing to me, Aby."

"Seducing you."

"All right, maybe you do know. But what if it doesn't turn out the way you want it to?"

"I have no expectations, Max. I know what you are, what you do. You've already said love isn't on the table. Why don't you stop worrying about everything for a while and just kiss me?"

"Because I need you to understand how I work. I could kiss you all day, Aby. I'd like to make love to you. But you have to realize if we start something and I suddenly walk away, it's because I have to."

"Is it the shadow?"

"Yes and no. It's something I can't talk about. Not yet."

"All right. But if you want to shadow, just tell me. I'm cool with it."

He drew her head close and kissed her forehead.

They must have kissed for ten minutes when Aby decided she wanted to feel Max's skin against hers. She pushed her hands under his shirt that strained at the buttonholes. His muscles tensed but he didn't break the kiss. Everything about him was hard and hot. Gliding her fingers lower, she counted the ridges strapping his abs.

So that's what they meant by a six-pack.

She shifted and the shoulder strap of her dress slipped, exposing her creamy skin. Max's hand cupped her bare shoulder, then slid lower, dragging the fabric down to expose the top of her right breast.

"I love your skin," he murmured. And she loved when he kissed her there. His kisses there always made her squirm with ridiculous joy.

A lazy, wanting groan accompanied the slow glide of his tongue. His murmurs hummed in her being, becoming as much a turn-on as his touches. Aby could gauge his rising desire as Max's voice grew lower and deeper, lingering across her flesh as he devoured it slowly.

The first touch of his tongue to her nipple sent delicious tingles up and down her spine. Clutching his shoulders, she dug her nails into his shirt. Arching her back, Aby drew up her leg and hugged his hip with her knee. She wanted to hold him in the worshipful position until she flew higher than this jet could ever take her.

"Max, that's better than kissing with our mouths open," she said.

He stopped suddenly and bracketed her head with his hands. Putting his forehead to hers, he then said, "What would happen if you…you know?"

"Came?"

He nodded. "You wouldn't accidentally—"

"An inability to control the bridging only happens with first-life familiars. I can't bridge a demon all by myself. You need a spell or summons. We're safe."

"Just checking."

His concern gave her little worry. He was the Highwayman. Of course, he'd be wary of any chance a demon might apport to this realm.

Aby traced her tongue down the center of his chest. Max spread out his arms and took in her ministrations with another lingering moan.

He tasted wonderful. The movement of his muscles beneath her tongue and fingers forged liquid iron and she could command its shape with a stroke of her finger.

Seven hours until landing? This was going to be a blissful flight.

He could strip her bare right now. He needed to. She was giving him all the go signals. But Max restrained himself from tugging Aby's dress over her hips and slipping it off her.

Wrapped about him, her ankles crossed behind his back, her arms about his shoulders, she dropped kisses to his chest and neck and mouth and sparked a long-lost desire he'd once thought dissipated in his soul.

But he wasn't ready to claim her, to slip inside her. How could he when it would only result in disappointment? Sure, he could please her, get her off, but he wasn't prepared to explain why he couldn't in return.

He would have to tell her sometime. And then she would learn about what walking in her dream had done for him.

He would tell her later, when he figured how best to put it. Such knowledge would change things. It would complicate everything.

But, Christ, he wanted her. Much as it would

increase his ache, he wanted to glide inside her. To spill over and over. His erection was so hard, it was painful. After all, man was not created to withstand pleasure for so long.

If and when he ever did shuck the demon, would his next lovemaking see him coming endlessly? What a relief that would be.

But he couldn't deny giving Aby pleasure vicariously served his own unslakable pleasure. Every moan from Aby, every touch, every hug of her skin against his gratified him. It had been a while since he'd indulged in the physical flesh.

She would be his undoing, if she didn't drive him mad first.

"You're so hard," she said. Her fingers eased over his crotch.

Max caught her by the wrist. "Don't, Aby, please. It's tough enough to not take you right now."

"Then why don't you? I want this, Max. Don't you think I have needs? Don't you think I've been imagining what it would feel like to have you inside me?"

"Don't talk like that."

"Why not?"

"Because you said you wanted to go slow. Bleeding cowboys, this isn't right."

He pulled away and settled against the chair, panting, sweating. Shoving his hands through his hair, he struggled with the need to do as she asked and the need to maintain his own decorum.

Decorum? Hell, it was sanity he needed to cling to.

She sat curled on the sofa beside him, her breasts bare and wet with his saliva. The nipples were hard. Her mouth red, bruised by his determination to take what he could from her.

He'd kissed her so deeply. And there were other places on her body he'd like to thrust his tongue into for a deep kiss.

"Don't you want me, Max? Are you still afraid I'll bridge a demon here? Because I won't."

"It's not you, Aby." It was his damned curse. "You're gorgeous. I want you. Damn, but I want you." And he could have her—in her dreams. "What happened to going slow?"

She drew curved fingers across the luscious mounds of her breasts. "You've stirred me to a wanting tangle of need and now you think to pull away and it'll all be fine?"

Exactly. What a bastard you are, Fitzroy. And yet, he'd given himself an out.

"You're forgetting the one rule I gave you if we were to be intimate."

She crawled over and straddled him. The vixen in her glinted in her green eyes as she spread her fingers through his hair and tugged his head back against the chair cushion. "When you pull away, you mean it."

"I…I should have shadowed before we left. Things are…" So hard.

"Are what?"

"God, Aby, I need to shadow. Just to take the edge off, you know?"

"I don't know, but I promised you I'd step back when you asked." She pulled back from him. "Can I watch?"

"Nope."

Chapter 15

Curled into a ball, Aby was purring softly by the time Max returned from chatting with the pilot. Opening the overhead bin, he tugged out a blue thermal blanket and laid it over her body. He'd used the excuse of checking in with the pilot to get away, hoping Aby would drift into a catnap.

She did not disappoint.

He stretched and decided to go wash up in the bathroom. They'd be in Paris in a couple hours.

In the bathroom he leaned over the sink, staring at his reflection. The shadow had but two options to dream walk. The pilot had better not be sleeping.

Which left Aby.

He'd already peered into her dreams once without asking.

When had he ever asked before? It wasn't as though the shadow allowed the dreamers it walked a choice. But not until now had Max considered the dream walking an invasion. A step into the dreamer's private life. He had no right to take that from Aby.

Because, depending on the topic of her dreams, he could be taking more than she was willing to give.

On the other hand, she was the one who'd suggested they go all the way.

God, he wanted to feel that climax again. To know it was real.

"If I don't," he said with gritted jaw to his reflection, "I'll be testy and angry when we arrive. She doesn't deserve that, either."

He needed to confirm that first time had been a fluke. She couldn't possibly have been the catalyst to him climaxing.

"Time to find out."

With a nod, he rescinded his human shape and the shadow slipped under the bathroom door.

The dreamer lay beneath a blanket on the couch. He moved over her, cringing at the strange air that squeezed upon his edges. This did not feel like usual shadowing. Perhaps because of the different place,

different atmosphere. Retaining this form was difficult...

Instantaneous images flooded him with experience. Bodies entwined. Gasps, moans, fingers
scratching softly across sweat-glistened flesh. A
cry of immense pleasure.

The shadow shuddered, feeling the sensation on
a visceral level, but unable to grasp it for any length
of time. Only the dreamer climaxed. The other—
him—lay beside her, watching her pleasure.

The joyous cry of orgasm suddenly changed to a
scream. The dreamer clung to the other—yet slipped
away. Water splashed. Hands frantically slapped the
surface but to no avail. Glugging. Waves rippling.

Then silence.

Her green eyes flashed open. "Max?"

The shadow crept away toward the back of the
airplane.

Max held Aby's hand when the rough landing
made her nervous, and he held it again as they dis-
embarked and went through customs.

He lifted her hand to his cheek, brushing it over
his stubble, then kissed each knuckle tenderly. Like
a boyfriend.

She'd often wondered what it would be like to
have a boyfriend. A lover. A man who would have
sex with her for reasons beyond summoning

demons. Now she didn't have to wonder. They'd gotten close to making love.

Okay, so calling him her boyfriend was probably putting the cart before the horse, but they had something going on between the two of them. And Aby intended to keep it.

She hadn't been at all frightened to see his shadow upon waking. What a strange dream he must have seen. She only remembered the drowning part. But she'd never had portentous dreams so she dismissed it as a nightmare.

Maybe that was why he seemed so concerned for her now.

"It was just a nightmare," she offered, smiling up at him.

He nodded. "I shouldn't have intruded on your dreams again. I'm sorry. It was unavoidable."

She squeezed his hand. "I'm not angry. But I don't want you to worry."

He grimaced and led them onward.

Rain pummeled the sidewalk as they stepped outside the sliding airport doors. Max strode to the curb and searched for a cab. The drive before the B terminal was clear of vehicles, but he reassured Aby it wouldn't take more than a few minutes for a cab to arrive.

Sniffing the air, Aby scented meadow, tarmac and fuel. Beneath the veil of odor, she smelled old elegance. She observed Max rubbing a hand across the back of his neck. "Sore muscles?"

"No, I… It's a strange feeling I'm getting. Like a knowing. But what, I just can't tell. You feel anything funny?"

"Should I?"

"Nah, it's probably nothing. Just the air, you know?"

"Yes, it feels old here."

"Exactly. Ancient." He cast his gaze across the sky. "Dangerous."

"So, Paris," she said, sitting on her suitcase under the building's eave. If she stretched out her toes they would get wet. Because she wore her black strappy sandals, she kept them tucked close to the suitcase. "Bet you love it, huh? Isn't Paris where you're originally from?"

Stoic, hands shoved in his coat pockets, Max kept his eyes glued down the street, toward the curving entrance to the pickup port. "I haven't been here for any length of time since it happened."

"Really? You mean…?"

"I couldn't get out of the city fast enough after I'd realized what had become of me. I headed across the channel to England."

"That surprises me. So you've no lost loves here in Paris?"

He smirked. "None who are still alive."

"Right. It's been a while. How long were you in England?"

"Twenty years."

"What kept you there for so long?"

"My wife."

He'd been married? The stoic, nonfeeling man she'd had to practically attack to get to kiss her had shared his life with another woman?

Aby tugged Max by the coat sleeve. "Your back is getting wet."

With a step, he fit himself close to her. The heat of him electrified her senses, while the memory of his tongue gliding over her skin as they'd soared through the clouds stirred up a delicious shiver.

She wrapped her arms around his waist, inside his coat. "So, a wife. That's interesting. How long were you married?"

"Five years."

"What happened?"

"I'd rather not speak of it. It's been a while, Aby. But you should know, I married once more after Rebecca."

A name. Somehow that made it more real, personal. Yet Max didn't seem eager to expound on their life together. She supposed that made sense. He'd had enough time to forget her.

"And the second marriage? Can I ask about that one?"

"It lasted three days. I married Emiline in eighteen-fifty. It was one of those all-night-drunken-escapades-in-Las-Vegas kind of things when you wake up the next morning with a ring on your finger. Only it was in a little Welsh village, and I wore a diamond bracelet on my…er…"

He swiped a hand over his face and turned away, but Aby had seen him redden. She could imagine where the bracelet had ended up. Oh, Max, what a deliciously bad boy.

"She was a widow and looking for a good time. Neither of us had intended marriage. When I told her the truth about my profession, she couldn't run away fast enough. Unfortunately, when she ran… I don't want to talk about this. It's the past. I've moved on."

"Max, you surprise me."

"Why? I'm a man, Aby. We do stupid things like get married when we're drunk. It should only surprise you I didn't do it over and over again."

"You learned your lesson with the second marriage?"

"Haven't so much as had a girlfriend since."

"That's very sad."

He smirked. "Didn't say I wasn't keeping a little black book."

"I bet that's a thick book."

"I'll never tell. There's a cab." He thrust up an arm, but the cab pulled to a stop down the way where an elderly couple stood. "Let them have it. Give it a few more minutes."

"So, who was the most interesting woman you've ever entered in your book?"

"Why are you so interested in my love life?"

"I'm trying to get to know you better." She shuffled under the eave again, brushing the rain from her forearms. "I mean, your love life has got to be about as unique as mine. Unusual circumstances, and all."

"You can learn about a man without prying into his sex life. Why don't you ask me about my hobbies, my favorite television show or book? What about my political leanings? My religion?"

"Max, you're getting angry for no reason. I was making small talk."

"I'm just saying there's more to me than the women I've bedded."

"Yeah? Well, you brought it up. For a man who never sleeps, you've no doubt countless time to expand your horizons and…do whatever it is you do."

"What I do—" He leaned over and stabbed a finger at her as his voice took on a sharp edge. "Is hunt demons. All day, all night. I don't have time for anything else. I live, eat, breathe and die for demons. Got that?"

Stunned at his rising anger, Aby nodded silently. Somebody needed to shadow again.

"Demons, I'll have you know, that you summoned into this realm."

"Not all of them!" How dare he accuse her? Why was he being so cruel? After what they'd shared on the flight here?

"Cab's here."

Aby was tired from the flight. The rain was making her stuffy and grumpy. And now the one man she had trusted to protect her during this new and dangerous adventure was yelling at her.

Sputtering out a few tears, Aby balked when Max directed her into the cab. She didn't want to get into another tiny, enclosed space with him.

"What are you— Are you crying?"

She nodded. "Just go away."

"Aby, don't cry. Damn it."

Rain ricocheted off his long coat and hit her bare legs. Aby twisted her head away from him and snapped, "Go chase some demons!"

The soft touch of his finger along her jaw startled her and she looked up at him. His eyes seemed genuinely apologetic.

"It's miserable and wet out here, Aby. Get in the cab and I'll bring you to a nice dry, luxury hotel. Okay?"

No apology? She ducked her head and mined for the cell phone in her purse.

"Who are you going to call?"

"I should check in with Severo. He asked to let him know when I arrived safely." Safely, but not happily.

"When are you going to let go of him?"

"What?"

"That werewolf is like some kind of crutch to you, Aby. Christ, you're on life number four. Haven't you the courage to live on your own yet?"

"You are a bastard."

She darted for the cab and slid inside. At least in there it was dry.

In her ear the phone rang, but Severo did not pick up. With the time change he could be working, or out on a midnight lope across the countryside.

The trunk slammed shut, then Max slid into the backseat and gave the driver an address. He shook his head, which sprayed rain all over the vinyl seat.

"You're worse than an animal," she muttered.

"You talk to your wolf?"

"He isn't answering. And so what if I like to check in with him? And, yes, I have already lived three lives, but it's not as though I remember all I've learned from life to life. Severo was the first to ever show me kindness, to want me to learn and retain that information. So I'll call him all I like, Highwayman."

She turned to press the side of her head to the window and closed her eyes. What had she done, traveling across the ocean with this virtual stranger? What made her think he might be interested in her beyond what she could do for him?

Stupid kitty.

She felt Max touch his finger to her wrist, but she didn't open her eyes. He traced the tattoo that declared him her enemy.

While Max was tempted to find a room at one of the hostels in the city, he directed the driver to the corner of rue de Rivoli and the Place des Pyramids and followed a quiet Aby behind the footman at the Hotel Regina. It was ultraluxurious, as he promised, with marble floors and columns, gilt and damask and velvets.

The sigh of relief Aby gave when she walked into the room worked wonders for his guilt.

"I'm taking a shower," she announced, before the footman even left. The bathroom door closed.

Max hadn't had time to change American dollars for euros at the airport, but the footman wasn't fussy. He nabbed the fifty and tucked it away more deftly than a magician, then bowed out of the room.

It was early evening. He wasn't tired. He was never tired. But he suspected Aby would be.

Thinking to make up for his crass treatment at the airport, he dialed room service and ordered dinner. She could eat, then sleep. By morning she might see to forgiving him.

If you ask for forgiveness, idiot.

He hadn't said he was sorry. It just hit him now. "Asshole."

When was the last time he'd been concerned about his actions toward another person? He didn't do relationships. It was a waste of time. The person always died. And he didn't want the person to die sooner because of their association with a hunter.

Besides, did he really believe he could date a chick who could curl up in his lap and take a real catnap?

This thing—whatever it was—between him and Aby was like walking across broken glass. One wrong step, and blood would flow. He knew she looked to him for more than a mere business partnership. She wanted a connection. They'd had connection in the jet. He couldn't resist her allure, the tempting sparkle of her.

"Don't forget she's a tool," he reminded himself.

Find her, screw her and then kill her. That had been the plan. But he couldn't think in those terms anymore. Find her. Make love to her. And then protect her with every fiber of his being.

"Bleeding cowboys, I shouldn't have touched her."

And yet, he couldn't have not touched her.

Chained to her now, he realized Aby had become the anchor he'd tried to shun. Would she become his madness?

The shower stopped, and Aby emerged minutes later wrapped in a towel and trailing a fruity scent in her wake. She scrunched fingers through her wet hair and went to unzip the pink suitcase.

Max sat on the bed opposite hers, trying to keep his expression neutral. She wouldn't dress in the same room with him, would she? Of course, she must be comfortable being naked in front of strangers. And she'd already been half-naked for him.

"I'm sorry for the way I treated you at the airport," he said. "It was mean."

"Thank you. And I promise not to call Severo anymore."

"He asked you to call, so you should. I've no right to ask anything of you."

"I wish you would."

He turned and she stood at the end of his bed, a towel clutched to her breasts. Normally this situation could only end in one way.

To keep from reaching for her, Max shrugged his fingers through his hair.

"There's room service," he said, and gestured at the tray the valet had brought up. "Thought you'd be hungry and want to sleep after you ate."

"That was thoughtful. Will you join me? You can watch and I'll describe to you how everything tastes."

That didn't sound half-bad. "You're going to dress first? I mean, you're kind of naked."

"You noticed?" She trailed a fingertip along the towel. There her breasts were high and the remembrance of tasting them brought the saliva to his tongue.

"Aby, don't do this to me."

"Do what?"

"I'm not made of steel. I do have feelings and sitting in a room with a woman in a towel is going to push me over the edge."

"I thought we'd already spilled over that edge. Are you having second thoughts about what we did in the airplane?"

"No," he breathed. "Never." Yes. Always.

"But now that you've had some time to think about it…?"

She could have easily answered the open-ended question. But it was his burden to bear.

Hell. He needed to tell her, and if she couldn't accept him after, then he'd put her on a plane to Minnesota and try to forget he'd ever known Aby.

Impossible. She was a part of him now. The shadow had tasted her soul, just as he had tasted her flesh.

"There's something about me I haven't told you yet."

Could he do this? You've faced down demons, Max, you can face this harmless familiar.

"I think you need to know, but I don't want it to change the way you think about me, or the things you want from me."

She sat beside him and clasped his hand, so tender and once again eager to please him with her open acceptance. "Go ahead. It can't be much worse than having a demon shadow inside and not sleeping or eating."

His voice rasped as he confessed his darkest secret. "Try not being able to have an orgasm."

"What?"

"It's the final nail in my coffin. No sleep, no food, no sexual satisfaction."

"But—"

"I can have sex. Hell, I can bring a woman to orgasm, and it's great for me. And the women, too, as you've learned. Pleasure is pleasure, after all. But I can't…get off."

"Seriously? All these years?" When he shook his head she asked, "Why didn't you tell me this before?"

"I didn't want to put you off me." He stood, but she wouldn't release his hand. Closing his eyes and inhaling, Max pushed back the strange fear riding his spine. He turned and knelt before her. "I like you, Aby. I like holding you, kissing you, touching you, and I want to do a hell of a lot more with you. It's a problem of mine, but it doesn't have to affect the way I make you feel."

"But if you can't take pleasure from being with me… Oh, I've been so awful."

"Aby, I take immense pleasure from you." Bracketing her face with his hands, he kissed her. Her lips had been made for his pleasure, no matter how fleeting. He nuzzled his forehead against her breast. "Sex doesn't always have to end in orgasm."

"I suppose." She stroked his hair. He could kneel before her forever and never wish release from her tender embrace. "But for a man denied it for centuries, I bet that's all you can think about."

"Most of the day and all through the night."

"That's about as much as I think of it, too. Except I'm always wondering how it would be to make love and not have just sex. You made love to me in the airplane, Max."

"Mostly. I couldn't go all the way with you. I didn't want you to think something was wrong with me."

"Oh, you poor man." She stroked his cheek. "Then we've got to find Rainier. You need to have an orgasm."

He chuckled quietly. "I should have told you

this right away. Maybe you wouldn't have been so indecisive about wanting to help me."

"Maybe."

He kissed her at the base of her throat. "We'll find Rainier. I can feel him."

"You can?"

"Yes, that feeling I had at the airport? Since we set foot on French soil, I've just…known. It's like it was in the old days. I might have been riding the high roads, pistol held high and eyes on the prize, but I always instinctually knew my partner was near, even when I couldn't see him."

"Do you think you can track him with that feeling?"

"No. It's not that tangible. But I know of someone who might set us on the right course."

"Good. Then after we've found Rainier, I want to be your first."

"My first?"

Her jewel eyes sparkled brightly and she stroked a finger across his lips. "The first to make you come after two hundred fifty years."

She was taking this well. There was no reason for her not to—save for one detail.

"Aby, there's something else."

"What else can a man be deprived of?"

"I think sex, food and sleep about covers it. It's about the dream walking."

"You've seen my sex dreams. I've accepted that."

"Right, but I told you I've never felt anything from them, that I couldn't get off watching another person's dreams."

"That makes me so sad for you."

"Yeah, well… The other night in your room as I stood over your bed, watching you dream of me making love to you, I, uh…got off."

Her mouth open, she waited with what Max hoped was expectation, but it looked more like fear.

"I don't know what happened, Aby, but I felt everything in that dream. I felt you kiss me, felt your hands gliding over my flesh, and I actually climaxed while in shadow form."

Her brows rose, though she sat there, still silent.

"I didn't think it possible. It's never happened before. But after I shifted out of shadow form… there was evidence." He searched her unreadable gaze. "You gave me pleasure in your dreams. It was the most incredible experience."

"And you're just telling me about it now?"

He bowed his head. "I wasn't sure how to tell you."

Aby stood abruptly and tugged the towel tighter across her breasts. She prowled across the room.

"I mean, I thought you'd feel…violated."

"Whew." She blew out a breath. Looking aside, she

clasped her arms high about her chest. "So you experienced an orgasm while I was dreaming about you?"

He nodded.

"And it's not something you've had for over two centuries?"

A shrugging nod was all he could manage. Had he said too much? He had. Stupid, Max, why didn't you just keep your mouth shut?

"I think I need to think about this one. I'm not sure how I feel right now."

"It wasn't purposeful. I swear it to you."

"And on the airplane? You shadowed again. Did you do so knowing you might climax again?"

"No, I—" Yes. "It was just the nightmare. You were initially dreaming of us again, but it didn't go so far that time." He winced, knowing he sounded like the voyeur of the century. And what kind of creep did that make him?

He avoided the truth now—that he had wanted to see if her dreams could make him feel again. How did he put into words the pining for a sensation that he'd not had for so long?

"I need to be alone," she said, still unable to meet his eyes.

"Of course. I've some contacts to make. I'll do it in the lobby. Aby?"

A shudder trembled her shoulders and she

looked away from him. He felt her rejection stab his heart.

"I didn't do it thinking I could get something from you without asking. It surprised the hell out of me. And you have to know, it was the best feeling I've known for centuries. Thank you."

He walked out and closed the door.

In the hallway Max hung his head and exhaled. Had he just lost the girl?

Chapter 16

"Where are we walking?"

Max hooked his arm through Aby's. She didn't balk. All morning long she'd thought about what he'd revealed to her last night. He'd been genuine. She believed he honestly hadn't gone into her dreams on some kind of voyeuristic quest. And that he'd actually climaxed should make her feel great. He'd gotten something from her he hadn't been able to achieve for centuries.

But that he'd gotten it without her knowledge still bothered her. She didn't want it to bother her. She wanted to embrace him and kiss him and say, "Way to go! Let's try that again."

She needed more time though. Dream sex was a new one for her.

The Seine flowed quietly to their right, and he'd pointed out the Eiffel Tower in the distance as their destination. The day was overcast, dreary, but walking alongside the Highwayman lifted her spirits.

She wanted him, but on her own terms. Terms they were both aware of, awake or sleeping. Was there anything wrong with that?

"The seventh arrondissement," Max finally answered. "In the Eiffel Tower's shadow, and down the street from Les Invalides, an old military hospital and veterans' home. Ginnie told me about a seer who can track auras, and I trust her judgment."

"Ginnie?"

"A friend of mine."

"I thought you didn't have friends."

"I met Ginnie in Berlin at the turn of the twentieth century. She's a financial whiz, and has been helping me with my portfolio ever since. I guess you could call her my accountant, but she'd prefer Total Lifestyle Rescuer. She pulled me out of some hard times."

"Sounds like a smart chick. But old." They paused to let a silver Smart car pass on the cobbled street before crossing it. "The turn of last century?"

"I didn't mention she's a vampire."

"That explains a lot. So you never had the desire to hunt her? I mean, you hunt all sorts, right?"

"Yes, but Ginnie has never been a threat. She lives under the radar. She's good folk. I think you'd like her if you two ever met."

Aby doubted it. She disliked longtooths, Severo's word for vampires. In fact, it was Severo's dislike, now that she thought of it.

Perhaps she was due for meeting the vampire and forming her own conclusions about whom she liked and whom she did not.

"Let's cross here."

They skipped across a wide street and Max filed down a neighborhood featuring three- and four-story houses and larger buildings. Over the rooftops, Aby spied the spire of the famous iron tower. "I want to go up there while I'm here."

"This is a business trip."

Right. Back to all business then. Max fluctuated from business to pleasure so quickly, she was beginning to get dizzy.

He stopped at a street corner and drew up her hand to kiss the back of it. A wink and his sexy, secretive smile with the dimple dove into her heart. There was that dizzy feeling again.

"You think about what I told you last night?" he asked.

"Haven't been able to stop."

"So?"

She shrugged and slipped her hand from his. "I'm still thinking."

"You're by my side today. That's got to count for something. I'll take what I can get."

She was changing him. Making him tolerant. More—damn, he hated to admit it—gentle. Max was happy to please his sparkly thing.

And what was wrong with that picture?

Nothing, actually. Most normal red-blooded men did enjoy a good flirt with a sexy woman. Many pursued them and had girlfriends. It was what men did. It made them happy. It was that whole circle-of-life thing.

Max couldn't deny he wanted to be normal. He'd tried with Rebecca to touch normality. It had worked a few years, and then had failed miserably. Did that mean he had to swear off relationships ever after?

Nope. And yet, his brain still hadn't caught up to his body. The ol' cerebrum clung to the darkness, forming dismal ideas of the future.

He should stay in the now and enjoy what he had with Aby.

But that was much easier said than done. Especially after he'd revealed the big one last night.

Could she get beyond what he'd done to her and

accept she had been the catalyst to the greatest pleasure he'd had in centuries? He wanted to celebrate that with her, not worry it might wedge them further apart.

Max threaded his fingers through Aby's.

Please, God; just give me this one thing. Haven't I sacrificed enough?

The seer's home was a narrow two-story set between two larger buildings, almost as if an afterthought.

Max pushed open the iron gate. Aby skipped in first through the small garden fronting the property, her attention drawn to a tall pink flower. The small plots of land on either side of the cobblestone walk were lined with flowers Max didn't have names for. Bees buzzed about ruffled purple blooms and birds chirped at hanging feeders.

"It's magical," she said, eyeing a particular yellow bird and licking her lips.

"Don't even tell me," Max said, noticing her interest in the bird.

"Hey, a cat's got to eat sometime."

He'd remember that next time they were in a restaurant. Chicken for his bird lover.

Aby strode up the porch to ring the buzzer. Before she could touch the button, the door opened to reveal a tall, slender woman with kind blue eyes.

"Oh, lovely," she said at the sight of Aby.

Aby smoothed at her wrinkled dress. "*Bonsoir,* I am Aby."

"Maximilien Fitzroy," Max offered from over her shoulder and held out his hand to shake the woman's. "Ginnie sent me. She said you could help me locate a missing friend."

"You've traveled far," the woman said. "Come in and I'll make tea."

Seating her guests in the front porch, the seer then excused herself to collect tea.

Aby plopped onto the wicker love seat and twined her fingers into Max's. He leaned in to kiss her quickly. She tasted like the champagne and orange juice that room service had delivered for breakfast. He'd never eaten an orange, but the sweetness on Aby's breath made him crave the fruit.

"Is it okay I still kiss you?"

In reply she kissed him back, this time tracing her tongue over his lips. "Yes, it is. But no dream walking for now."

"I can live with that. I want you to be happy for me, Aby. Happy that together we achieved something I haven't known for so long."

"Don't push, Max. Just give me time." With a sigh, she dismissed the conversation and looked about the porch. "This is the neatest place, all the flowers and this cozy porch. I think I need to plant flowers when I get home."

He stroked her hair and she nuzzled against his shoulder. "This coming from the chick who refused the gift of a plant in favor of a kitty toy. Maybe you should hire a gardener. That seems more your speed."

"I could deal with that. Mmm, your hand is warm." She opened his palm and traced his lifeline. "It goes past your wrist."

"A lot different than yours."

"I've never seen anything like it." She kissed his palm.

The tiny moist touch stirred him, and Max knew if he didn't end this flirtation he'd be very uncomfortable when the seer returned.

Thinking of the devil... The old woman popped in with a silver tray loaded with teacups and a plate of tiny frosted cakes.

"I'm Beatrice, by the way. I haven't seen Ginnie for a few years. I hope she is well?"

"*Très bien,*" Max reassured her, finding that he utilized his long-abandoned French when he was around those who spoke it. He refused the tea with a polite nod.

Aby sipped the warm brew, while Max drew in the scent of chamomile. Pure, sweet and fruity, like Aby.

"You've come for insight," Beatrice said to Max. She glanced expectantly to Aby. "You've all you need if you accept her for what she is."

Max's jaw dropped, but he resumed his calm when Aby noticed. What was with all these psychic witchy sorts? They all wanted to wheedle into his love life.

"It's not about Aby," he said with forced casualness.

"It is, Maximilien. You will learn that soon enough."

Accepting her advice with a tight-lipped grimace, he then said, "I've a former partner—"

"In crime," Beatrice finished knowingly. "Yes, you rode the high roads in the eighteenth century."

Ginnie had said this woman would blow his mind.

"You mustn't be frightened," Beatrice said to Aby. "You are strong."

"Oh, I'm not frightened. Just out of sorts to be in a new city. But I have Max to protect me."

"Yes. Ahem. Don't suffer fools." She said the last with a glance to Max.

If she could see the trouble he and Aby were having right now… Nah, she couldn't. Could she?

"About my partner," Max insisted. "I believe he may still be in France, possibly Paris. I need a fix on him."

"You don't feel him?" Beatrice asked. "Since setting foot on French soil, you've not noticed the tug within you?"

Max clutched his chest. "Those weird sensations? Yes, a sort of knowing. But I can't follow it
by any means."

Beatrice smiled and shook her head. "I'll need
something that belonged to your Rainier."

"It's been centuries. I don't—" Max tugged open
his jacket. "Maybe."

He produced the small silver disk from an inside
pocket.

"A silver *demi-écu.*" He handed it to Beatrice.
"Rainier and I both held it at one time."

"Before someone shot at you," Beatrice finished.

No points for the seer on that one. It was pretty
obvious from the hole in the coin.

Aby set down her teacup and leaned forward to
examine the coin Beatrice held between two
fingers. "What happened to it?"

"A bullet went through it. I've carried it with me
since seventeen fifty-eight." Max smirked. "'To
danger, to adventure.' That was our motto."

"Cool." Aby smiled at the seer and the woman
nodded sagely.

Beatrice closed her fingers over the coin and
stared straight ahead. "Rainier Deloche," she said.

"Yes," Max agreed. "Do you get a vision of
him?"

The old woman closed her eyes tightly, winced
then opened them wide. She looked beyond Max

and Aby, as if seeing into eternity. "He's half a foot shorter than you are. Brown hair and bold brown eyes. Freckles?"

"Yes, he had them on his nose." She was impressive. "Can you get a fix on his location?"

"I see him…"

"Yes?"

The screen door creaked, and in walked a man with brown hair and bold brown eyes set above a freckled nose. "Hey, Max, long time no see."

Chapter 17

"I knew the moment you landed in Paris," Rainier said.

The trio had bid Beatrice adieu after Rainier's surprise entrance, and now stood across the street from her home, arms leaning on the bridge railing overlooking the Seine. The Trocadero loomed across the river. A short jog to the right of the famed hotel bloomed the Tuileries.

Aby stood at Max's side, and Rainier to his left. The breeze from the Seine wasn't pleasant, but Aby took it all in. She might never get back here.

"We're connected," Rainier continued. "Today's the first time I felt you near. I couldn't get to town fast enough. Took me a while to track you though. Had to use a spell. How the hell have you been, Max? Damn, it's good to see you. Are you going to introduce me to the little lady?"

"Sorry." Seeming to surface from a daze, Max rubbed Aby's shoulder. "This is Aby. She's a friend."

Despite the noncommittal label of *friend,* Aby offered her hand to Rainier. He had the whitest teeth and a sexy smile. A charmer, she felt sure. He wore his brown hair shaved military short and the trace of a goatee edged a square jaw. He didn't smell as clean as Max, but human toxins didn't taint him, either.

In fact, she thought she smelled brimstone on him. But it couldn't be. It must be Max.

"Not vamp or were," Rainier said, as he held her hand in a firm handshake. "But I'm not sensing human, either."

She looked to Max. "Familiar," he offered.

Rainier nodded knowingly. "Good for you, man. Business partner?"

"She's just a friend."

"Uh-huh." Rainier winked at Aby. "That's not the vibe I'm getting from her."

"Still the same old Rainier," Max said. "Look, I'm at the end of my rope. Seeing you, and confirming your immortality answers some questions. I know the two of us each carry a half of that damned deprivation demon within us."

"Deprivation demon? I've never thought of it as that."

"That's what it is, I'm sure," Max confirmed. "Gandras? Though I've never found it listed in demonology texts."

"Whatever. Been an interesting few centuries," Rainier replied as he turned to look over the river. "The whole immortality thing is pretty sweet, eh?"

"I just want to sleep," Max said.

"Sleep? I get more than enough. You, ah…have the, er…sex thing?"

"Yes."

"Man, that rocks."

"It rocks?" Max's fingers tightened over Aby's hand. "Not being able to climax is your thing?"

"Not climax? Hell, Max, I can't come enough. It's like a disease. I *see* a woman I nearly shoot the wad. Er, sorry, mademoiselle. Wait, you mean, you…can't?"

"Sounds like you got the complete opposite package I did. You sleep, have sex. Can you eat?"

"All hours of the day. It's like I can never get full, you know? Don't put on any weight, either. Still got the same ripped abs I had in the eighteenth century."

"Max can never be fulfilled," Aby said, "and Rainier's become a glutton. That's interesting."

"Come now, I wouldn't go as far as gluttony," Rainier commented. He slid a sharp eye across her face, then clamped a hand across Max's back. "Hell, man, I'm glad I wasn't dealt your hand. Hey, you figure out the shadow thing? You do that, don't you? The dream walking?"

"Yes. It's as close to staving off the madness I'll ever get."

"True, so true. There is a certain madness to getting all you want. LSD works, too, you know."

Max smirked. "So does absinthe."

Aby lifted a brow at that statement. There was so much she didn't know about him. But every morsel she learned was like a gift, something she wanted to hold and keep to herself.

But the demon couldn't be the deprivation demon Max suspected it was if it had gifted Rainier with all he wanted. What, exactly, was it, then?

"So what?" Rainier said. "You want to exorcize this thing?"

"As quickly as possible."

"Uh-huh. Gotta tell you, Max, I'm not seeing a need. Sure, if I was in your pitiful predicament. But my life? It's sweet."

"You mentioned that a few times," Max said blandly.

Tension tightened the muscles in Max's arm resting along hers. He was so close to what he wanted. And she wanted it for him. Rainier had got it all, and Max had been deprived.

"You bring her along to bridge the demon?" Rainier asked.

"Aby's the best."

Rainier's gaze found Aby's and she had the distinct feeling he had already undressed her and was running his fingers over her body. Not a pleasant feeling. There was something about him, beyond the brimstone, that put up her hackles.

"So we going to do the double-dating thing again? Max, I gotta tell ya, when you show up for a visit, you really know how to bring the treats."

Max gripped the man by his lapels and shoved him against the cement railing so hard, Rainier's jaw clacked. "You won't lay a hand on her, Deloche. She's not for you."

"So she is yours. How does that work if you can't get it up?"

"I can still—" Max released him with a shove. "Can we do this?"

"This is sudden, Max. First reaction would be a resounding hell no. But I can understand your agony. No reason we can't discuss it further."

"Further?"

Rainier shrugged. "Like I said, immortality rocks."

Max swiped a hand over his face.

Aby felt his distress. To come so far, and find his only hope wasn't on board with him had to be devastating. If she were more skilled, she'd unhook the whip from Max's side, wrangle the bastard with it, and force him to agree to whatever her lover wanted.

Rainier crossed his arms high over his chest. "Where are you two staying?"

"The Regina," Aby started, but Max shushed her.

"Nice digs," Rainier said. "Why don't we all head over there and discuss the possibilities?"

"Sounds like a plan." Max threaded his fingers through Aby's. "But not right now. I've, uh… promised Aby we'd do the Eiffel Tower."

She flashed him an incredulous look, but he avoided her gaze. He was so eager to lose the demon within. Why take a break to do the tourist thing now?

"Why don't you stop by later, after ten?"

Rainier checked his watch. "It's eight now. The Tower will take you a couple hours if you're going to the top. How about midnight?"

"Appropriate," Aby said. She allowed Rainier to kiss the back of her hand, before he said goodbye and crossed the street to the black Hummer that waited.

"We're really going to do the Tower?"

Max put an arm around her shoulders and watched as the limo rolled away. "Nope. Plans have changed. We're going to see if Ginnie is home."

He punched a fist into his palm. His jaw pulsed.

Aby could smell the aggression. If he were a cat his spine would be arched right now.

"What is it?"

"He got it all," he muttered. "That bastard got it all."

She would finagle a trip to the Eiffel Tower before they left Paris. Aby was determined. But the alternative—visiting Max's vampire friend—was equally as intriguing, if not more. Now was her opportunity to meet a vampire.

He led her to an apartment building fronted by gorgeous gold-and-silver-mirrored tiles edging a huge park he called the Bois de Boulogne.

"Used to race the horses through that park," he commented as they entered the building. "And take pretty jewels from around women's necks."

Aby touched the diamond necklace he'd given her. She'd rather experience the taking than the gifting, she decided, because having him steal anything from her could be sexy fun.

So why hadn't she come to terms with him stealing her dreams?

There was something a little twisted there she couldn't quite embrace. And yet, he'd been honest with her, and she didn't want to lose him.

Was there a way for her to experience his walking in her dreams?

But really, this would all be taken care of as soon as they exorcised the demon from him and Rainier. If Rainier would cooperate. She crossed her fingers, and whispered a plea as they entered the foyer.

They were buzzed inside after a soft French female voice verified Max as the Highwayman.

A short woman who barely topped Aby's shoulders greeted them at the door. Her sleek blond hair was tugged into a ponytail. A pale-pink silk suit emphasized her generous curves, and a strand of pearls gleamed at her neck.

She hugged Max for the longest time.

It surprised Aby to see him express emotion—and to a vampire. She was the last person Aby expected would want an emotional hug.

They said a few things in French, exchanged kisses to cheeks, and Max turned to Aby and spoke in English to introduce her.

Ginnie kissed both her cheeks. She smelled like lavender and lemon.

"Are you on your way out?" Max asked.

"I am. Oh, Max, *mon cheri,* and it's been so long since we've visited. But I've an appointment at Versailles *tout de suite.* I'll be absent the entire weekend. Will you be in town longer than that?"

"Not sure. I've found Rainier."

"Oh?" Something flashed in her dark eyes. Recognition. Or perhaps, compassion. "Oh, come inside for a bit. I have a few minutes. Aby, you're so beautiful. I love the color of your hair."

"Thank you." She beamed at the unexpected compliment. Usually Aby received glares and snotty looks from other women. She didn't like it when people judged her by her appearance.

The vampiress dug in her huge Dolce & Gabbana bag for a pair of dark sunglasses and a scarf, which Aby suspected would see her to the curb and into the back of a cab or limo with enough protection from the sunlight.

"So, Rainier Deloche after all these years? Does it feel real, Max?"

"It won't until I've slept my first night. But I found out he's been experiencing the opposite as me."

"He can sleep and eat?"

"And have satisfying sex."

So Max had told Ginnie everything. Apparently they were closer than Aby had thought. Then again, Max had lived so long, and had so many more experiences than she could know of. In a way, that made him all the more appealing to her, and she wanted to learn all those experiences, even if it took five more lives to do so.

Very well, so she was being hard on him. He had confessed everything to her, and no doubt faster than he would have liked. He deserved a second chance. Not necessarily at dream walking her, but certainly at being her guy.

Because she wanted to be his girl.

"We plan to meet later, which is why I've come to you. Do you think Aby and I could stay here a day or two?"

"But we have a room, Max."

"We're not going back to the Regina. Rainier was lying. I know him too well. And something didn't feel right."

"Brimstone," Aby said. "I smelled it on him."

"So did I." Max cast her a curious look that told her they were on the same wavelength. "Which means we need to reassess. Play it cool. I'd rather relocate and keep a low profile until I figure what's up with Rainier."

"He wasn't being honest," Aby added. "Why do you think so?"

"I've heard things about him." Ginnie tilted her wrist to check her watch.

"And you never told me?" Max asked her. Aby could see his fingers itching to clutch the whip beneath his duster coat. "Ginnie, you know I've been searching for him a long time."

"But not until a few years ago did you start to seriously consider you might be able to exorcise the demon, *mon ami*. And you've never suggested that you needed Deloche to do so."

"What have you heard? Do you know where he lives?"

"Not in the city, but close. I've no clue where. I've heard whispers that if you need a demon to work black magic, Deloche is the man to go to."

"Black magic? Rainier is summoning demons? Why would he want—" Max rubbed his fingers over his jaw. "To make a buck. Always after the easy money. I can't believe it. Isn't his life satisfying enough with a gluttony of pleasure? But if he's summoning demons, he must be working with a familiar."

"I don't know about that." The vampire tied the scarf over her head and under her chin. "But I do know you need to be careful, Max. If you and Rainier get in the same room, and the demon is exorcised, what's to say he won't turn it on you?"

"It will have to be a controlled bridging. That's why I have my own familiar."

Ginnie gave Aby a less-than-pleased look. "You trust her?"

Aby straightened her back. But she didn't protest. It probably wasn't wise to argue with a vampire.

"Aby's on my side."

"I certainly hope so. Well, I have to run. I wish you would have called, Max, I could have rearranged my schedule. But I'm happy to offer my place to the two of you for the weekend. Just wash the sheets when you're done, *très bien?*"

She kissed Max on the cheek, and pushed around him to enter the hall. "There's an extra key under the bathroom sink, and the walls are thin as paper, so be warned."

With a wink, the vampire skipped down the stairs.

"She thinks we're lovers," Aby said as Max closed the door. She leaned against the wall and spread her palms across it. "I like how that vampire thinks."

Max smirked audibly. "Do you? What's that twinkle in your eye? You change your mind about this dream walker?"

"Maybe. Not about the dream walking, but I still like you."

"I'll take like." He hugged her and kissed the corner of her mouth.

"But what about Rainer? What are your plans now?"

"Not sure." The change in subject seemed to set him back. He wandered the living room that lay behind the long, black leather couch. "I know Rainier is up to something."

"So we're not returning to the Regina at all? But my clothes…?"

"I'll buy you new stuff. You want to run to the

market across the street? I'll guarantee you there's no food in Ginnie's fridge."

"I'm not hungry yet. But if you're trying to get rid of me, I can go for a walk."

"I don't want you going anywhere alone, Aby. Just stay, but give me some room to think."

She could do that. After all, he'd done the same for her.

He strode across the living room. The wall-to-wall window offered a spectacular view of the Tower, which, though twilight barely grayed the sky, now twinkled brightly.

Aby walked to the window and clasped her hands before her mouth. "It's beautiful!"

"They light it up at the top of every hour. Can you be satisfied with this view? I'm sorry, but I don't see a way to run over there when I've so much to think on."

Aby sighed. "I'll survive. If you're here to keep me occupied."

Aby closed her eyes as he stroked the base of her neck. Was he getting romantic?

"You confuse me, Aby," he said, not quite in a whisper, but achy and low.

"I don't mean to."

"I know, and that's another conundrum to wrestle with about you. You are what you are. You don't put on false airs. If you want something you say so."

"Like you?" She turned and leaned against a huge metal support beam before the window. "You are this dream that walked into my life."

"Actually, it was I who walked into your dreams."

"Yes." And she was glad he'd seen what she desired from him. "I forgive you for walking in my dreams."

"Thank you."

"And I'm glad you were able to experience the climax. I did that for you?"

"You did, Aby." He leaned over her, his bangs dusting the crown of her head. "You have some kind of power you're not aware of."

"I like having power."

"Over me?"

"I don't need it over you. But I don't know about you walking in my dreams again. I want to help you find Rainier, so you can exorcise Gandras and then we can make love and you can feel everything. With me awake and you like this—a man, not a shadow."

"I'm with you on that one hundred percent, kitty cat."

She roused herself to her tiptoes and slanted her head to kiss him, but she immediately retracted before their lips could touch. "No. You have some thinking to do. I'm going to freshen up."

She skipped away from him but felt his gaze follow her all the way into the bedroom.

The Highwayman was interested.

Now, to snag him.

Max kicked back on the leather sofa and listened to the shower beat against the glass doors. The walls were paper-thin, as Ginnie had warned. He imagined Aby slicking her hands over her body, sliding through the soap bubbles, and him cupping her breasts and sucking her nipples.

He sat upright and swung his legs onto the floor. Scrubbing his hands over his face, he shook his head to obliterate the titillating thought.

"No thinking about sex right now," he told himself. "Think of what to do about Rainier."

Right. But the naked woman in the next room certainly did seem a better think. All those water droplets glistening on her skin like liquid diamonds. An easy nab for a thief who couldn't stop himself from stealing.

"Rainier," he said aloud, forcing his thoughts to the point.

Max had his work cut out trying to convince his former partner that a life of unending gluttony wasn't worth it.

Damn, he'd drawn the wrong card.

On the other hand, much as it hounded him, he

had accepted this lifestyle. He'd become what he must to survive. Rebecca had been the one to convince him his sacrifice was worth it for the people he saved.

And he had to admit he'd saved a bundle on food and pillows over the centuries. Not to mention condoms. Not that he would mind fathering a child.

He shook his head. Not with his lifestyle. That wouldn't be fair to the child. But someday, when this was over, and he was no longer immortal.

Someday loomed close. He felt it.

He heard it in the scatter of water from the next room. Aby was his future.

She had to be.

Okay, so a plan. He wouldn't miss the proposed meeting at the Regina. Yet, he wouldn't actually meet with Rainier. He'd lurk outside, and then follow Rainier home when he realized he'd been stood up.

That gave him a couple hours to kill.

Max swung a look over his shoulder. Steam crept out on a thin mist from the bedroom. She'd forgiven him. And she hadn't forbid him from pursuing her—when in human form.

That worked for him.

Heeling off his boots, he then shrugged off the leather coat and tucked the whip under the couch so Aby wouldn't accidentally touch it and get cut.

He padded into the bedroom and knocked on the bathroom door. The water sprayed the glass shower door. She probably couldn't hear his knock.

Bleeding cowboys, he'd never wanted a woman so much. He'd experienced what he and Aby could be like together in her dreams. Now he wanted to make it a reality. Be damned the frustration.

Opening the door a crack, he called, "Aby? Can I come in?"

"I was wondering when you'd ask. Take your clothes off, Highwayman. It's lonely here in the nice hot shower."

He stripped off his shirt and had his pants around his ankles before he made it across the threshold. Peach-scented steam misted the room. He could taste the flavor at the back of his throat. Instead, he'd taste Aby.

Kicking off his pants—he wore no underwear, meaning less laundry when living on the road— Max slid aside the shower door and stepped inside.

"I was wondering if you'd sit out there the whole time I was in here." Aby touched his chest. The move seared through him. Marked him. Max bent to kiss her under her jaw. "I was clean five minutes ago, but thought I'd wait…"

"Sneaky, but effective. We have time before I meet Rainier, and I can think of nothing I'd rather do than make love to you."

"Oh, Max, really? I want that, too. But will you be all right with it if you can't climax?"

"More than all right. I'm all about your pleasure, Aby. And I'm going to enjoy giving it to you."

Her fingers slicked down his abs, and she touched the head of his erection. "I've never had opportunity to really look at a man before."

"Are you telling me you've never…?"

"Nope. All business with Jeremy, remember? So let me look, Highwayman." She tentatively touched his erection.

"It's not going to bite. Take it gently, and then firmer. Yes, that's— Ah."

Water splattered his eyes, but he forced himself to stand and let her study him. It wasn't a trial by any means.

"Nice. So big. The head is smooth."

She slicked a fingertip over his length and it bobbed against his stomach. When she curled her fingers about it, he moaned deeply. "You don't have to be so delicate with it. A good firm— Oh, yes."

He stepped closer, putting his shoulder under the shower flow. Kissing her gave him the taste of peaches. He slicked his hands over her breasts, and tight nipples skimmed his palms.

Aby squeezed his hardness. "This doesn't make the frustration worse?"

"A little, but the good outweighs the frustration, trust me. It's like the best massage in the world."

Emboldened, she gave him another squeeze and a few rapid slick strokes. When she touched the thick vein on the underside, he moaned. If this was as close to heaven as he might get, then he'd gladly forgo an invitation from Saint Peter.

They tumbled out from the shower, patted each other off with the big thick towel, then made a stumbling, kissing, wall-slapping and laughter-filled path to the bed.

Max laid Aby on the bed and she scrambled to pull away the counterpane and top sheet. Kneeling, her legs spread, she crooked a finger at him.

She would kill him with her wicked innocent sensuality. It was a death he'd succumb to over and over.

Max laid her flat and drew up her arms, gliding his hands along the inside of them until he reached her hands. Clasping fingers with hers, he pinned her loosely, hands above her head.

She giggled as he nipped at her breasts, but quickly those giggles changed to moans and that soft low purring he liked.

"I want to be on top," she decided, and struggled against his hold.

Max set her free, perfectly willing to roll to his back and have her mount him.

"I've never been on top before," she said. Stroking her clawed fingers less than gently down his torso, she wiggled her bottom and moved to fit her warmth directly over his pulsing erection. "I like it up here. Now to take my Highwayman for a ride."

"Hold on tight." He lifted her by the hips and she directed him inside her. "Because it's going to be a good one."

Biting her lip as he slowly entered her, Aby closed her eyes. Her fingers clenched the sheets near his head. Her spiky hair glistened with watery jewels. A fine sheen of water glittered across her breasts and collarbone.

She hugged him tightly as he filled her. Inside Aby was an amazing place to be. He gasped at the intensity of rising emotion. He felt so right here, with her, in her. Silently he thanked her for the gift.

Her motion slicked her wetness up and down him and soon they began to glide. Each movement tugged the flesh on his erection, a tremendous sensation.

"Max, this is incredible. I can feel you deep inside me."

Her voice hypnotized him. She said things any man would like to hear.

"I wish we could stay like this always. Locked together. One."

Her breaths rasped, as did his. She rode him as she desired, and he thought it best to give her the reins, for this was her first time. She'd made love to no man for pure and simple pleasure.

"I love those purrs of yours." He clenched his jaw. Release loomed so close. "Aby, you're killing me."

"You want me to stop?"

"No, never, keep going."

He felt it all, every stroke of her, every glide, every squeeze. That much he'd never lost, thank the gods. The heat of her weakened him. Her daring stirred him. Her moans and gasps matched his own.

"I've a birth control spell on me, so you needn't worry."

"It's not going to matter much, Aby. No climax, remember?"

Words fled. Rational thought faded. Even as he regretted his own frustration, he was able to enjoy Aby's pleasure. There was no denying, he felt awesome. And when she came, it was like a song he wanted to play over and over again.

Chapter 18

"You said you were going to meet Rainier at midnight?"

Max nuzzled his cheek against Aby's breasts. A weary exhaustion lengthened his muscles, but a giddy grin had permanently fixed on his mouth. "Mmm."

"It's quarter of."

"Hell, I have to get out of here." It took all his resolve to move away from her warmth and separate himself from heaven.

"Take me along?"

"Too dangerous. And pouting will get you nowhere." He tensed as her hand found his semihard erection. "That will get you somewhere, but not right now, Aby. Besides, you need a catnap, yes?"

"Sounds blissful. But not as sweet as lying naked next to you." She rolled to her back and stretched her arms across the sheets. Moonlight through the window gilded her bare skin. "I wish you could come with me, lover."

"Where are you going?"

"I mean, when we're making love. Maybe I should take a nap and let you dream walk again. I hate knowing you're left unsatisfied."

"Aby, holding you is the most satisfying thing I've done in a long time. And don't worry, I'll find Rainier soon enough. And when this shadow is gone from me, you won't be able to get me out of your bed. Ever."

"I like that. I can't wait to hear you come for me, Max."

"Mm, I will. Soon."

He leaned in and kissed her. It seemed impossible to get his fill of her. But he was the master of dissatisfaction, so with but a twinge of regret, he gave her one last kiss. The clock was ticking.

"Stay inside until I return. Promise me."

"Promise." She purred, a soft satisfied trill.

Max slid off the bed and retrieved his clothes from the bathroom floor. He bounced on one foot as he slid his other into the pant leg.

"Max, tell me, what we are now."

He knew what she wanted to hear. Did he believe this could go somewhere after Paris? Did he want it to? Of course he did. But the label she was looking for—boyfriend and girlfriend—didn't work for him.

"We're lovers, Aby. It's all I can offer."

"I'll take it. I'll miss you the moment you walk out that door."

He kissed her neck. Aby's trusting warmth bruised his soul. "If I find out you've skipped over to the Eiffel Tower alone…"

"You'll punish me?" The cat's mouth curved wickedly.

"Until you beg me to stop." A kiss at the top of her breast nearly changed his direction, but he forced himself to step away. "If you can be patient and not leave, then I promise we'll go to the Tower when I get back."

"Really?" Giddy delight sparkled in her emerald eyes. That was the Aby he adored.

"Promise."

Paris was a large, but compact city, easy to negotiate by paralleling the Seine. Max headed north toward the rue de Rivoli. It was ten minutes past midnight. Smoke billowed in the sky in about the area where the Regina was.

Cars honked at him as he dashed across the busy main street. The late-night crowd was thick. The city never slept. A red fire engine was parked before the hotel. Max wasn't allowed to pass the police tape cordoning off an area at the front of the hotel. Guests loitered outside in elegant gowns, some in night-robes, all looking shaken. But he'd yet to sight an ambulance.

"What happened?" he asked the gentleman standing next to him. He wore the hotel livery with gold epaulets.

"Fire broke out on the second floor in two rooms, monsieur. It is contained. They're moving the guests to the Bourgogne for the night."

"Was it arson?"

"Who knows? Someone may have gotten lazy with a cigarette."

Max watched the fire crew climb a ladder to an outer window and tracked the hotel layout in his mind. The room ablaze was his; he was sure of it.

Had Rainier hoped to catch Max and Aby asleep inside the room? It was a nasty play on Rainier's part, and Max found it hard to believe his former partner wouldn't have simply faced him in a battle of fists, instead of taking a coward's choice.

Maybe he'd known the room was empty and he'd wanted to leave a warning? That was the likelier choice.

Stalking away from the scene, Max scanned the street. He saw the obvious—people watching the fire, cars being redirected—but focused beyond them. His eye was drawn to the dark shape that lurked behind the brown Renault down the street.

He took off in a sprint, and the dark shape fled.

"Thrill me." Max slapped a hand against the brick wall and swung around the corner. He smelled sulfur, and followed it. In a short distance he caught up, which meant the dark figure was just a man, occupied by a demon. Inside a human, the demon was always constrained by the abilities of that mortal shell. And this guy was in no shape to run a marathon.

Overtaking him before the alley ended in a *T*, Max shoved the guy and he collided with the brick wall. He hissed and flashed a blue gaze at him.

Smashing his head against the wall, Max cautioned his strength. He didn't want to kill the human. Veins bulged on his face and neck. Demons could never pull off the façade without some clue to their presence.

Whipping him around by the shoulder, Max barred his forearm across his chest. "Did you start that fire?"

"I do not know what you are saying!" the man protested in French. "No English!"

Max switched to French and repeated the question.

The demon wearing human flesh shook its head frantically. Blood trickled from his temple from Max's rough treatment.

"Who started it?"

"The demon wizard," the thing replied.

"Would that be Rainier Deloche?"

"I do not know his name. He brought me to this realm and set me free to find a body. I was summoned and binded to start the fire. That is all I know!"

"Where's Deloche?"

The demon struggled. Max kneed him in the groin, which subdued him nicely.

"I do not know."

"So you apported right here before the hotel? I don't think so. Where were you summoned?"

"I do not— East! East is where I came from, but I do not know the place. I pay little attention. I was so glad to be free."

It was all he was going to get from this idiot. Max grabbed his whip, but couldn't kill the thing yet. Instead, he slipped a hand inside his coat and brought out a hematite rosary. He pressed the silver cross against the man's forehead. It smoked. The demon yowled.

Max recited the exorcism in Latin.

Demon dust poured from the man's body, slipping out beneath the pant legs and from the fingertips, mouth, nose and ears. The human body slumped at Max's feet. He'd be catatonic for days, but it was a better fate than the demon's.

Lashing out the whip, Max snagged the bewildered entity by the neck, slicing off its head.

Aby stirred and woke with a moan. She blinked at the brightness in the room. It was morning.

Had Max come home last night and left her to sleep alone?

His side of the bed was bare. A peek in the bathroom found it silent and dark.

He hadn't returned.

As she gripped her throat, her heart pounded against her forearm. Had something gone wrong? What if he was…

She wouldn't think it. Couldn't. Max could take care of himself. Wherever he was, he must be following a lead on Rainier. He'd return soon.

Slipping a jersey sundress over her head, Aby strode out to the living room. She stared out the window for a long time, tracing the city's landmarks from the Eiffel Tower to the Arc de Triomphe, to Notre Dame. There were many distinctive buildings, but she hadn't a clue what they were.

The urge to sightsee was strong. But she knew

better. That would come after Max had gotten what he desired.

"Will he give me what I desire?" she mused aloud as she wandered into the kitchen.

He had already given her what she wanted. Him. At least as much as he was able to give. What kind of man would do so much for a woman when he could not have his own satisfaction in return? A selfless man.

"I love him," she said, feeling the word out and liking its shape on her tongue.

Love was one of those words that had so many meanings, and could be used in different ways. Appropriate for her feelings toward Max. Different from how she regarded Severo. Max devastated her heart when he was not around. And when he was he owned it.

Crossing her arms over her chest, she gave herself a hug, wishing it were Max hugging her. Max kissing her. Max tracing the line of her muscles and following with his tongue. Max capturing and, in turn, owning her.

Shaking her head, Aby realized daydreams would get her nowhere and would leave her in a frustrated, pining mood.

"I want him to be able to feel as I do when we make love. We must get his partner to agree to the summoning."

Tugging open the fridge, she pouted to find Max had guessed correctly. Not a crumb of food. But there were three bottles of vodka.

Vampires and vodka? Couldn't be a good mix.

Closing the door, she padded out to the living-room window and scanned the street below. She thought she'd seen a grocery store earlier. There. Not even half a block away. "He won't know I left the apartment."

Decided, Aby dug out the credit card from her purse and headed for the store.

After twenty minutes strolling the aisles and marveling over the fascinating foods and jars with bright labels in a language she could not understand, Aby selected some fresh fruit from the refrigerated aisle. But the small shop didn't take MasterCard, nor American dollars.

The storekeeper said in English that a cash machine was up the way.

Heels clicking in a pleasing rhythm, Aby wandered the cobbled street checking the buildings. She and Max had passed an automatic teller on the way here; they were set into the building fronts, but not marked with a telltale Cash Here sign.

Not that she could read the French signs.

The cobblestone street narrowed and forked off

at angles. No streets were left or right, just heading more slightly to the right or veering off to the left. It wouldn't be difficult to get lost.

As long as she could see the top of the Eiffel Tower—which she could—Aby was confident she'd find her way home.

"Finally!"

She rushed to the teller, inserted her credit card and selected a hundred euros. She wasn't sure about the exchange, but that should be more than enough to tide her over for a few days.

The machine spit out crisp colored bills that she marveled over. European money was so pretty. Artwork, really. She'd have to save one as a souvenir.

Tucking the cash into her skirt pocket she retraced her steps, but, as expected, when it came to a choice between veering and angling she couldn't recall which she had previously chosen.

She scented the river to her right, and so chose that direction. This wouldn't be difficult at all, thanks to her homing instincts. She could find her way back blindfolded.

Brimming with renewed confidence, Aby turned the corner and collided with a tall leering man.

"Excusez-moi," he said as his fingers closed about her wrists.

She tried to disentangle from his firm grip. "Let go!"

"This way." He tugged her down a narrow alley, still gray with shadows because the sunlight hadn't yet crept between the buildings.

He was strong and there was no way she'd manage to loosen herself from his tight grip.

"What do you want?"

"You, *cherie*," he said brusquely. Slamming her against a brick wall, he pressed the length of his body against her.

Aby choked on a scream. It tangled in her throat, becoming muffled, insignificant. Instinct kicked in. As her pupils widened, his face sharpened before her peripheral images blurred. She clawed at him, but he held her wrists above her head so her fingernails cut nothing but air.

She recalled Max's warning that the demons would merely laugh at her silly kicks. Far as she could tell, this was but a man.

A man, not a demon. She wasn't afraid of a man.

Aby aimed her knee for his groin. The direct hit resulted in hot, nasty breath chuffing across her face.

Her wrists free, she pressed her hands to the wall behind her for stability, then kicked out her foot. As it connected with his chest, the pain brought him down. Blood scented the air and he stumbled against the opposite wall.

Aby spun and kicked high, landing her foot

against his gut. He let out a groan and hit the ground, knees first. He swayed, probably more surprised that a woman had brought him down than actually hurt.

Knowing she had to act quickly, Aby delivered another kick under his jaw. The knockout punch. He went down on his side, out cold.

"Right, then." She clapped her palms together once, and skipped through the shadows in search of the light.

A portion of the shadow clung to the wall above the fallen man, then peeled away and formed a human shape in the center of the street. The gray figment shivered and began to solidify, taking on color and flesh and clothing.

With a deep inhale, Max resumed his human form, his head bent over the man's body. He had been knocked out. A gash under his chin, from a spike heel, still bled.

"Impressive," he muttered. But he couldn't manage a smile.

He'd come upon them as the man held Aby against the wall. Prepared to shift out of shadow form and lash out with his whip, Max had paused when Aby's first kick had taken the attacker by surprise. She did pack a wallop with those killer high heels.

Sexy and dangerous, she'd defeated her opponent with little fanfare. Yet, Max suspected, she'd surprised herself with her skills. But it hadn't been a fluke. She was strong.

Severo had sheltered her for so long that perhaps now, out on her own, Aby would finally learn her true strength and come into her own. Max liked the idea of watching her grow and get stronger, more independent.

He hadn't realized how much he needed a woman's company until Aby. But had he stolen her innocence to satisfy his needs? Until Aby he'd not considered the emotional implications of his actions. He'd become unfeeling.

She was teaching him self-awareness—lost long ago following Rebecca's death—and he was glad for it.

He wondered if she'd tell him about this encounter.

He did not like the smell of fried eggs. Max grimaced as he entered the apartment and found Aby sitting on the divan, finishing a plate of fluffy yellow eggs and melon.

"You went out for food?"

"Just the market across the street. You can see it from the window."

He eyed the grocery store from the eagle's-eye view at the window. Aby had run into her attacker a quarter mile to the north down the twist of streets that led to the eighth arrondissement. "No problems?"

"What problem could I have, running out for eggs and fruit?" She strode past him. "I'm fine, Max. But you've been gone all night."

The plate clinked as she set it in the sink.

The soft swish of her skirts played a musical tease as she came up behind him. Hugging him, she pressed a hand across his heart.

"Did you find Rainier?"

"Yes and no." Clasping her hand over his chest, he pointed with his other hand toward a neighborhood across the river. "See the smoke?"

"Did a building start on fire?"

"The Regina. Just after midnight."

"You think Rainier started it?"

"He sent a demon lackey. A few rooms took the damage, including the one registered in my name."

"So he tried to kill you? That makes little sense. If Rainier wants to summon the deprivation demon, he needs you to do so."

He nuzzled his face against the top of her head. Her hair tickled his nose.

"I don't know what his game is. He's not as keen on losing immortality as I am. Why would he be? And I tracked a demon from the hotel. It confessed to starting the fire."

"You think Rainier controlled it?"

"I know he did."

"Takes a powerful witch or wizard to do something like that. The only way Rainier could control a demon is if he's learned magic."

"But it's possible?"

"Sure. Any man can learn the craft, if they dedicate themselves. I can't imagine they'd ever be as good or accomplished as a real blood-born witch."

"Maybe he's got a witch working for him? And yet, the demon did call him a demon wizard. Never heard the term before."

"Neither have I."

"A wizard who summons demons, who is also immortal and unkillable. How do I fight something like that?"

She turned and offered her gaze to his. "You'll have to do more research on Rainier so you know exactly what you're dealing with."

"I don't have time."

"Why? Is the demon shadow inside knocking to get out? What's a few more days, Max? You've waited two and a half centuries."

He dropped their embrace and paced the living-room floor. She could never understand. A few more days were a lifetime after his wretched centuries.

While Aby lived many lives, they were so short

and she forgot from one life to the next. She couldn't fathom what his life was like. Without sleep. Without care. Without satisfaction.

"I love you, Max."

The simple words startled him. Aby stood before the window, her hands straight at her sides. Her mouth didn't quite smile, but hope glittered in her green eyes, promising the freedom he quested for.

He didn't know what to say to that. He knew what he should say. That she was a fool. That love didn't come so easily. That he was the wrong man to love.

Because women who loved him died.

But those reproofs didn't land on his tongue. She was his. His sparkly thing. Instead, he splayed out a hand and silently entreated—for what, he wasn't sure.

"I knew it this morning when I woke and you were gone," she explained. "You're like no man I've ever known. At least that I can recall. You're frustratingly closed and difficult to squeeze the smallest bit of emotion out of. But you're Max. Bold. Secretive. Strong. Lonely. Handsome. And sometimes too cautious when it comes to me. I wouldn't love you any other way."

It was hard to listen to someone sing his praises. But at the same time, Aby's words penetrated the armor Max had fashioned long ago. She knew him because she wore her own sort of protective armor.

"You're handsome and sexy. An amazing lover. So giving, even when you can never take."

Her voice permeated his flesh, glowing through his extremities and wrapping about his soul.

"And when you look at me like you are now— kind of lost, but wanting direction—I want to show you the way. But I don't know the way any better than you do. Together we're a complete map. Does that sound strange?"

He still couldn't speak. Visions of Rebecca flashed across his mind. She'd understood him. She'd accepted him. She'd made him a better man. She had changed his perception of the world and pulled him up from a darkness he hadn't realized filled his every pore.

And then he'd watched her die.

He'd watched Aby come close to being hurt today. His pause, that moment when he should have rescued her, could not be excused. Though she'd successfully gotten out of trouble, would he have been able to save her had she not?

The touch of her fingers to his chin bowed his head, and Max pushed her away. He turned his face and sniffed back the tears.

"Max, what is it?"

Why he cried, he didn't know. He hadn't cried

after Rebecca's death. He hadn't cried after Emiline's death. He never shed a tear for any who had fallen at his whip.

He put out his arm, to keep Aby back. "Don't love me," he said.

"But I do. I can't unlove you now, Max. I don't want to."

"No, you'll die. Like Rebecca. Like Emiline. Anyone I love always dies. They'll kill you, Aby, the demons. I don't want to watch that." He sank to his knees and bowed his head into his hands. "Not again."

Chapter 19

Aby knelt over Max and cradled his head on her shoulder. His long legs stretched out before him, he sat on the floor with his arms around her. He sobbed softly.

This strong man had opened up to her. She didn't want to push him away by asking too many questions. That he trusted her to show this intimate side of him was immense.

Now she understood why it was so difficult for Max to get close to another being. He'd watched two wives die. And though he hadn't given particulars, she could guess their deaths had been delivered by demons.

He'd suffered. She could feel it in his body as it shuddered against hers.

There was so much pain inside this man. And when had he a moment, in all his centuries, to trust and release it into the world? Denied every bit of pleasure, he could only forge ahead with hope while he walked his never-ending immortality.

Though she gave him comfort, Aby wouldn't fool herself into believing that a simple embrace would ever come close to healing Max's broken heart. It was a pain she had never experienced. A pain Max would carry every day of his life.

Severo had his own history, his own pain. Trials had made him a strong man, yet sensitive to certain emotions and memories. She knew why he despised the vampires—they'd murdered his family—and understood his angst.

Herself, she had no history. At least none that she remembered. Yes, she could die again. And Max might witness it. She didn't want that to happen, the same as she never wanted to lose memory of Maximilien Fitzroy.

She eyed the tattoo. It was wrong. Max was no longer her enemy.

"I love you." She hugged him tighter, burying her face against his shoulder and hair. "I will love you no matter what."

"I don't want to watch you die, Aby."

"I won't."

"You can't know the future, or even what the day will bring."

"Don't think like that, Max. I'm here right now. Do you want to talk about it?" She knelt and brushed aside the hair from his eyes. Stroking his lips, she traced away a teardrop. "I like to listen."

"There's not much to say. I've told you about my wives. One was a mistake. The other, Rebecca, I loved deeply."

He managed a faltering grin.

"Love is better than sex," he said. "That's something I've learned. It's maybe why I've been able to come to terms with the whole not-climaxing thing. Memories of Rebecca remind me there are more precious things in this world than momentary satisfaction. She taught me to look beyond the shadow and to want more for myself."

His tone darkening, he clenched a fist upon Aby's thigh. "She and Emiline were both killed by demons. Because of me. I attract them—they seek me out. If there's someone in my life I care about, then they become collateral damage."

"I'm experienced with demons, you know that, Max. I know when to get the hell out of the way and hide my furry little tail under the bed. Or your car."

He smirked. "But as I've said—"

"I'm not strong enough to fight them," she finished for him. But he was wrong. She could take out a slippery-handed mortal man. "My going out on my own is what upset you."

He nodded. "I don't want to be like the werewolf. I don't want to control you, to treat you as a pet who must be kept on a leash."

She'd never heard her relationship with Severo put quite that way before, but it rang true. Devastatingly so.

"I can't be there for you all the time, and I know you're capable. I was there when the man attacked you in the alley, Aby. In the shadows. I was the shadow. But you handled the situation well. I didn't want to interfere. I like to see you growing into yourself, gaining independence. You don't need the leash."

"I was scared, but not nervous. I beat that asshole. But now that I know you were there, it makes me feel much better. You would have protected me."

"I would have."

"It's not like a real leash," she said, unsure herself. "I need the companionship, Max. I have this great dream of being independent, but I'm fooling myself. Familiars do best when they have someone close to protect and care for them. I'm not like those wild cats that roam the plains. I've been domesticated."

That realization, always at the back of her mind, now blossomed, and she couldn't deny it. She'd never be truly independent, able to survive without the help of others. Could she accept it?

"Aby, I love you. And if you want it, I will protect and care for you."

She did want his protection. Was there a way they could be together without either of them feeling as if she were the one to be kept on a leash and constantly cared for?

He bent to kiss her before she could reply, his mouth tasting hers, owning her lips, her breath, her life. The tender connection ached in her heart. A kiss had never been so wanted, yet so bittersweet.

He gripped her shoulders fiercely. "You have to know it would kill me if anything happened to you."

"Things happen to everyone, Max. If I die, it wouldn't be the end of the world. It would be the beginning of life number five."

"You wouldn't remember me." He kissed one eyelid then the other. Warm hands bracketed her face.

"No. And I couldn't bear that. But you'd keep me, wouldn't you?"

"You're not a pet, Aby. No leashes. But if something ever did happen to you, I'd love you still, even if you didn't know me."

"Hold me."

They tumbled together to the floor.

He loved her. He would be there for her. It was a different kind of love than she had known. This one went beyond borders of skin, body and breath. This love felt like something she could stand in, no matter where she walked, and she would always know it was there.

Max pushed up the hem of her skirt and kissed her thigh, there, on the inside. Shimmers of desire tracked her veins.

"I've gone beyond my safety zone," he said. "I was determined to remain at a distance from you. Not fall in love again."

"Are you sorry for it?"

"No." He blew softly over her nether curls. "I just don't want you to be sorry."

"Never."

"Aby, you're so perfect. And I…well, I'm complicated."

She tipped up his chin so she could look him in the eye. "Let's take it day by day, yes?"

He nodded, kissed her palm. Then he nudged aside her fingers and pressed a kiss above her mons.

The trace of Max's tongue tickled all the way to her toes, and Aby arched her back. "I love how you touch me. Mmm…"

"I love when you purr." Spreading his wide hand over her mons, he blew softly upon her reddish-brown curls. "You want me to stroke lower?"

"Yes, please."

His tongue slicked across the apex of her sex. The hot, brief touch mastered her. She arched her back more, striving to take as much as he would give. Aby dug her fingers into the rug. Her purring increased.

He stroked her with a measured pace, kissing her and flicking out his tongue to service her doubly.

"Oh, yes, that's perfect."

"A little faster?"

She could but mumble an affirmative noise. The man did know how to bring her to orgasm with a deftness that impressed. It was as if he'd known her body for years, and found a rhythm—her rhythm— so easily.

If only she could do the same for him.

She would. They'd summon the deprivation demon and exorcise it from Max. Then she would give him the same pleasure he'd gifted her.

When she came it was soft and trembling, as if a butterfly hovering over the tops of bright flowers. Aby clutched him and fluttered, endlessly, sweetly into oblivion.

Max put his cheek to her belly and hugged her. "Is it good for you? I mean, better than…"

He was wondering about Jeremy. But that had

been business sex. Unfeeling, unemotional. "Twenty times better, Max. I love you."

Max had laid out an arsenal on the living-room floor. It was a cache of treasure that satisfied his need to take things, even though he would not keep them.

He traveled with his whip, but decided backup necessary. He'd found the weapons in a safe at the back of Ginnie's closet. He was the one who'd taught the vampiress the value of a few defensive stakes, silver bullets for the werewolves and salt rounds for the demons.

Aby sat curled on the couch, observing over his shoulder. Having her close put the world right. He felt their connection even when they were not naked, their skin rubbing slickly against the other.

God, she came exquisitely. Purring and moaning and fitting her body against his as if not making that connection was the worst thing in the world.

She'd brushed away the cobwebs and opened the gates to his heart. And while he was yet regretful for letting her in, the more he thought on it, the more he wanted it.

Feeling made him a better person. If not supremely frustrated.

Would he ever be able to put himself inside her

and achieve climax? Could he be happy with one woman and not have an orgasm? He'd been happy with Rebecca for five years. Just knowing her pleasure had been enough.

He'd never dream walked Rebecca. He hadn't dared. Could he have had an orgasm if he'd walked in his wife's dreams?

Didn't matter now. Aby had offered to let him dream walk her again, but he would not. He was confident they'd convince Rainier to give up the demon.

"What's that one for?" She pointed to a weapon.

He tilted the iron object. Holding it by thumb and forefinger on two of its three spikes, he displayed it to Aby. "Caltrop. They were used back in my time by nefarious sorts to injure horses and bring carriages to a halt. Toss them on the ground and it lands, spike up. Horse gets one of these in its hoof, and it brings them down."

"How cruel. You used them when you robbed people?"

"Which would make me a nefarious sort." He winked at her over his shoulder. "But not overmuch. I like horses as much as the next guy. These are modern renditions. No horses required. Toss one of these into a wall or at a demon and it spews out holy water. Hear that?" He shook the weapon and liquid jiggled inside.

"But how do you carry them? They're prickly."

"I just take a few along in my pockets. The pistol, with some salt rounds will serve, too. And with my trusty whip, I'm ready for action."

"Who made that whip for you? It's intricate, with the razors woven into the leather."

"A wizard who lives in Montana. Amandus Muldron designs all my weapons. I've known him for sixty years. He puts the binding wards into the leather. He's pushing ninety now, and training an apprentice." Max smirked. "Amandus doesn't like the boy's new ideas. He's not all that into technology. Neither am I."

"I couldn't imagine you whipping out an iPhone to talk to your agent or lawyer."

"I do have a cell somewhere in the trunk, but Ginnie's and Amandus's are the only numbers on it."

"I'll have to change that when we return to the States. I'd hate for you to forgot how to contact me."

"I won't ever, Aby."

He leaned back, resting his head on the edge of the couch. She stroked his hair. It made him feel respected and loved. Two things he hadn't had for too many decades to count.

"I'm going out alone again tonight. Promise me you'll stay inside?"

"Promise. I bought enough fruit and some cream

to keep me happy. Though I could go for salmon. Or sushi. Mmm…"

"I'll bring you out for sushi after we've found Rainier, okay?"

"You staying out until morning again?"

"However long it takes. Don't worry about me."

She kissed his cheek. "I have to worry. If I thought you were all right, then you wouldn't be in my thoughts."

"Well, then, think only good thoughts."

"Like what you'll do with me when you get back in the morning?"

"That'll work."

The transistor radio above the refrigerator crackled, and Aby danced to the beat of a French group, though she couldn't understand a word. She shimmied through the living room.

There wasn't much else to do while Max was gone. She'd attempted to figure out the washing machine to do the sheets as Ginnie had requested, but it was beyond her. Max would have to interpret the dials when he returned.

Thinking Ginnie might have a laptop so she could do a little online research, she had opened her bedroom drawers and closet to look for one. Much as she enjoyed snooping, she hadn't poked way into the depths of the closet.

The vampire had no computer, which surprised her, if she were Max's financial advisor. Maybe she'd taken it with her.

Another surprise was that Aby had found nothing untoward during her snoop. No strange vampiric items. Though as she danced around the room, she couldn't decide what she would consider vampiric. A dark cape? Vials of blood? An Elvira dress? By all accounts Ginnie was as normal as the next mortal, except she drank blood.

Relieved she hadn't found blood drops at the back of the closet where the vampire might have stowed a victim, Aby spun around when the doorbell jangled.

She wondered fleetingly why Max didn't just walk in, but headed to the door anyway.

The doorknob twisted just as she touched it. Aby spread her arms to welcome Max, but instead saw a familiar face—an unwelcome familiar face.

It was the man she had beaten in the alley. He lunged inside, fitting his hands about her neck. Her vision blurred, her legs buckled. A foul-smelling handkerchief came over her mouth and nose, and darkness overtook her senses.

Chapter 20

A definite demonic trail led east of the city. Max had encountered a fire demon in the fourteenth arrondissement. It hadn't been the friendly sort, rather inflammatory actually. Instead of taking a talon to the face, Max had snapped the demon's head from its body with a crack of the whip.

Just beyond the old Salpêtrière building—a world-famous teaching hospital—he ran into another demon. The greedy demon was trapped within a chain-link fence rolled on the ground. She'd apparently thought the fence was platinum and had wanted it all for herself. He'd set her free, but held her firmly, the whip wrapped about her throat, sigils glowing. He choked it to death even as it pleaded ignorance of her arrival in this realm, leaving behind a pile of demon dust.

The Métro wasn't the best means for tracking demons, though Max thought sure to find many below the city. But this trail led beyond the road that circled the city, so he needed to rent a car.

Within twenty minutes Max had a Renault gassed and cruising the road. He'd traveled this way on horseback many times with Rainier during their heyday. This road led to the Château Vaux le Vicomte, once traveled frequently by the king's financier in the seventeenth century. Lavish parties were still held at the grand estate even centuries later.

Perfect hunting grounds for a thief.

Max gripped the steering wheel. The Highwayman had returned home. Men, secure the coffers! Women, hold on to your jewels!

He scoffed. Not so much anymore.

There was but one woman Max could think about. What was it Rainier had once said about his choice in women?

You always need that other something.

"That other something," Max said with a smirk. "Yeah, she's it."

And it only took him two and a half centuries to find her.

Max stepped on the gas and passed a convoy of cars. Five kilometers out, he veered left, sensing the path he should take.

It wasn't Vaux le Vicomte, but a splendid field-stone mansion that topped the horizon to the west. Two pepper-pot turrets hugged the front façade. Twelve-foot hedgerows surrounded the iron gates fronting the estate. It was impossible to see the grounds, but Max sensed no activity outside.

He parked the rental before the gate. There was not a gateman, nor an intercom, and the gate was overgrown with a wide-leaved vine dotted with frilly white flowers.

Max stepped out and noted the new tire tracks impressed in the gravel. Someone had been here recently.

He gripped the iron gate and released the bars with a hiss. Flapping his hands alleviated some of the sting. He drew his gaze up to the insignia topping the gate. It was no family crest or coat of arms.

"A sigil."

But to ward off what? Demons? Isn't that what Rainier did—summon demons?

It was a guess. Max had no idea what Rainier was involved in. For all he knew the man could be inundated by the dark denizens and was merely trying to fend them off.

They had become opposites by fate. If Max had spent his life pursuing demons it made sense Rainier may have spent his avoiding them.

But if Gandras wasn't a deprivation demon, as he'd always guessed, what the hell was it?

The sun blinked on the horizon. Crickets chattered in the tall grasses. Max shook out his shoulders but paused before shifting from his human form. The shadow couldn't get past any wards his human body couldn't penetrate.

"Guess I'll have to do this the hard way."

Uncoiling the whip, he snapped it once, high. The tip gripped the top bar. Giving it a tug ensured the whip held securely. Then he climbed the whip.

He'd done this before; the razors braided within the leather had been spaced to allow handholds. The sigils on the whip reacted to the warded gate, glowing fiercely. Each step shocked through Max's system as if he treaded a high voltage line. He gritted his teeth as the clash of wards cut like a blade through his nervous system.

Reaching the top, he grabbed the iron. It hissed and smoked. His flesh burned. Kicking against the crossbar, he swung his body wide and high and managed to lever himself over the top. With a cry of pain, he pushed away from the warded iron and dropped.

He landed sprawled, half on the gravel drive,

half on grass. The cool thick grass soothed his burned palms. He winced at the remnants of electrified warding that shimmied through his veins.

Had he been completely demon the wards would have reduced him to sulfur dust. Rainier was not a stupid man.

Retrieving the whip and coiling it but keeping it in his hand, Max strode up the gravel drive.

Now to discover what made Rainier Deloche tick.

"I was wondering how long it would take you to find me."

Max stopped at the bottom riser of a half-dozen limestone steps that ascended to the front entrance. Massive stone urns sprouted wild nightshade, spilling their violet blooms across the grass. Demonic gargoyles leered down from the rooftop, sooted and streaked from rain.

Rainier leaned in the doorway, a long, black velvet robe open over his bare chest. Striped pajama bottoms and bare feet said he'd either been sleeping or lounging.

Ah, the glamorous life of a gluttonous playboy.

"You tried to kill me and Aby."

"Me? Nah. I just wanted to smoke you out. Pity, that was a pretty hotel. It opened during the World's Fair in 1900, I believe. That was one hell of a party, man."

The guy must have never left Paris. And Max had never returned. No wonder he'd not sensed Deloche was alive until now.

"What's up, Rainier? Not keen on getting rid of the shadow that's been riding you for centuries?"

Rainier smoothed a hand over his bare abs. "Not particularly. Kinda like sucking the dreams from people, you know? I'm sure you do, too. Still a kicker that you can't get it up though."

"I can get it up with the best of them."

"Oh, right, you just can't complete the transaction."

"Never realized how big of an asshole you are, Rainier."

"Yeah, well, I was always the one who shed caution and jumped into life feet first. See what happens when you pause to think things through? You go without an orgasm for centuries."

The man laughed uproariously.

Max splayed out his arms, showing his lack of humor. "We are at an impasse, Deloche. I need this thing gone from me. You want to keep it. One of us will have to surrender."

"I agree. Doesn't do one or the other any good to carry only half. Imagine what we could do if we possessed the whole damn thing?"

Rainier glanced over his shoulder but Max couldn't see what he looked at inside the mansion.

His former partner fashioned an evil grin. "I'm all for sport."

That grin was the same one Rainier had always delivered to those he'd robbed, cheated or tricked. And now Max stood on the receiving end.

He'd known this wouldn't be easy. Might as well get into the mood.

"To adventure!" Max rallied.

"To danger!" Ranier replied.

Rainier stepped back and, as Max suspected, a dark shape gushed out the doorway toward him.

Whip already in hand, Max seized the malformed demon about the chest with the razored leather. The sigils glowed. It took but a yank to cut the thing in half. Sulfur dusted the air.

Max ran over the settled dust and kicked at the closed door through which Rainier had disappeared. It wasn't locked. He hadn't expected it to be. Rainier loved a good chase.

"To the best man go the spoils," he muttered.

He had to admit, he loved a good chase, too.

Once the door closed, the interior settled to darkness about Max. Floor-to-ceiling windows were covered with heavy damask drapery. No artificial light glowed from behind shades or glass globes. It took a moment to adjust his sight to the darkness, but Max did not stop walking.

The odor of brimstone was so strong he could

not pick out a specific demon or know if it were a residual scent from the summonings Rainier must perform.

The whip cracked on the marble floor. "Deloche!" The echo of his voice sang longer than the whip's bite.

His hackles prickling, Max spun swiftly to see a demon soaring toward his head, its blue eyes the only thing visible. He ducked. Talons clawed his scalp, lifting his hair.

A brimstone hiss preceded the next blind attack. This time the talons drew blood. Wincing at the wound to his thigh, Max swung the whip and captured the unseen enemy. It struggled, jerking Max's arm roughly until his shoulder socket popped audibly. The demonic bastard was strong. Max heaved and managed to swing it around. Moving in a circle, he used momentum to throw the demon against the wall.

Stunned, the demon couldn't comprehend the snaking whip quickly enough to save its head.

Two demons down.

Max popped his shoulder bone back in place. "Hell to go."

He entered the ballroom cautiously. Candelabra lit the center of the room. Dozens of lit candles dripped wax, forming stalagmites on the parquet floor.

Tinny strains of a harpsichord coerced him to search the dim shadows of the empty room for the source. He recognized the tune, a Scarlatti fugue...

Max chuckled. "The Cat's Fugue." How oddly appropriate.

Visions of frock coats, wide panniered dresses and fancy wigs flashed in Max's mind as he strolled the vast ballroom. It was as if the ghosts of his past awaited his arrival at the soirée.

The room was not empty, except for the sensations of evil that prickled his flesh. They were everywhere and nowhere.

He could not kill what he could not see. Yet, neither could they kill him if he were but a shadow.

Shucking his mortal shell, Max shadowed and slid across the floor and up against the wall. He skimmed the flocked paper higher. This room had not been changed for centuries for dust crusted on the paper.

And indeed, there were ghosts. He moved through their ectoplasm, cold and gooey, some sticking at the edges of his shadow. Touching the cold death made his shadow shiver.

He'd not dealt overmuch with ghosts. Much as he knew they could not harm him, he didn't look forward to touching them now.

Below, the room grew darker with swirls of black smoke. Demons formed, stirred up by the evil resonance that coated the room like a shroud.

The entities were aware of him, he knew. Sliding out of the room and seeking Rainier seemed the better option than trying to fend off the dozens of demons he now counted. Some opened their maws, tilting their heads to catch the hot wax dripping from the candelabra. Others joined hands to dance a hideous quadrille. Most stared directly at him— a shadow clinging to the wall, gliding slowly along the ancient paper until it found position directly over the ballroom doors. He couldn't hold form long before the shadow would overwhelm and he'd be off in search of dreamers.

The doors slammed shut below him, causing Max's shadow to temporarily lose its grip on the wall. Below, the coven of demons ceased their mad machinations and bowed to the man who walked to the center of the room.

Rainier's mad, Max decided. Or else he would surrender his half of the demon's shadow.

"My people!" Rainier, arms held wide and velvet robe splayed, greeted his minions. "Bring in the distractions!"

The doors at the far end of the ballroom opened and a macabre band of demons and ghosts danced inside. Three particular brutes—menace demons, Max guessed from their switchblade grins— pushed a huge iron cauldron on a wheeled tumbrel that looked as if it had been stolen from the eighteenth century.

A spinning ghost whirled in and around Rainier, tipping its head to its eerie master—literally, for it must have been beheaded. It tucked the head under its arm and glided off into the crowd.

A cavalcade of women in grand dresses with wide skirts and tattered lace, dust-coated diamond necklaces and mouse-infested wigs, shimmery figments of their former selves, ghosted across the floor and mingled with the demons as if at an elegant event.

"You ready to join the party, Maximilien?" Rainier did not turn toward the door, over which Max still clung. "It's going to be a wild one! Where's that kitty cat?"

Max's shadow cringed at that query. He slipped down the wall and puddled on the floor, but did not transform. Not yet.

A tall ghost who was mostly corporeal and only partly ectoplasm glided forward, her grand skirts dragging a trail across the dusty floor. She bowed exquisitely before Rainier.

"You were my favorite," Rainier announced. He stroked the woman's cheek. Rainier's hand slid through flesh and bone and she winced as if the touch were painful.

Max had always believed ghosts could feel no pain.

"What did you bring me today?" Rainier asked.

The woman slid her palms over her frayed skirts.

Bits of lace separated and fell, but dispersed to dust before touching the floor. She parted the folds of fabric, and it opened to reveal no feet, only bloody stumps. As she moved backward, the thing she had concealed beneath those generous skirts was revealed. A cage.

Inside sat a reddish-brown cat.

Chapter 21

Max shifted to human form. The shadow relented grudgingly, tugging at his soul. Like the wards in Aby's home, it sensed the darkness to come and wanted to remain, to stick around for the macabre events.

He solidified before Rainier, his hand about the man's neck. "Release her!"

Legions of demon and ghost loomed over them. Blue eyes glowed, talons clicked in anticipation. Incorporeal bodies shimmered, craving the life they once possessed, and tasting it in the room.

Rainier put up a hand to stop his troops' advance. Max did not relent his chokehold. He knew how

easy it was to bring death to those who did not give
him what he demanded.

Behind him the cat meowed. Aby's plea crept
through Max's flesh and touched his soul. His
breath huffed out. The desire to destroy faded,
seeping out like the shadow he had just been.

Maximilien Fitzroy did not give death unless it
was warranted. Not two hundred fifty years ago and
not now.

He released Rainier and put up his hands in pla-
cation. He knew his partner well enough. When he
wanted something, he would stop at nothing to get
it.

Rolling his head, Rainier made show of puffing
up his chest and setting back his shoulders. He had
no physical weapons that Max could see, except for
the hundreds of demons drooling for a chomp at
Max's intestines.

"Funny how we both settled in with kitty cats of
our own, eh?" Rainier nodded to the left.

The ballroom inhabitants parted to reveal a tall,
slender woman with long white hair, clad in a
barely-there beige sheath of a dress. She slinked
across the floor, feline smooth, her catty glances
piercing the crowd. Wax droplets spotted her hair
as she passed beneath the candelabra. Her bright
green gaze was focused solely on Rainier.

A familiar, Max assumed. His fingers itched for

the whip, but he had to play this game right. He was outnumbered, and his opponent treaded insanity.

Yet so do you.

Indeed.

Max laughed, releasing a hearty chuckle. He was aware the room gazed in awe upon him, as did Rainier. The familiar flicked a bored gaze over all.

"So you have a collection of demons and ghosts due to your nefarious sex life with a demon conduit?" Max shook his head. Laughing held back the urge for violence. "Good old Rainier. Always the Lothario."

Rainier smirked. "Yeah, well, you can't climax? I have to bed whatever comes my way."

The white-haired familiar hissed at the cage. Max stepped before it, protecting Aby futilely. How she had gotten here from the safety of Ginnie's apartment, he could not guess. Didn't matter. He'd meant it when he promised the werewolf he'd keep her from harm.

But he wasn't about to play the hero so the wolf could claim the prize. Aby was his.

"Let me walk out of here with Aby," Max proposed, "and I won't return. You can continue to do…whatever it is you do, demon shadow intact. I won't bother you again."

"Maximilien Fitzroy." Rainier shook his head, then looked up from a tilted smirk. "You're lying. I know you."

"It's been a long time, Deloche. A man changes."

"His core remains the same. Once a thief, always a thief. Once a liar? Well. I'm surprised you didn't come after me a century ago. I know the shadow inside must eat at you. Yet, there's no way you're going to sacrifice your freedom from the shadow for a woman. A familiar, Max. The very creature you've spent your life destroying."

It disturbed him that Rainier knew more about him than he knew of his former partner. Had Rainier tracked him through the decades? He had garnered a certain unwanted fame as the Highwayman.

If he were so eager to have the complete demon himself, why hadn't Rainier come after him sooner?

"You going to kill mine, too?" Rainier hugged the familiar to his side. She snarled an unhappy mewl. "She's a tough one. You don't have a hello-how-do-you-do for an old acquaintance, Max?"

The familiar's eyes glinted like stolen emeralds. Max studied her face. He'd met her before? But that would make her… The original familiar with whom he and Rainier had shared that disastrous night.

"She's a survivor," Rainier added. "We hooked up about a month after the big night. Her old man—who was a witch, by the way—kicked her out."

The familiar pushed out of Rainier's precious

hug, obviously annoyed. Preening her hair, she eyed Max coyly.

"You head off to do your thing now, sweetie. Max and I have business to discuss," Rainier told her.

"We have no business."

"I say we do. You want to save that pretty Abyssinian? A fine breed. Rangy but devoted. Had one of those once. Demon ate her."

"Have you been collecting familiars over the centuries?"

"Someone has to keep them safe from your vengeance. Ain't that right, sweetie?"

The familiar meowed from the lush sofa she'd climbed onto over by the wall beneath a pair of dusty portraits. Max marked her position from the corner of his eye. He slid his foot back, the rowel of his spur connecting with the cage.

"What kind of business do you propose?" If he could keep Rainier talking that would give him time to plan. Their conversation kept the demons and ghosts at bay, as well. He and Rainier provided a macabre spectacle. "Riding the high roads for good old times?"

"Stealing is so gauche."

"So you've not been afflicted with the need to take things?"

Rainier smirked. "If you've got a problem,

buddy, maybe you should see someone about that. I'm into charity."

"You can't be serious."

"Sure I am. Gave over a million to the Helping Hearts Foundation last year. They love me."

Irony at its finest. This kept getting better and better in no way that appealed.

"So back to business. You know demons?" Rainier said. "I know them better. But a summons doesn't always conjure the ones I can use or control. I need an exterminator for the unruly ones. Someone who won't blink an eye to slicing off heads."

"And that would be me?" Max crossed his arms high on his chest. "What do you summon them for, Deloche?"

"Clients. The highest bidder. Gotta write those charity checks somehow. Mostly for the fun of it." He gestured at a particular ghost, the one who'd had the cage under her skirts. "Most take on a human shell as soon as they arrive. But their stolen mortal forms stick around forever after they die. It's a bitch."

"Fitting. You destroy them, so why shouldn't they haunt you ever after?"

"You have trouble with the ghosts of your destruction, Max?"

"I don't kill innocents. Only the bad-ass demons you've been setting free to this realm."

"Oh, it's not just me. You know damn well it's the familiars that have all the power. Speaking of which…you almost ready, sweetie?"

An agitated meow rent the air, followed by a gasp for breath. A particularly lusty gasp. As if someone were close to—

Max spun and eyed the familiar stretched on the couch. Her back arched as she panted, her shoulders pressed to the cushions. "What the hell?"

Rainier cocked a wink at Max. "You don't know about the ninth life? When a familiar hits good old number nine they develop a sort of tantric sex power to summon and bridge demons all on their own. Freaky, if you ask me. But it keeps me from having to satisfy her myself. Takes less than ten minutes. And, since we're both here, I figure it's time we met the demon who's been clinging to our insides, don't you?"

The familiar was bridging a demon on her own? Though amazed, Max gave it no more than a few moments' thought. If she were bridging the deprivation demon—or whatever the hell it was—then he had to increase his odds of survival. Chaos was never a day at the park.

Swinging the whip high above his head put off the encroaching demons, but not the ghosts. Sigils didn't keep them back, and the leather glided right through the ectoplasm, leaving them undamaged.

But he didn't worry about the ghosts. They couldn't harm him.

Rainier tromped over to his familiar and began to chant what Max knew was a summoning spell.

So Max began the ritual chant that would exorcise demons. "Depart then, transgressor…"

Of Exorcism and Certain Supplications. When all he had was time a man had opportunity to memorize the document put out by the Roman Catholic Church.

He was able to swing the whip, nabbing demons in a tight clutch, and break their necks while keeping up the chant. It must be repeated over and over. Power increased with repetition.

Already, the lesser demons were dissipating, shattering or exploding into sulfur clouds. Some surrendered their mortal shells, leaving collapsed bodies sprawled on the parquet floor.

Rainier's voice increased. The familiar writhed on the couch, close to climax.

Whip extended fully, Max dodged, but an incoming demon hit him square on the chest, stopping his chant. He landed on the floor, arms splayed, his whip skidding across the marble. Kicking high, he brought down his boot on the forehead of the charging demon. The spur cut through the black muscle and flesh and tore its face wide open.

Resuming the chant, Max got to his feet. He tugged the hematite rosary out from a pocket and dangled the silver cross before him. The wounded demon disintegrated to demon dust.

A swirl of female ghosts in high wigs and low décolletage clapped and swooned before him. Max stepped through the figments, ignoring the cold tug of their ectoplasm.

The air in the room changed. From the darkness a blue-eyed demon charged, clamping its teeth into Max's bicep.

Max hissed out, "I command you out, unclean spirit!"

He managed to clamp the hand holding the rosary over the demon's leg. With a whimper, the demon pried out its teeth and fled, taking all other demons in a hysteric scatter to the far side of room.

It was then Max noticed the ghost who hovered over the iron cauldron. From its hand dangled the cat cage holding Aby.

"No!"

Heedless to his plea, the ghost dropped the cage. Water splashed over the cauldron lip. Aby clawed at the wire mesh. Her hysterical meows cut through Max's heart. The last time he'd walked through her dreams…

She'd dreamed of drowning.

Max raced for the cauldron.

The air in the ballroom grew thick, much like the wax he slipped on. Candles flickered to darkness. The scent of brimstone and smoke spiced the air.

Max bounded and leaped for the cauldron as light snuffed out. Chest colliding with the iron rim, he groped in the tepid water, snagging his fingers in the cage, and tugged it out.

Stumbling, he landed on his knees and the cage clattered to the floor. He fumbled with the latch, opening it and reaching inside to touch the shivering wet creature. Shivering meant she was still alive.

Limbs flailing and claws striking blindly, she struggled as he pulled her out and tucked her to his chest. The poor thing mewled.

Still, the woman's climactic moans echoed behind him.

Max shrugged off his coat. "Hide," he directed Aby, and tucked her under the coat. "Get out of here if you can."

Max could barely make out shapes and shadows in the vast ballroom. He stepped forward, avoiding the fallen bodies. They were innocent mortals, once inhabited by demons.

"I need you over here, Max!" Following Rainier's shout, the familiar moaned loudly.

"I don't do the tag-team thing anymore, Deloche!"

He glanced across the floor where he'd set Aby. The coat was gone. No cat, either.

Through the mire of demon dust, a thick fog of charcoal and sulfur particles, Max stomped across the floor and found Rainier standing before the couch. The undulating familiar contorted in near-orgasm behind him.

In Rainier's grasp, a knife to her neck, stood Aby in human form. Max's coat hung on her bare, wet limbs. One of the ghosts must have nabbed her for its unholy master.

Rainier tilted back Aby's head with a fist under her jaw. "You really want to save this one, Max?"

"Let her go, Rainier. We can come to accord on this."

"I don't think so. You know what? I'm thinking I want to break what's yours and take what's mine."

"Not very charitable of you."

"Yeah, well, much as stealing kills you, you gotta know charity gets frickin' boring after a few centuries. You think I want to give all my money away? There are much better things to do with it than fixing some orphan's cleft palate or feeding a starving family of ten."

"Go ahead and summon the demon. Your familiar seems close."

"She's close all right, but I need you."

"I don't understand."

"I can't summon the demon into this realm alone. It needs to connect with its shadow."

"I still don't get it. You have part of the shadow."

"Yeah, but that doesn't leave me the freedom to exorcise the thing from myself. So I call it into you, then I can get a wrangle on it."

"You'll let Aby go if I agree?"

"Of course I will. I'm not that big of an asshole. I just want the demon, Max. I'm genuinely sorry that means you've got to give up the ghost for it, but that's the only way I can figure to do it."

Even in the darkness Max could see the brilliant green eyes pleading with him. Green for freedom. She'd given him as close as he'd ever get to elusive desire. He'd been foolish to have entertained the dream of escaping a fate he'd earned well and good.

At least he had known pleasure. And Aby had given it to him.

"All right. Use me as you see fit. But release Aby first."

Rainier shoved Aby away from him. She stumbled over to Max. "No, Max."

"It's the only way you'll get out of here alive."

She clung to him, whimpering. He wanted to clasp her hand, stroke her hair, to whisper promises of forever to her. Or maybe just the simple promise of love.

Max forced those futile thoughts out of his brain. "You swear to her safety, Deloche?"

"You have my word."

"But you'll die, Max. You can't leave me alone," Aby implored. "I love you."

"Ah, now isn't that special?" Rainier nodded over his shoulder toward the familiar. "Clock's ticking, Max. Kiss her and send her off."

Not needing to be told twice, Max swept Aby up. He kissed her hard. He kissed her as if he'd never see her again. He kissed her as if she were the only woman for him. Because she was. And he couldn't see a way out of this.

"I'm sorry, Aby. I love you. The wolf will take care of you."

"No, I don't want him to. I'm not leaving!"

Into the darkness Rainier shouted, "It's happening now, Max, whether or not she's out of the room!"

The familiar convulsed on the chaise and Rainier leaped around to recite the Latin words Max had memorized for decades. The spell to summon the demon to this realm. A spell that would call the demon to collect its shadow.

The familiar cried out. "Ready!"

Before his eyes the demon manifested from her pores. It clouded above her, but did not take shape.

"My liege!" Rainier called to the demon.

The demon resembled a monster beast of dark

fog. It couldn't completely form until it claimed its shadow from Max and Rainier. And once formed…?

If Max took out the demon now, he couldn't know the results. The shadow may live on in him ever after, or it may be struck out with the demon's exorcism. But doing so could also kill him.

A week ago he would have done so willingly to ensure the world was not plagued by the deprivation demon.

His world had changed since then. If Max died, Aby would be alone. And while he'd seen her gain independence he didn't want to end it now. He needed more time with her. Time to fall deeper in love. Time to know her.

He wanted time to begin anew.

"Max, please." Her green eyes pleaded with his.

"The vessel is open to you, master," Rainier announced. He pointed to Max.

"Yes," Max agreed.

The demon cloud turned to him as if it had just realized Max stood there. Blue glowed in the area where its eyes might be. Its cloudy form ever changing, the muscles shifted and bulged, trying to find shape.

"Aby, shift now."

"No."

"If you love me, do it!"

He shoved her away from him. She stumbled, casting a hurt look at him.

"Just do it! Get safe."

The demon moved over his head. Rainier's wicked smirk sickened. He had always been the one to go for it all, no matter the cost.

Out the corner of his eye, Max saw the russet cat scamper toward the doors at the far end of the ballroom. Thankfully she'd done what he'd asked. Now she would be safe. The wolf would care for her.

Damn him, but he didn't want the dog to take care of her!

Turning from the one thing he wanted more than life, Max thrust out a fist. "Take back your shadow," he called. "If you dare!"

The demon grinned at the challenge. The glimmering dust coalesced and formed a maw that roared. The noise put Max back a few steps. He stepped into Rainier.

"'Bout time you came around," Rainier said. "Let's do this!"

Doing this, Max knew, did not involve a friendly reunion or brotherly hug after their shadows had been yanked from their insides. Doing this meant Rainier would have to slice Max's head from his body to allow the demon escape, because he suspected the man wasn't going to take the time for an exorcism.

Before Max could protest his unwise choice, he felt icy fingers grip his heart. The demon had plunged a fist into his chest. Now it lifted him bodily from the floor. Boots kicking, he bent backward, his arms swinging at the agonizing pain. The fist opened and the sensation of his insides moving toward the splayed fingers twisted Max's limbs in agony. He growled, the noise wrenching from his very soul and becoming a battle cry against the heavens that would never admit him.

Yet, the demon did not enter him, as expected. Instead, it yanked out its fist. Blackness scurried over the demonic cloud, taking away dimension and increasing its size. Was it the shadow?

Before he could tell, Max fell to his knees in a near-lifeless heap.

Chapter 22

Aby sought safety beneath the heavy Highwayman's coat. Shivering, she listened with fear as the demon tore into her lover. There was nothing she could do to help Max. Not in cat form.

So she shifted, stretching out her human limbs beneath the coat.

Shuffling her arms into the coat sleeves she then scampered toward the far doors. Buttoning the coat to her thighs, she relished the scent of Max surrounding her. But it wasn't enough. She needed his arms about her.

But how could she save him from the demon?

"I've been waiting for you."

Aby stepped right into the white-haired familiar. The naked woman smiled, then slashed at Aby's cheek with razor-sharp claws.

"You bridged the demon." Aby darted deftly from the woman's attack. She put her back to the wall and kicked, catching her in the gut. "Don't you know it'll kill Rainier, too?"

"Good." The familiar pounced, fitting her clawed fingers to Aby's shoulders. "I've longed for freedom from that monster. He'll get his due tonight."

"He's kept you prisoner?"

"Five lives long." The woman yanked Aby forward, and they tumbled to the floor.

Aby's claws grew out and she slashed defensively and kneed her opponent, gaining moments of freedom before the wily thing pounced again.

"If you help Max get out," Aby said as her hair was jerked and her head smashed into the floor, "he'll let you go."

"How stupid are you? You think he'll let you live? The Highwayman kills familiars. If he does not, he'll imprison you like the other highwayman. They are two of the same cloth."

"No, Max isn't like that."

"He's killed hundreds of your sister familiars. We are a disappearing breed because of the Highwayman. Would you really show them respect by taking him as your lover? You were merely a tool to lead him here."

"He didn't need my help to summon the deprivation demon. You did that. You are the one who put us all in danger."

"That demon is not a deprivation demon. It is a marauder that feeds on the weakness of mortals. It can deprive those most moral or overwhelm the immoral ones with their greatest desires. Either way, the mortal suffers. The demon will sooner kill both men than be trapped whole within one forever."

She could not accept either fate for Max. She would not. Summoning her strength, she pushed the white familiar. "I have to get to Max. Get off me, bitch!"

Her strength was not enough. The familiar slapped Aby so hard, her head twisted sharply and her temple smacked the wall. She blacked out and dropped to the floor.

On his hands and knees it was all Max could do to lift his head toward the demonic cloud that expanded and coalesced over him. Indeed, the shadow was leaving his body but not without a clawing desperation to remain. It would not be had easily. That surprised Max even as he twisted in agony.

When it was done, he landed next to Rainier, who lay sprawled amid the wax droplets. Had the demon ripped out his shadow, too?

"Rainier?"

"That wasn't right. It…didn't enter you."

There was no time to lose. He reached for his whip. It wasn't at his hip.

"I do have a backup plan." Rainier chuckled. He pulled himself to a wobbling stand. "You lost, buddy. It's my turn now. You know what I can do with the complete demon inside me? Such delicious chaos."

He stalked to the center of the ballroom, crunching hardened candle wax with his feet.

Rainier thrust back his arms and head. "Come into me!" And he chanted the demon into his body.

The demon was having nothing of it. It hovered high in the ballroom, spinning. It assimilated the shadow it had wrenched from Max and Rainier, becoming whole, stronger. Once complete, it could escape.

Max spied his whip across the ballroom. He made a dash for it. The candelabra rumbled, the crystals tinkling. The demon soared through the iron structure of the candelabra, shaking the metal fixture attached to the ceiling—and the massive thing dropped.

Heavy wrought iron crashed into marble,

crystals exploded underfoot. The force knocked Max down and he landed on the floor once again.

He'd missed being crushed by a foot.

Much as the demon clawed in the air, trying to keep away, it could not resist the pull of the summoning chant that would enslave it within Rainier's body.

The snarl of a cat alerted Max. He closed his eyes, trying to pick up Aby's scent. She was no longer in the ballroom. He couldn't get a fix on her.

"Please let her be alive."

The demon clouded before Rainier. It was too late for Max to wrangle it. He'd have to do this the hard way.

He reached out for his whip, clutched it securely in his hand. Stomping across the ballroom, Max swung his whip high. He brought it around and around as the demon permeated Deloche's body, entering his pores.

Rainier turned a blue-eyed glowing gaze on Max. "To adventure," he growled.

The whip caught him about the neck. Blood spilled from the razor slices.

Rainier fought against the restraint, his palms opening at the razors. "Max," he choked. "Whatever happened to us? We were partners!"

With one tug of the whip, the razors sliced through flesh and bone. Rainier's head tumbled to the floor.

Max stood heaving over his fallen cohort in crime. "To danger."

Reaching into his pocket, he produced the silver *demi-écu* and flipped it through the air. It landed on Rainier's chest. Sulfur spewed from his body.

The demon formed, quickly taking shape. It was now complete, yet disoriented.

Max wielded the whip in dangerous circles, slashing through the form, cutting the demon into shreds that fell in a rain of demon dust to the floor and over Rainier's body.

One final crack of the whip took the demon's head and cut it in two.

It was done. The shadow was gone from him. The demon had been destroyed.

Coiling up the whip, he took but a moment to say a blessing over Rainier's remains. Then he turned and dashed for the opposite door. He had to find Aby. He searched the darkened hallway and found her body. Motionless and cold.

Falling to his knees, he lifted her head gently. She didn't rouse.

"Aby, no. Please don't be dead. Oh, God, I couldn't protect her."

He held her against his chest, his hand supporting the back of her head. Her arms hung slack at her sides; he couldn't feel her chest moving against his.

"No, don't do this, Aby. Not now. If you die— No, you can't start over! I don't want you to forget me. Please."

Tears rolled over his cheeks, hot and stinging, but not so unbearable as the pain ripping his heart. A new heart. A mortal heart?

A heart not worth a single beat if he had not the love that made it beat.

"I love you." He squeezed her against him, as if he could take her into him and never let her go. "I need you."

A meow sounded from down the hallway. It was the white cat. Rainier's familiar. She had done this to Aby. He should strike out with the whip and take her head from her body.

But the breath against his neck stopped his hand from moving to his hip.

He felt fingernails digging into his thigh, then a gasp followed by a deep inhale of life-redeeming air. "Max?"

She was alive!

He pulled back and looked at her.

"Aby?" She'd said his name. She knew him. She was still on life number four then.

He pulled her close again and felt her smile curve against his eyelid. She kissed him there.

"I thought you were dead," he whispered as he looked into her eyes.

"I'd still come back to you."

"Not knowing me. I'm not ready for you to move on to number five, Aby. I want you in this lifetime. You're too precious to lose. I thought I had lost you when that ghost dropped you in the cauldron."

"That was nasty. I hate water. Did I tell you that?"

"I think you mentioned it once or twice."

He kissed her and her mouth was cold, but open to him warming it. Drawing her fragile limbs onto his lap, he hugged her, endlessly.

"The white familiar said you'd kill us both," she whispered. "You would never harm me, Max."

"I thought she'd killed you."

"She's on her last life. Let her be. Rainier was keeping her prisoner. She's free now. Are you? Did the demon manifest? What of your shadow?"

"I think it's gone. I won't know for sure until I try to shadow. But I'm too tired right now to attempt it. Let's go home. I want to hold you in my arms until I can't hold you anymore."

He tugged his coat around her shoulders and helped her to stand. Halfway down the hall the howl of a ghost stopped them both in their tracks. Max turned and saw an approaching line of long-dead bedraggled warriors wielding muskets and maces. Behind them charged ranks of demons.

"Max?"

"Reach in my coat pocket, Aby," he said.

He released the whip and snapped it in the air.

"The caltrops," she said.

"Toss them at anything that moves. You okay with weapons?"

"Are you kidding? You should see Severo's arsenal."

"Good girl. Stay close and I'll get you out of here."

"I know you will." She fit the weapon into her fist, prepared to throw it. "Let's do this."

Three hours later, Max held Aby against the wall in the vampire's bedroom. There was no time to make it to the bed. They'd begun stripping their clothes as soon as they'd plunged through the front door.

With Aby's legs wrapped around his hips, he hilted himself inside her. A fierce instinct to find his way into her world now increased his rhythm. She moaned, deep and throaty.

"Max, I love you. Come to me, lover. I can feel you shake against me…"

His body trembled. Part of him was ready to leap, to surrender; another part wasn't eager to be let down yet again.

He slammed a palm against the wall near her head. "I don't know, Aby."

Gritting his teeth, he strained, trying to hold on to the feeling of utter abandon that simmered beneath his skin, wanting release.

Aby tensed her inner muscles, squeezing him like a hand. He gasped out a growl. "Can I do this?"

"Just let go," she whispered at her ear. "Give yourself to me, Max."

Her body, hot with perspiration, slid against his skin. He'd never thought to know love again. Never wanted to take the chance of losing her. Now he thought differently.

At least he'd have known her.

Sighing, Max relaxed against Aby's body. Her breasts, hard and slick, conformed to his chest. Her fingers trailed up his spine.

And with his surrender, came salvation.

He came hard and forcefully, bucking her against the wall, clinging to her and moaning. Two hundred and fifty years of frustration died in the fierce Paris dawn.

They made love all morning. Both spilled onto the bed lusting, wanting, needing. After they climaxed many times, Aby settled into a much-needed catnap.

Bright morning sunlight woke her. She guessed she couldn't have slept more than a few hours because she was achy and her head foggy. Next to her lay Max, his eyes closed, his soft breaths relaxed and steady.

Aby leaned over Max. "Sleeping?"

She marveled at him. The man didn't stir. He was actually sleeping.

A touch to his bare chest, and she traced down the center to below his belly button where the dark hairs tempted her to go farther. His erection sprang to attention.

And so did Max. He startled to sit upright. "What the—?"

Aby giggled. "I'm sorry. I woke you up."

"You…woke me?" He shook his head, as if to knock away the sleep.

"Max." She kissed his chin where rough stubble formed a dark shadow. "You were sleeping."

"I was? No, I…I couldn't have been. We were making love. You come so sweetly, love."

"So do you. Well, not sweetly, more like a man, so ferocious and spectacular. Like you've been waiting to do it for centuries."

"You can call it sweet, because it was, Aby. So sweet." He exhaled into a big grin. "We need to do it again, in case that was a fluke."

"Sounds like a plan. Unless you want to take another nap?"

"I was seriously sleeping? All I remember was

us making love…and then…I don't know, it was weird. I lost account of things."

"Sleeping," Aby crooned.

"Impossible. I haven't slept for over two centuries. And…I saw you. And me. We were walking hand in hand. On a beach, I think. There was white sand and palm trees."

"Max." She sidled up to him and kissed his chest. "I do believe you've had your first dream in a long time."

"A dream?" he said on a gasping sigh. "Amazing."

He tugged her to lie prone on top of him. "It's really gone. The demon's shadow. I can sleep."

"And eat. You want me to go make breakfast?"

"Hell, yes. I want to eat. But first…" He rolled on top of her and eased himself inside her. "You did wake me up."

They made the top of the Eiffel Tower by evening. After a day spent making love, catnapping and eating all the fruit Aby had gathered in the fridge, he finally took her to see Paris.

Then, at a fancy restaurant Max ordered sushi for Aby, steak for him. And potatoes. And gravy. And the veal looked interesting. And even the escargot. He ordered half the menu before the night had turned to morning.

* * *

Their first stop in the States was a tattoo shop on the corner of a small town's main street. Max perused the clientele while Aby sat in a booth at the back. The artist bent over her and decided she'd need a magnifier to do the task.

Ten minutes later, Aby left, hand in hand with Max.

I am: Aby
USB AG: 2790456318
I trust: Severo 65470
Jeremy Stokes
My ~~enemy~~ *love*: The Highwayman

* * * * *

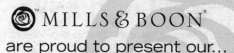

INTRODUCED BY BESTSELLING AUTHOR KATIE FFORDE

Four fabulous new writers

Lynn Raye Harris
Kept for the Sheikh's Pleasure

Nikki Logan
Seven-Day Love Story

Molly Evans
Her No.1 Doctor

Ann Lethbridge
The Governess and the Earl

We know you're going to love them!

Available 20th August 2010

www.millsandboon.co.uk

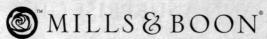

FREE BOOK
AND A SURPRISE GIFT

We would like to take this opportunity to thank you for reading th
Mills & Boon® book by offering you the chance to take A special
ly selected book from the Nocturne series absolutely FREE! We'r
also making this offer to introduce you to the benefits of the Mills
Boon® Book Club™—

- **FREE home delivery**
- **FREE gifts and competitions**
- **FREE monthly Newsletter**
- **Exclusive Mills & Boon Book Club offers**
- **Books available before they're in the shops**

Accepting this FREE book and gift places you under no obligatio
to buy, you may cancel at any time, even after receiving your fre
book. Simply complete your details below and return the entire pag
to the address below. You don't even need a stamp!

YES Please send me a free Nocturne book and a surprise gift.
understand that unless you hear from me, I will receive 3 super
new stories every month, two priced at £4.99 and a third larg
version priced at £6.99, postage and packing free. I am und
no obligation to purchase any books and may cancel m
subscription at any time. The free book and gift will be mine to kee
in any case.

Ms/Mrs/Miss/Mr _____ Initials _____

Surname _____

Address _____

_____ Postcode _____

E-mail _____

Send this whole page to: Mills & Boon Book Club, Free Book Offe
FREEPOST NAT 10298, Richmond, TW9 1BR